I0614718

Gravity

by

Mona Sedrak

Gravity

Cover Art by *Jennifer Greeff*

The Wild Rose Press, Inc.
PO Box 708
Adams Basin, NY 14410-0708
Visit us at www.thewildrosepress.com

Publishing History
First Mainstream General Rose Edition, 2020
Trade Paperback ISBN 978-1-5092-3132-4
Digital ISBN 978-1-5092-3133-1

Published in the United States of America

Relationships were difficult enough when the individuals involved shared a common language and culture. Leila knew of only a handful of couples who succeeded in mixing cultures. Even if she made peace with her family, she knew they would never accept Aiden. In their eyes, he would be an American—an outsider—who couldn't understand their ways.

She took a deep breath and filled her lungs with his heady masculine scent mixed with the ocean breeze. His intoxicating scent swirled around her brain and quieted her fears—silencing the voices of doom and crumbling the final vestiges of her defenses. Leila sagged against him. She opened her eyes and met Aiden's steady gaze.

"Gravity," she murmured.

"Hmm?" Aiden raised an eyebrow and smiled.

"No matter the barriers my brain conjures, it's useless." She shrugged.

"Baby, I'm not following you. What's useless?" Frowning, he tilted his head.

"I can't stay away." Leila looked away. "We are as different as two people can be. You are the sun and I the moon." She met his gaze. "Gravity has me in its grasp, and I can't defy it."

Aiden kissed her forehead and settled back against the lounger.

She sat between his legs with her back resting against his chest.

"Me neither. From the second I met you, I was drawn in ways I couldn't explain." He circled her with his arms. "Don't fight the gravitational force."

Dedication

To my beautiful family.
Each of you has filled my life with immense joy.
Family is everything, and you, my loves,
are the reason I rise each morning.

—Gravity—

Gravity is the force that attracts two bodies toward each other, the force that causes apples to fall toward the ground and the planets to orbit the sun. ~Tia Ghose

Chapter One
Brave

Each year on her birthday, Leila Solomon gave herself a present. Utilizing all her might, she unsealed the steel-reinforced concrete vault she buried the details of her twenty-fifth birthday in and allowed the memories to escape and ravage her. She wielded each painful, humiliating detail and shored up any cracks in the dike she built around herself. When the movie reel reached the day she boarded a plane in New Jersey bound to Florida, Leila seized the calamitous runaway memories and secured them into the vault to be re-gifted the following year.

Although the rules, boundaries, and moral code of her people were drilled into her from the second she took her first breath, she dipped her toes into a forbidden river. Dark and murky, the river harbored dangerous, bottom-dwelling creatures that attacked the innocent and ignorant. Those ugly memories reminded her one bad decision could forever alter the fabric of a person's life.

Wrapping her arms around herself, Leila gazed at the turbulent Atlantic Ocean. Over the last half hour, the wind picked up. Sand peppered her face and whipped her long curls into a frenzy. Leila captured the tangled mess, ran her fingers through it, and braided her hair down the side of her head. She glanced over her shoulder and studied her daughter. Although thunder rumbled in the distance and clouds gathered on the horizon, above her and Mia, the warm Central Florida sun stood its ground, refusing to be dimmed even in the slightest. Still, Leila shivered.

She closed her eyes and summoned the image of her mother. No matter how far Leila ran or how many years passed, she never forgot Karima's kind face, unusual colored eyes, or heartwarming smile. In truth, Karima's image greeted her each time she studied her own reflection in the mirror—olive skin, midnight curls, and hazel eyes with gold flecks fringed by dark, thick lashes.

Nightly, Leila struggled to find peace until she allowed her childhood memories of Karima bidding her goodnight to lull her to sleep.

Cradling Leila's face in her palms, Karima had gazed into her eyes. "Every day counts," she whispered. "Always remember, every second we are on this earth together is a blessing. Family is everything." She'd tucked Leila in bed and kissed her forehead. "Sleep now, my child, and know yesterday, today, and tomorrow you are loved."

Leila believed every word her mother said and every promise she made until hurricane force winds battered her world. Then, like leaves ripped from trees and petals snatched off delicate daisies, Karima's promises scattered to the wind and were trampled beneath ugly words and accusations, leaving the landscape of Leila's life altered beyond recognition.

"Mommy. Mommy. See?"

Mia's excited squeals broke into Leila's foray into the past. She crouched and threaded her fingers through the child's wispy blonde hair. Mia's hair was unlike her own thick, inky curls. Other than her heart-shaped face, Mia didn't resemble Leila. At times, Leila noticed strangers scrutinizing them. People probably assumed she was Mia's nanny or babysitter. But when they heard Mia call her *mommy*, they glanced from her to Mia—searching for a resemblance.

In all the ways that mattered, Mia was a part of Leila. Mother and daughter were bound by the blood running through their veins, nurturing their vital organs. Often, they were in perfect synchrony—every heartbeat and breath aligned. Mia was Leila's—only Leila's. She filled Leila's thoughts during the day, and visions of the petite pixie floated in her dreams.

"What is it, my love?" Leila kissed the top of her daughter's head. "What did you make your mommy?" My love—*habibtee*. The words held the same meaning, yet each time *habibtee* echoed in the recesses of her mind, pain, followed by a deep sense of loss, sliced through her. That single word reminded Leila of the woman who'd carried her under her heart for nine months, loved and nurtured her for twenty-five years, and then promptly put her out with the trash in the middle of the night.

Leila never uttered a word of Arabic in front of Mia, and she never would. Arabic, the people who raised Leila to speak her native tongue, and the world those people inhabited didn't exist for Mia. For as long as Leila breathed, she would protect her child from pitying glances and judgmental comments spewed from wagging tongues. Mia would always be, *my love*—never *habibtee*.

"Cake." Mia padded the mound of sand in front of

her and flashed Leila a toothy grin. "For your burf-day."

"You made me a sand-cake for my birthday?" Leila smiled.

Giggling, Mia nodded.

"Thank you very much." Leila pulled the child into her arms and squeezed. "You did a wonderful job. This cake is the best ever. Why don't you get some shells to decorate it before we go? The hour is late, and rain will fall soon."

"'kay, Mommy. I'll make it pretty for you."

Leila helped Mia stand and brushed the sand off her bottom.

Wobbling across the sand, Mia made her way to the water's edge.

Leila gazed at the sand. Maybe Mia's sand-cake could be a new birthday tradition. The sand-cake wasn't *baklava*, but at least it wasn't chocolate cake. As she gathered Mia's beach toys, she remembered the week before her tenth birthday. A smile spread across her face. "What will you make me this year for my birthday?" Leila had asked Karima as they prepared dinner one evening.

Karima rested her chin in her hand and brought an index finger to her lips. She straightened and smiled. "Hmm. You're having a big birthday so I will make you something special, my American girl—spaghetti and meatballs and a big chocolate cake."

Frowning, Leila scrunched her nose. Spaghetti and meatballs? Why would she want that meal? She loved her mother's home-cooked Middle Eastern food. And chocolate cake? Unlike many children, she hated chocolate. How could her mother forget? Leila opened and closed her mouth.

Karima had burst out laughing and gathered Leila in her arms. "Only you, my child, would think chocolate cake was a punishment. Don't worry. Mama knows what you need—grilled *kofta kebab* with onions and parsley, yogurt with cucumber, mint, and garlic, creamy macaroni with ground beef and extra béchamel sauce, and *baklava* for desert."

Leila wondered what her mother was doing at this moment. Did she remember today was her twenty-ninth birthday? Did she think of and pray for her as she promised, or had Karima, like Leila's father, brother, grand-parents, cousins, aunts, and uncles, erased Leila from her memory and forbidden her name from being uttered?

Struggling to keep the tears at bay, Leila took deep breaths in and out. She didn't have the luxury of giving in to her emotions. At three years old, Mia was a sensitive and perceptive child easily swayed by her mother's moods. Although many days Leila longed to indulge in the full latitude of her feelings, she wrestled with her demons and harnessed her emotions. With Mia in her life, she couldn't wallow in anger, bitterness, and grief.

In the months before Mia was born, Leila surrendered to those destructive emotions. But on the day she pushed Mia into the world, she vowed she would no longer spend her days filled with resentment—crying over the people she loved and lost and the world that condemned her existence. Gazing at her daughter with adoration, she promised Mia a life filled with immeasurable joy and a mother's unconditional love and unwavering devotion.

Shaking her head, Leila straightened her spine and pushed away the memories. She walked to where Mia played in the water—her sand-cake all but forgotten. "Mia, baby, time to go. The sun has said its goodbye for the day, and we must do the same."

Mia jutted out her chin, and her lower lip followed in a pout. "Mommy, no. I swim."

A temper tantrum was imminent. Leila scooped Mia into her arms and started the long walk to the cottage they shared with Leila's childhood friend, Deena. "We live here now, my love. We can come to the beach any day you wish after I finish work."

"But I swim now." Mia's voice rose, and her eyes filled with tears.

"Hush now, baby girl. Lay your head on Mommy's heart and listen to the secret message it's sending you."

Mia stilled. She tilted her head until her bottomless aquamarine eyes focused on Leila's hazel ones. "Secret?"

"Yes, my love, a secret message just for you," Leila whispered. "But be quick and listen hard."

Wrapping her legs around Leila's waist, she stuck her thumb in her mouth and settled her head against Leila's chest.

They played this game hundreds of times, yet Mia never tired. Leila silently repeated the words Karima used to whisper in Arabic when Leila was distraught. She instructed her heart, with its strong, sure beat, to drum out the words she longed to utter but never would. Each precious word of the Arabic missive was permanently etched in every wave and curve of Leila's brain. When translated in English, their meaning was lost. Some promises could only be relayed from heart to heart.

Leila gave her heart free rein to share the covenant passed from mother to daughter—from generation to generation. *You are more precious to me than my next breath. Rest now. Rest easy, my love…my heart. You are safe in your mama's arms. Nothing can harm you. I'm a part of you, and you're a part of me. Link your heart with mine, and together, we can move mountains and part seas.*

Rubbing circles on Mia's back, Leila repeated the words until Mia's eyelids fluttered shut and her breathing deepened and steadied. Mia's heart rate and rhythm synchronized with Leila's own steady beat. Message received. She kissed the top of her daughter's head.

Leila dug her toes and heels into the sand, stopped, and turned once more toward the tumultuous ocean. Lightning cut through the clouds, illuminating the horizon. Buoyed by the wind, her long curls flew behind her like a superhero's cape. Despite the depressing thoughts plaguing her most of the day and the troubled waters before her, she smiled.

A part of her mama was with her. Although Karima shoved Leila out of the nest, she hadn't completely abandoned her. Often a gentle breeze, coming from the fluttering of Karima's wings, caressed Leila's cheeks. Time and again, Karima's voice filled Leila's ears, urging her to stand tall, hold her head high, and be a better mama than Karima was allowed to be.

Closing her eyes, Leila breathed in the humid, salty air and released it slowly. "Okay, Mama. I'll try harder." She opened her eyes and studied the ocean. The sea undulated, inviting and enticing her to lose herself in its midst. If Mia wasn't in her arms, Leila wouldn't hesitate. She'd throw herself into the sea, letting her troubles float away.

If nothing else, Leila's father gifted her with the ability to swim without fear in the deepest, most turbulent water. Swimming and a love of the wild Atlantic were the only things they shared. Perhaps if her *baba* put half as much effort into understanding and loving his only daughter as he did instructing her to swim, their lives might have turned out differently.

With a tremendous thunderclap followed by an array of lightning inching dangerously close, Mother Nature cried out on Leila's behalf. For the most part, the residents of Florida's Treasure Coast enjoyed beautiful weather year around. On occasion, a storm hit fast and furious. Mother Nature's show of force was best enjoyed from indoors.

Mia startled and whimpered. Her tiny fingers, with their sharp, hot-pink colored fingernails matching her mother's toes and nails, dug into Leila's back.

"Shh, my love. God and his angels are moving their furniture," Leila whispered. "Easy. Mommy has you. Nothing will harm you." She turned from the churning and spewing sea and picked up her pace, continuing her journey to the cottage.

As Leila approached her favorite stretch of the beach adorned with large estates built in the architectural design of the French and Caribbean Islands, she frowned. The wind carried the faint echo of piano music. She strained to hear the haunting melody accompanied by the crashing waves, crying seagulls, and moaning wind.

With every step, she heard the music louder and

clearer. Soon, she stood in front of Harbor House, listening to a piano arrangement of Garth Brooks's *The Dance*. Over the last month, whenever she had a chance, she explored this stretch of the beach, admiring the majestic white-washed house with sky blue shutters. High above the sand and ocean, the house rested on tall stilts and stretched toward heaven. Dozens of wooden steps led from the sand to the deck.

Like many of the large beachfront estates bordering the affluent community, the house was immaculate. But where the other dwellings appeared cold and impersonal, Harbor House wasn't just a house, it was a home. Towels hung off the deck railing, chairs, bikes, and umbrellas sheltered underneath the deck, and children's toys scattered over the sand. Often, Leila imagined the family living among all that beauty. Sometimes, she included herself and Mia as part of the fantasy.

Deena found Leila's obsession with Harbor House amusing. Although Deena hadn't met the owners, she told Leila Aiden Stone, a well-known photographer, owned the house. Like Peter Lik, the Australian native known as the Thomas Kincaid of photography, Stone was a self-taught landscape photographer who documented the natural beauty of the world—oceans, waterfalls, glaciers, deserts, and forests. Apparently, he owned a rather impressive gallery in Vero Beach. Leila loved Peter Lik's work and one day, when she had a free moment to herself, she hoped to visit the gallery.

A door slammed.

Leila startled. A tall, dark blond-haired man stood on the deck. Much like how Mia rested against Leila, a child wrapped around the man's torso. The man swayed to the music—head down, face buried in the child's cinnamon hair. His muscular arms sheltered a precious bundle. In all the time Leila walked this stretch of beach, she never spotted the people living in Harbor House. The remnants they left outside created her fantasies.

Rooted in her spot, Leila was mesmerized. The roaring of the ocean and the wind faded. Piano music accompanied by the rhythmic crescendo of her heart filled her ears. The man and child dominated her vision and stole her breath. Other than Mia's face, Leila never witnessed anything quite as beautiful as the picture the man and child made.

A tall woman with mocha-colored skin and a head full of braids cascading down her back joined them.

The man raised his head and wrapped an arm around her shoulders, drawing her into his embrace. With the child sheltered between them, they swayed to the music.

Man, woman, child—together *they* were the most beautiful image Leila ever witnessed. A wave of longing hit her with such force, it threatened to pull her out to sea and consume her. She swallowed hard against ragged breaths. Pulse galloping, she tensed, her heart threatened to break free from the confinement of her ribcage and take off.

For three-and-a-half years, Leila operated on autopilot, working her ass off, taking care of Mia, struggling for survival, and breathing in and out. She existed only for Mia. In all that time, she rarely stopped to think about all she lost.

A few weeks after Leila arrived in Florida, she came face to face with her new reality. She was an orphan—worse, an alien. Nothing in this new world resembled the one she was driven out of. One way to survive existed.

With superhuman strength and a spine made of newly tempered steel, Leila gathered her memories—good and bad. She locked them away and visited as infrequently as possible. Next, she collected her girlish dreams amassed over twenty-five years. One by one, she flung them into the sea. However, she allowed hope to reside within.

But the family dancing on the deck was magnificent. Leila's heart ached in the best of ways. Long-forgotten dreams of a loving husband, family, friends, and a home of her own floated to the surface. The churning sea hurled her childhood dreams to shore, and they landed at her feet, demanding to be recognized. For the first time in years, she was tempted to reach for her dreams once more, wash away the salt and sand, and scrape off the barnacles.

The family swaying on the deck signified all the things Mama swore she'd have one day. A pang of jealousy ran through Leila. If she could bottle and run away with all that perfection, she wouldn't think twice. Packing was unnecessary. All she needed was in her arms and swaying before her eyes.

Shame slammed into Leila, and she lost her balance. She stumbled backward before she found her center. Voices from the past taunted her. Their words pierced and shredded her flesh—unworthy, disgraceful, and sinful. Thundering and vehement, the barbs and jeers she normally blocked roared in her ears, reminding her she could dream and pray, but her efforts would be futile. She wasn't worthy of beauty and grace.

She ducked her head, heat invading her cheeks. Her mother's voice rang in her head. "Stop, Leila. You chose this road. Stand straight. Walk proud. Be brave. Do better."

Shaking her head, Leila took a deep breath. Often, she wished she could scream—why didn't you stand straight and do better? Why weren't you brave? What kind of role model were you? How am I supposed to do and be all those things, when you never showed me how? Rebuking a ghost, however, was fruitless.

Mirroring the family above her, Leila rested her head against Mia's, closed her eyes, and swayed. The music soothed her troubled soul. When she gagged the tormenting voices, she opened her eyes and shifted Mia, holding her even tighter.

Leila hadn't kept all the promises she made to Mia. She still harbored anger and resentment. If she wasn't careful, one day she would wake and find life passed her. Mia would grow and build a life of her own, and Leila would be alone—still pretending to be happy but never experiencing the true definition.

"Mommy will make you proud," she murmured. "I'll not only tell you to stand straight, walk proud, and be brave, I'll show you."

Leila straightened—standing tall, shoulders squared. The time had come to stop hiding in Florida. To go forward, however, she must be brave enough to step back, confront her demons, and find closure. No more would she be a victim. She wouldn't spend her life blaming all her adult problems on her troubled childhood. For Mia and for herself, Leila would grow a backbone and find her voice. She would run headlong into the fire and pray she wasn't incinerated.

Chapter Two
Closure

The next morning, Leila stood in a zombie-like state in her kitchen, staring at the teapot, begging the water to boil. Before she could function, vast amounts of caffeine pumping through her veins were required. Since she detested the smell and taste of coffee, tea and diet soda were her lifeblood. Although she reached for sleep throughout the night, it eluded her. Like a thief in the night, doubt slipped in undetected, stole the little peace she enjoyed, and fled, leaving her with trunks full of insecurities.

In the light of day, she stood straight, hiked up her big-girl panties, and decided to go home and confront the entirety of her gene pool. But in the dead of night, her panties were too constricting and fashioned from cheap polyester, making her itch all over. At three a.m., her imagination stretched then performed death-defying acrobatic stunts. Specializing in inflating problems, her cerebrum twisted reality and threw in untrue facts and fictitious characters. Leila had bolted up in bed and gasped for air. Her limber brain deserved first place in the sport of nocturnal mental agility.

Leila poured bubbling water into a hand-painted, owl tea mug, adding a healthy spoonful of honey. Although as a child she was taught owls were a symbol of death, destruction, and bad luck, the notion was ungrounded in reality and ridiculous. Irrational superstitions conjured and spread from generation to generation no longer held a place in her life. Caught between what she was taught—folklore, cultural taboos, and rituals rooted in fear and tradition—and the life she longed to live, Leila often struggled to stretch beyond her comfort zone.

Tiptoeing through the kitchen to the deck, she eased open the heavy glass door. Muggy darkness engulfed her. Soon, the sun would rouse, yawn, and travel to its designated place in the hemisphere. This first day of May would be sweltering hot and soupy.

Leila relished the heat. Her curly hair soaked in the humidity, twisting into tight corkscrew curls that were the envy of many of her American friends. Absorbing the abundant moisture in Florida's subtropical climate, her olive skin glowed all year around.

Leaning against the deck railing, she closed her eyes, inhaled the salty air, and savored the stillness and peace of the wee hours of the morning when Deena and Mia where lost in the depths of dreamland. She envied their ability to push their yesterdays, todays, and tomorrows to the recesses of their mind and surrender—floating in contented slumber. The gift of peaceful submission to the night was stolen from her years ago.

Since childhood, Deena possessed the ability to fall asleep and stay asleep, no matter the circumstance. Deena and Leila grew up in the same Jersey City neighborhood, residing side by side in a duplex with thin walls. Leila awoke daily at six-thirty a.m. to the sound of Deena's mother hollering every fifteen minutes for Deena to wake up.

Three years older than Leila, Deena Hanna was a bit of a wild-child. To the chagrin of Leila's parents, the girls formed a steadfast friendship in elementary school and kept in touch even after Deena, at the age of eighteen, made her great escape. When her life fell apart, Leila washed up on Deena's doorstep.

Deena was Leila's life-raft and lighthouse in the gargantuan storm ripping through her world. Leila smiled. The woman was certainly a force to be reckoned with. Turning away from the ocean, Leila went into the house and grabbed her laptop. On her way back to the deck, she switched on the lights and settled on a deck chair. She had plenty to do and only a few hours to get things done. Concentrating, Leila answered all of Deena's realtor business emails, checked her social media accounts, and prepared the brochures for the day's open house. At the sound of Mia's voice, she turned off the computer and rose to start the day.

For the last two years, Leila juggled two jobs. By day, she worked as a medical assistant at a pediatric clinic, and by night and most weekends, she functioned as Deena's part-time assistant. Thanks to Deena, she discovered her passion—a career in real estate. Once she was fully credentialed and built a healthy clientele, she and Mia would gain a measure of financial security instead of the paycheck-to-paycheck existence they now led. Leila dreamed of the day she closed her eyes at night and opened them in the morning without financial worries.

Sundays were prime open house days. Sellers primped their homes, hoping to lure buyers with shiny wood floors, vibrant flower bouquets spread throughout the house, and home-baked cookies and brownies. Leila loved every aspect of real estate. Decluttering and staging homes were her forte, and people were naturally drawn to her. Each house she entered told a story about its inhabitants. Some stories were happy while others were tragic.

Over the last two years, Leila built important relationships in the community. She possessed an eye for interior design and was genuine and trustworthy. Her list of roofers, builders, electricians, landscapers, inspectors, attorneys, cleaning services, and contractors of all kinds was endless and enviable. Word spread a magician worked for Deena. Weekly, competing realtors offered bigger bonuses and spun tails of a lucrative, worry-free future. But Leila wasn't enticed.

A few hours later, Leila dropped Mia off at the babysitter and drove to Sebastian. Once she reached the neighborhood where the open house was located, she set up signs advertising the event. By the time she joined Deena at the house, five couples had toured the luxurious beachfront estate. Leila was in charge of crowd control and keeping prospective buyers interested and happy until Deena gave them individualized attention.

By noon the open house wound down. Leila glanced toward the bright kitchen window, her brain foggy from lack of sleep and a dwindling blood level of caffeine. Face aching from forced smiling and shoulders drooping, she glanced at her watch. When she heard Deena usher out the last potential client, she strode from room to room, blowing out candles and turning off lights and music.

Forty-five minutes later, Leila sat across from Deena at The Swimming Seagull, a trendy restaurant in

Vero Beach, the County Seat of Indian River County. Located one hundred and thirty-five miles north of Miami on Florida's East Coast, Vero Beach boasted over twenty-six miles of white sandy beaches. The affluent community was well-known for its excellent golfing, historical sites, offshore fishing, and upscale shopping and dining. The area was rich in culture and was featured in *USA Today* and the *Huffington Post*. Deena's house at Skyland Beach was less than ten minutes from Vero Beach.

The Swimming Seagull was not a restaurant Leila could afford, but after a well-attended open house, Deena treated her to one of Vero Beach's many delectable eateries. Leila often brought Mia to Vero Beach to feed the seagulls clustered around the docks, and she wanted to pick up Mia from the babysitter on their way to lunch.

Deena, however, insisted they needed a private lunch without little ears picking up every word said—even when the word was spelled out. Despite the busy lunch crowd, they snagged a table on the outdoor patio facing the water. After giving the waitress her drink order, Deena ran to the ladies' room.

Closing her eyes, Leila tilted her head to the sky and basked in the warmth of the sun. She dreamed of owning a home near the ocean. In the wee hours of the morning, she often jogged on the beach and gazed at its wild beauty. Her troubles diminished and sometimes even dissipated. Although she lived in Florida for several years, she still felt adrift. But she was hopeful one day she'd sail into a safe harbor, drop anchor, and enjoy life fully.

Leila took a long swallow of her iced tea, set down

the glass, and concentrated on the condensation dripping down the side of the glass. All morning she completed the tasks expected of her on autopilot. Her heart wasn't in the work.

Despite her reservations about moving in with Deena, she was pleased her concerns about peaceful cohabitation were wasted. Leila worried the harmony wouldn't continue once she informed Deena of her plans to contact her family. She twirled a long curl around her finger and frowned. Perhaps she worried for nothing. She was wrong before.

Two months ago, Deena and her lover, Jesse, separated and sold the home they shared for almost nine years. Since the separation, she was often emotional but refused to speak about the sudden separation. Instead, Deena rearranged her life, cutting Jesse out of every aspect. She bought Breeze Bay Cottage and begged Leila to move in.

Leila was hesitant. They'd lived together for three short weeks before Mia was born, and she wasn't certain Deena was ready for a rambunctious child underfoot night and day. Deena, however, was a savvy negotiator. She argued Leila could save money on rent and take classes in photography, interior design, or staging, and earn her real estate license. Then she could build a career that gave her and Mia financial stability.

Leila gave in. She must think of Mia. The child grew fast and every other week required new shoes and clothes. Leila shopped in thrift stores, but she wanted better for Mia. Recently, Leila's elderly neighbor became too sick to watch Mia, and Leila enrolled her in an expensive pre-school.

Leila sat straighter as the waitress approached.

Surveying her surroundings, she glanced at Deena standing near the entrance, speaking on her phone.

Deena mouthed, "Sorry." She shrugged.

Smiling, Leila shook her head. Unexpected calls and sudden changes to plans were an expected part of a realtor's life. Even though she normally possessed a healthy appetite and loved greasy cheeseburgers, the thought of food nauseated her. She ordered a Cobb salad for each of them.

Leila squeezed lemon in her iced tea. Her decision to contact the family who disowned her would impact Deena. Spurred by a series of fierce arguments resonating through both their homes, Deena fled her family home. She never saw or spoke to her parents or extended family again, shunning them before they destroyed her.

Chewing on her lower lip, Leila recalled the promise she made Deena never to discuss her family or the events leading up to her departure. No choice existed but to break her promise and pray Deena forgave her. Splashes of cool water hit Leila's face. She gasped and glared, noting Deena's mischievous smile.

Laughing, Deena dried her hands on a napkin. "Look alive, woman. You haven't heard a word I've said."

"I can't believe you did that." Leila ran a hand over her face. We're in a nice restaurant. Behave."

"Don't ignore me, and I will." Deena smirked.

"Sorry." Leila shook her head. "I've been pre-occupied. Anyway, you ignored me first and because you did, I've ordered Cobb salads for both of us—yours without the avocados, of course. You're a pain in the ass, but I don't want you dead."

"Why are you punishing us with salads?" Deena wrinkled her nose. "With all the brooding you're doing, I thought you hit the grease and booze stage. You were up before dawn, and you've been lost in your head all day. Spill, sister."

Leila cleared her throat and prayed for strength. "I've been doing a lot of thinking."

"Yeah…and?" Deena reached for her iced tea.

"I'm stuck, Deena." She hung her head. "I can't move forward until I look back and find closure. I must stop hiding, and…I must face them."

Deena's smile fell, and her eyes widened. Her hand shook as she lowered the glass to the table. "What did you say?"

Swallowing hard, she met Deena's gaze. Sweat formed at the base of her skull and ran down her back. "You heard me," she whispered.

"Say it again." Deena gritted her teeth and narrowed her eyes. "I can't believe my ears."

Leila took a deep breath, releasing it slowly. She hated hurting Deena, but she was resolute in her decision. Perhaps the time had come for them both to go home, face the past, and the people they loved and trusted—the people who ripped out their hearts. But Leila could only make that decision for herself. She learned the hard way what happened when Deena was pushed and didn't want to live under the same roof in silence for two weeks.

"I owe you my life, my dear friend. I'd do anything for you, but I need to face my family. If you want to stay hidden, I promise I'll do everything in my power not to reveal your whereabouts. But, Deena…" She raised her chin. "For more than three years, I've been in hiding, behaving like I've committed a crime. I internalized all those painful words they threw at me—immoral, shameful, sinful."

Deena shook her head. "But…"

"No, I know I'm not, but those words still ring in my ears." Leila squared her shoulders. "For me and for my daughter, I must stand up to them." She clasped Deena's hand between hers. "Maybe even for you. They took so much from us." She blinked back the tears. "I won't let them take any more. How will Mia learn to hold up her head high, if her mother never does? One day, she will want to know her heritage. She'll ask about her father, grandparents, aunts, uncles, and cousins. Even if I fail at reconciliation, I can honestly tell her I tried everything to give her a family. Do you understand?"

"I'm trying to." Deena sighed. "But I don't need my family or want them in my life. They no longer have any hold on me." She pulled her hand from Leila and clenched it in a fist. "And Leila, I'm not sure you'll get what you desperately want. Are you looking for acceptance and validation?"

"I'm not sure what I expect." Leila shrugged. "But I have many questions, especially for Mama. Now that I'm a mother, I don't understand her actions. What kind of mother shuns her child? Am I not a part of her and she a part of me?" Leila's voice cracked. "Despite the pain they inflicted, I can't stop loving or missing them. I'm not strong like you. I've tried to write them off, but…" A knot lodged in her throat, and she looked away. "They're my people. I don't know how you closed off the part of you longing to be loved and accepted by those who gave you life." She shook her head. "I don't have an off switch. I wish I did. In many ways, my life would be easier."

Deena took a long drink of iced tea. She focused on something in the distance. "You think I woke up one day, packed my things, and, like a heartless bitch, walked away from everyone I loved without ever looking back? You think I flipped an emotional switch deep inside and never felt the agony of their disapproval or the loss of their love?"

Leila widened her eyes. God, she spoke without thinking. "I'm not saying…"

"Uh-uh." Deena shook her head. "Listen up. I know I don't talk about why I left, but you know. It's not a secret, and the details don't matter anyway. But did you know I went back like you're planning?"

"What? When?" Leila gaped.

Deena glared. "Five years after I left, Jesse talked me into returning for the same reasons you touted. Closure. Well, I got closure all right." She clenched her teeth. "Do you want to know what happened?"

Swallowing hard, Leila shook her head.

"No, of course you don't. You're happy to sit making assumptions and passing judgments. But you started this, so let me clue you in on what my loving mother did. She opened the door, the smile on her face disappeared, and she froze. Although the temperature was in the nineties, ice formed in her veins, and she stared at us with such coldness and disregard. Without a single word for the daughter she hadn't seen in five years, she slammed the door in my face. Guess what, Leila?" Deena slapped a hand on the table, rattling the dishes and silverware and sloshing the iced tea and water onto the white tablecloth. "I got closure."

Leila gasped. Dear God, would her mama react as Deena's had? Would her family rip out her heart once again? She worked hard to build a new life and achieve a bit of happiness. Was her deep desire to be loved blinding her to reality? Perhaps she was dreaming of the impossible. Do families really love one another unconditionally?

Chapter Three
Strangers

AJ stacked sausage, eggs, and fruit on top of the English muffin on his plate. Instead of swallowing any nourishment, he constructed a jiggling food fort that continuously tumbled over, littering the breakfast counter with food particles.

No matter how hard Aiden pleaded or what he offered in the form of a bribe, he couldn't convince his boy to put a morsel in his mouth. Although the child didn't appear sick, he was fooled too many times in the past to trust his judgment. One day, the kid would be the death of him.

Stalking to the staircase, Aiden summoned the one person on Earth, other than himself, AJ minded. "Ty," he bellowed up the stairs. "Need your magical powers before you go, please." No doubt, Tyra would be down in a matter of minutes. Where AJ was concerned, he never asked her twice. Since the day they welcomed him home from the hospital six years ago, they made AJ their first priority.

Throughout winter and spring, AJ battled various ear infections, stomach viruses, and respiratory illnesses exacerbated by a congenital heart defect and a poor immune system. For a child with Down syndrome, minor ailments often resulted in complications. Over the last six weeks, he lost a significant amount of weight due to pneumonia, leading to a two-week hospital stay. His appetite never recovered. He was a picky eater, and every meal turned into a battle of wills.

In tiny denim shorts and a lime green tank, Tyra strutted into the kitchen. Her long braids dangled in a ponytail high on her head, showcasing her graceful neck and trademark massive gold-hooped earrings. "Hey, little man. Whatcha building?"

Long and lean with flawless mocha skin, a confident strut, and a mighty attitude, Tyra was a walking contradiction. Sexy, spunky, and sassy on the outside, she was chocolate pudding on the inside—soft, sweet, and soothing. Her sexy-as-sin body, combined with her exquisite features, scrambled men's brains and stopped conversation. Strangers probably assumed she was a supermodel or an actress, having no idea her beautiful, yet aloof, exterior guarded a magnificent creature with a tender heart of gold. Aiden was one lucky sonofabitch to have Tyra Campbell in his life.

"Hi, Mama Ty." AJ grinned.

"Not hungry?" She sat beside him, stroking his hair.

"Uh-uh."

"Little men must eat so they can grow into big men. Can you take a bite for Mama Ty?"

AJ shook his head and turned to his plate.

"Do you feel sick? Do your ears hurt?" Tyra furrowed her brows.

He shrugged.

Sighing, Tyra slid her gaze to Aiden.

Mimicking his son, Aiden shrugged then glanced at his luggage stacked in the corner. He peeked at his watch. He was scheduled to board a nonstop flight out of Orlando International Airport to Costa Rica in four hours. "Peanut, look at Daddy."

AJ raised his head and stared at his father.

"Do you remember what happens when I go on a trip?"

Again, the boy shrugged.

Aiden frowned. "Remember, you call me on your tablet, and we talk every morning before school and at night before you sleep?"

AJ nodded and hung his head.

Exhaling loudly, Aiden ran a hand through his hair. AJ was accustomed to him traveling. Aiden set a routine which, in the past, never failed to put AJ at ease. He showed AJ pictures of the various locations he planned to visit. Together, they planned his itinerary. The night before his departure, Aiden allowed the boy to help him pack, and in the morning, he attempted to make pancakes in the shape of the island or continent he visited. In the past, separation anxiety never reared its ugly head.

AJ's behavior concerned Aiden. Due to AJ's precarious health, Aiden ceased traveling for eight months, and he rescheduled this trip twice already. Working fulltime from a desk wasn't possible in his line of work.

Running her fingers through AJ's cinnamon hair, Tyra touched his forehead with the back of her hand in the process. "How about instead of going to Miles's house, we drop off Daddy at the airport and spend the entire day on the beach? We can build sand monsters and eat hotdogs and snow cones. I can go out with Jay another day. What do you think?"

AJ glanced at Tyra. A slow smile spread across his

face, and he launched himself into her arms, wrapping his too-small, six-year-old frame around hers. He laid his head on her shoulder and sighed.

Rubbing the back of his neck, Aiden pushed aside his frustration. Although he longed to lose himself in his art, he'd wait a few weeks then attempt the trip. He wasn't going anywhere. His boy needed him.

Dr. Klein had assured Aiden and Tyra AJ was fully recovered, and his appetite and energy would return in time. Aiden wasn't convinced. He studied his luggage once more then swung his gaze to AJ. His face was buried in Tyra's neck, listening to her soft whispers. "Know what guys? I've changed my mind. I'll go to Costa Rica in a few weeks."

AJ raised his head and grinned.

Tyra shook her head. "No need to cancel your trip. I can handle AJ."

"I know you can. But the timing is off. I'll go in a couple of weeks. AJ, you and I can go to the beach, or you can go to Miles's. First, though, we have to see Dr. Klein to make sure you're okay."

AJ's smile fell, and he stiffened. "No. No." He struggled in Tyra's arms.

Racing to Tyra's side, Aiden took AJ out of her arms before the boy hurt her or himself. The child was terrified of hospitals and doctors. He held his boy in a tight embrace. "Stop now, son. I know you're scared, but we're not going to the hospital. We'll go to Dr. Klein's office—the one with the giant fish tank filled with red sharks and blowfish that make funny faces. No one will hurt you."

AJ ceased struggling and peered at Aiden. "No hopstikal?"

With his fingers, Aiden wiped the wetness off his boy's face. "No hospital. Just Dr. Klein's office. We can see if he has any new fish in his tank."

"Fish for me?" AJ tilted his head, and a small smile formed on his lips.

AJ's speech might be delayed, but his negotiation skills were advanced. Thanks to Dr. Klein, he was fascinated with tropical fish and often begged for a tank of his own. He wasn't ready for the responsibility of a pet of any kind.

Gazing into his son's luminous green eyes, Aiden noted the dark shadows underneath made more prevalent by his creamy skin and the freckles dotting over his cheeks and nose. His resolve crumbled, and he kissed AJ's forehead. "Okay. You got it, Peanut, but only a small tank with two fish."

"Four." AJ held up four fingers.

Laughing, he shook his head. "Three, but you have to drink a shake right now."

AJ held up his palm and giggled.

Aiden high-fived him.

"Deal," he shouted.

Tyra raised an eyebrow. "You know that kid has you figured out, right? He's a master manipulator at the age of six. Can't wait to see you handle him as a teen."

Aiden shrugged. "No meltdown plus a shake in his system. I'm pretty happy with the results of the negotiation. I hope Klein solves his eating issue. He's wasting away."

"He's fine, A. Don't cancel your trip. I'll take him to Klein."

"My decision is made." He shook his head. "A few more weeks won't change anything. Hopefully, by the next time I leave, his eating habits will have improved, and he won't feel as vulnerable. We'll talk nightly about the trip until he's comfortable. I won't leave until he is."

She threw up her hands. "Fine. Call Klein's office. Give me fifteen minutes to put on clothes that won't give the old man a stroke and to call Jay and cancel. I'll be right down."

Straightening, Aiden squared his shoulders. "Take all the time you need. You're not going. You won't use us to cancel again. You've planned this day for weeks. With Jay's crazy work schedule, he rarely has a Saturday off."

Tyra planted her hands on her hips and cocked her head. "Aiden Stone, you're thirty-five years old— nowhere old enough to be my father. Do *not* tell me what I can or cannot do, you foolish creature. My boy is sick, and he needs me. Besides, Jay and I are only going to lunch and a movie."

"Our boy is probably fine." He rubbed the back of his neck. "We both know that fact. While we always need you, we can survive a day without you. Stop using us to distract you from getting some much-needed and well-deserved R&R."

She glared and huffed.

Enough was enough. Aiden met her glare with one of his own. He loved Tyra. She was his best friend— and a lifesaver. But she needed more than he and AJ in her life. She deserved a man and a family of her own. Even if she refused to admit it, Tyra was Jayden's. He was a gifted emergency room physician and a damn fine man. For several years, she rebuffed all his advances, but a year ago, she capitulated.

Early in Aiden's friendship with Tyra, he considered a romantic relationship, but he wasn't attracted to her or she to him. They agreed to preserve their friendship and co-parent and co-love AJ. Tyra often harassed Aiden to open his battered heart, and he hounded her to do the same. Neither was successful, using AJ as their excuse to stay cocooned in their safe little world.

Tyra raised her chin. "I'm not having this conversation. I'm fine."

"Good." He smirked. Turning, he picked up his cell. "Go, be fine with Jay. You're not invited to our party. I'll call if anything comes up."

An hour later, Aiden, with AJ strapped in his car seat, was on his way to Dr. Ash. Klein was out of town on a family emergency, and Dr. Ash covered his practice. Aiden hated taking AJ to see a doctor he didn't know, but his choices were Ash, urgent care, or the emergency room. The problem was, Ash's office was across town, and his distrusting son was on the brink of a tantrum.

Aiden parked, opened the back door of his SUV, and regarded his son. "Peanut, you need to come out of the car now. Dr. Ash is a nice doctor. I promise." He prayed he wasn't lying. AJ's memory was remarkable, and if Ash wasn't as gentle and kind as Klein, he would make his displeasure clear. Aiden would have to purchase a forty-gallon tank and enough fish to fill it.

"Are there fish?"

"I don't know, son. Let's go inside and find out." He unbuckled AJ's car seat.

"No." AJ scrambled out of the seat and huddled near the opposite door. He crossed his arms and puckered his lips into a pout. "I want Mama Ty. Where's her?"

Aiden closed his eyes and pinched the bridge of his nose, pushing aside his frustration. As much as he wanted, he couldn't grab AJ. In the past, he'd tried that maneuver, but it was a huge mistake of meltdown proportions. Rather, he crouched to AJ's level. "Come on, Peanut. Take a deep breath. Mama Ty is with Jay. Remember? We can call her when we're done with the doctor."

"No. Stop it, Daddy. Stop." AJ wailed and kicked his feet.

Aiden extended an arm. "Peanut, take my hand. Come to Daddy, and let me hold you. We'll see the doctor together."

AJ shrank away farther. "I want my mama. Call my mama. Please, Daddy."

Rubbing AJ's leg, he waited for the child to calm. "Easy, son. Daddy wouldn't let anything bad happen. This visit will be quick, and then we can go to the pet store, buy an aquarium, and fill it with all kinds of fish."

He hated forcing AJ to do anything. Since AJ's recent string of illnesses, meltdowns played a significant part of his life. Whenever he was frightened or pressured, he called for his mama, causing a vice to tighten around Aiden's heart.

"Excuse me. Can I help?"

Startled, Aiden peered over his shoulder. A petite woman with black curly hair stood behind him. She was dressed in navy scrubs and a colorful nursing jacket. Straightening, Aiden glanced at his son's tear-streaked face then back at her. He took a deep breath and released it.

"Hi, I'm Leila Solomon." She smiled and extended an arm. "I'm Dr. Ash's medical assistant. I assume you're here to see him since we're the only business open in the building on Saturdays?"

After blinking a couple of times, he stared into exquisite hazel eyes fringed with dark, thick lashes. He scanned her face, noting her tiny nose, full lips, and flawless olive skin. Then he beheld the wild mass of dark curls cascading down her shoulders and halfway down her back. Transfixed, he gaped.

She cleared her throat.

Flushing, Aiden shook his head and clasped the woman's outstretched hand. What the hell was wrong with him? He made a total fool of himself ogling a perfect stranger. She was an exotic beauty. Unlike Tyra who dressed to accentuate her looks and capture attention, Leila's clothing, jewelry, and makeup accomplished the exact opposite. Didn't she realize her natural beauty couldn't be suppressed—even under baggy scrubs?

He sucked in a breath. "Ah, hello. Yes. I'm…I'm Aiden Stone." He nodded toward the car. "This is my son, AJ. He usually sees Dr. Klein, but Klein is dealing with an emergency, and Ash is covering him today. AJ is anxious around healthcare providers. I'm trying to convince him to get out of the car, but I don't think Ash has fish, and that's a big problem. I even promised to buy fish afterward, and that's an even bigger problem 'cause Ty's gonna kill me." Aiden shook his head.

Extracting her hand from his, she tilted her head to the side. "Fish? Ty?" She furrowed her brows and opened and closed her mouth.

Damn it. He was a rambling idiot. Aiden's neck and face fired up. He'd crushed Rapunzel's tiny hand. Rapunzel? He clamped his mouth shut before he made a bigger fool of himself. This conversation went to hell—fast. He was relieved Tyra wasn't in hearing distance. She would enjoy seeing him flustered and tripping over his tongue. "Never mind," he murmured and ran a hand through his hair. "We'll be in soon."

Grinning, Leila peeked inside the car. "Can I try? I'm pretty good with kids."

Aiden scrutinized Leila. Compared to Tyra or his own six-foot, three-inch frame, she was tiny—five-feet, two-inches of curves and curls. She didn't speak with a prominent accent, but a lilt existed in her speech. English wasn't her primary language. He doubted the average person detected the accent. He was well-traveled and spoke several of the romantic languages. On first glance, he guessed she was of Italian or Spanish heritage. But upon hearing her name, Aiden was certain she was Middle Eastern.

Normally, he would be annoyed and suspicious of a stranger interfering. But something about Leila, maybe her sweet smile or the kind, patient way she listened to his ridiculous rambling, chased away his usual response. He doubted she would have any luck with AJ. Aiden opened his mouth to decline her offer but then…*fish*. Leila's nursing jacket was covered in a variety of cartoon drawings of smiling fish—swimming, water-skiing, and canoeing. Closing his mouth, he stepped aside, allowing her access to his son but staying close to watch AJ's reaction.

Leila bent—hair tumbling around her. "Hi, AJ. I'm Leila. I'm Dr. Ash's helper."

Widening his eyes, AJ curled farther into the seat.

"I know you're scared, Brave Boy. I don't blame you. Sometimes, coming to the doctor is no fun. My little girl doesn't like coming either. Want to see a picture of Mia?" Leila plucked her cell out of her pocket and showed AJ a series of pictures, describing each one.

Absorbed in the pictures and the funny stories she told, AJ relaxed his tense frame and leaned forward.

"Do you want to know what helps Mia feel better when she comes to the doctor?"

AJ glanced from the cell phone to Leila. He nodded.

"Well, Dr. Ash gives all his patients their own Care Bear, Cuddly Kitty, or Dear Doggy. You can pick one and hold it while he examines you, and then you can take your animal home. Does that plan sound good?" Leila smiled.

AJ studied her for a minute and smiled. "Any fish?"

"Fish?" She tilted her head to the side then glanced over her shoulder. She flashed Aiden a quick grin then turned to AJ.

Aiden was as mesmerized as his son.

Nodding, AJ pointed to her jacket. "Do you gots sharks and blowed fish?"

Eyeing her jacket, she burst out laughing.

The symphony of her laughter, accompanied by his son's giggles, floated through the air and washed over Aiden. He smiled, and the anxiety he experienced right along with AJ eased. Leila wasn't good with kids, she was brilliant.

"No, Brave Boy." She shook her head. "I'm sorry.

We don't have fish, but I think you will love the doggy or the kitty. Did you know some fish are called catfish and dogfish?"

AJ's face lit up, and he scooted toward Leila. "Really?"

"Yup. Come with me." She opened her arms wide. "Let me show you all the animals I have in my zoo, and you can choose one."

AJ scooted into her arms.

Using her hand, Leila protected his head and straightened, kissing the top of his head.

Bewildered, Aiden observed his shy, distrusting boy wrap his legs around her waist, and his thin arms wound around her neck. Leila cuddled him close, cradling him as if he belonged in her arms. A weight, Aiden didn't realize he carried, lifted off his chest.

"Now"—she said, as she marched toward the clinic—"tell me why you like fish."

The next hour passed better than Aiden anticipated. Dr. Ash was competent and thorough, listening to Aiden's concerns. He was gentle with AJ and, at the end of the visit, declared him healthy. He encouraged Aiden to offer AJ a wide variety of food, giving him choices so he feels more in control. He was convinced, in time, the child's appetite would return. When he finished examining AJ, he stepped into the hall.

Leila followed.

Although the door to the examining room was closed, their conversation was clear.

"You're moving too slow. Do you have any idea how long you wasted in that room?" Dr. Ash huffed. "Your sloth-like movement has cost us. Hope you weren't planning to leave on time. At this rate, we'll be here well past noon."

"I'm sorry, but AJ Stone is new to the practice, and his medical history is complex," Leila explained. "He is terr—"

"Stop wasting my time with lame excuses," he growled. "I don't have time for nonsense."

Guilt flooded Aiden. She tried to elicit a family history, but he insisted the history was irrelevant and refused to engage in a discussion in front of AJ. On their way out of the examining room, Aiden and AJ ran into Leila.

She smiled, hugged AJ, and straightened.

Strain and fatigue showed around her eyes, and an overwhelming protective instinct hit him. He was tempted to draw her into his arms and ask what he could do to relieve the pressure she was under, but he resisted. No matter how kind she was or how attracted he was, they were strangers, leading separate lives that might never intersect again. But why was he so captivated?

When Leila heard Dr. Ash bellow her name from down the hall, she jumped, but her smile never wavered. "It was nice to meet both of you." She extended a hand. "Maybe I'll see you and AJ at the beach sometime."

Like a well-trained puppy ready to do his mistress's bidding, Aiden enclosed her delicate hand in his large paw. Unable to find the words to thank her, he opened and closed his mouth.

"Leila, I need you in here. Now," Dr. Ash yelled.

Snatching her hand from his, Rapunzel spun and raced off—her long tresses flying behind her. In a flash, she was gone.

Aiden stood with his arm extended and his hand empty. He should leave. AJ bounced from foot to foot, tugging him toward the door. But Aiden failed to convince his stubborn brain the interlude with Leila Solomon was over. Their interaction was brief and probably wouldn't be repeated unless AJ required medical care when Klein was unavailable. The thought of never seeing her beautiful smile again left him oddly bereft.

On his travels, he met thousands of strangers. Why was she any different? He shook his head and willed his feet to step toward the exit. Standing in the clinic pondering the secrets of the universe was pointless.

Endless miles of beaches traced Florida's coastline, and thousands of people—all strangers—inhabited the region. Aiden halted. The fog cleared from his brain, bringing clarity and an answer to the question plaguing him from the second he saw her. Leila wasn't a stranger. Although his analytical and somewhat cynical brain searched for clues and an explanation as to her importance, his heart and his boy recognized her and accepted her as someone special. Now what?

"Daddy, fish."

Aiden glanced at his impatient son then ran a hand over his face. He behaved like a love-struck teenager, and he didn't have that luxury. He was an adult with a special needs child who depended on him to make solid decisions. She had a child which could mean she was either married or in a relationship—taken. He shook his head and strode toward his son. Strangers were strangers, even if the heart attempted to pull a fast one and convince the brain otherwise.

Chapter Four
Sacrifices

Eyes closed, Leila stood under the spray of the hot water, swiveling her neck side to side, working out the kinks. She awakened early but lay in her bed, unable to find the will to move. Eventually, she dozed off and now ran late. Yesterday, she worked with an obnoxious and temperamental Dr. Ash until after four p.m., and by the time she ran to the pharmacy, grocery store, dry cleaner, and arrived home, she was exhausted. Still, she fixed dinner, played with Mia, bathed her, and collapsed in bed pleased she survived another busy Saturday.

If Sunday was anything like Saturday, Leila's energy stores would be depleted before a new work week began. The open house scheduled for the day was sure to be challenging given the continued silent treatment Leila received from Deena. Despite their differences, however, the women were pros and would don professional masks for their clients.

Leila opened her eyes. She had no choice but to wait for Deena to finish brooding. She hoped her friend found understanding and acceptance sooner rather than later. At times, Deena was as stubborn and willful as a toddler.

Finishing her shower, Leila dressed, fed Mia breakfast, and wrestled her into the car, dropping her off at the babysitter.

The open house was a few minutes away at a beautiful home adjacent to Harbor House. Oceanfront Manor was a four-bedroom, three-bath, and three-car garage dream. Recently updated with gleaming hardwood floors, a luxury master bathroom with a built-in hot-tub, and a chef's kitchen, the house drew a large crowd. She and Deena were busy with potential buyers for three hours straight.

Many realtors detested open houses, but Leila enjoyed them. She was in the kitchen putting out more cookies when a child's high-pitched squeal rang through the air. Smiling, she followed the sound of the child's infectious giggles accompanied by splashes and cheers. Stepping onto the deck, she faced Harbor House in time to see AJ Stone launch himself from the edge of the pool and into his mother's arms while Aiden snapped pictures.

Leila reveled in the sound of AJ's carefree laughter. He didn't resemble his exotic looking mother or his father in the slightest. They made a beautiful, if unusual, family. When she first met Aiden and AJ at the clinic, she didn't recognize them, but the address on AJ's medical history form clued her in.

For a few minutes, Leila closed her eyes and imagined a life filled with love, laughter, a home of her own, and a good man she and Mia could depend on. That man would adore Mia as Aiden Stone did his son. Perhaps, he would also hold Leila at night when voices from the past haunted her and stand by her side in the light of day—unashamed, loving her unconditionally.

A prickle of awareness ran through Leila. Although the day was exceptionally warm and humidity fogged her sunglasses the second she stepped out of the air-conditioned house, goose bumps sprouted on her arms. Knowing what she'd find, she opened her eyes. With a wide smile decorating his handsome face, Aiden peered through a camera which focused on her. Tall and tanned with caramel-colored hair and whisky eyes, he was impossible to resist. Her face heated, but she couldn't stop a grin from spreading across her face.

Leila wasn't drawn to him because of his outward appearance, though. Aiden Stone was a rare find. Although she hardly knew him, she was convinced he was a good man. Some would say she was the last person on Earth who could spot a good man. After all, she fell for fool's gold. But her past experiences with men were invaluable. Those experiences, and the years she spent dissecting every relationship she shared with the men in her life, were a testament to her credibility. Leila was an expert at mining for and identifying the male equivalent of gold—a man who loved with his whole heart and would sell his soul to spare his boy an ounce more pain. Aiden Stone was gold.

"Leila, can you show the Johnsons the house?" Deena called.

She blinked and straightened. Tearing her gaze from Aiden, she willed her body to turn, leaving her fantasy husband and his real family on the deck of her dream home. The great thing about fantasies is they were harmless. This man, and all the beauty surrounding him, was taken. She was raised with a better moral compass than to pursue a married man.

At the conclusion of the open house, Deena left Leila to close the house and went out for the rest of the day with friends. Leila picked up lunch and an energetic Mia and hit the beach. That evening, after Mia was safely tucked in bed deep in slumber, she barricaded herself in her bedroom and relished the silence. Time to pamper herself. After a long hot bath, she sipped from a glass of wine, listened to soothing music, and painted her toes a startling lime green.

When she finished, she eyed her handiwork and grinned. If her *baba* saw her, he would have a coronary. Often, he asserted refined women should not wear such vulgar colors. Leila examined the basket containing all her fingernail polish, wiggled her toes, and giggled. Every single color was vulgar—just the way she liked it.

That night, the beautiful, big-hearted Aiden Stone strolled through Leila's dreams, flashing his tantalizing smile and filling her head with delicious fantasies. When she awakened at the crack of dawn, she was disappointed and overwhelmed with the reality of her life, the long week ahead, and the steps she must take to reconcile the past with the present.

As all Mondays were at Skyland Pediatrics, the day would be long and busy. Leila rubbed her eyes and rolled out of bed. The time was five a.m., and although she was exhausted, she couldn't fall back asleep.

She longed to take a personal day but if she made the request, especially on a Monday, Dr. Ash would throw a massive hissy fit and possibly fire her. Leila couldn't take the chance. Mia depended on her. Like all single parents, she couldn't be frivolous with her vacation and sick days, and she must bank every day possible in the event Mia became ill.

After grabbing a cup of tea, Leila stepped onto the deck lost in thought, watching the sun shove its way through the clouds and dense fog and climb the heavens.

When Leila felt arms snake around her waist, she jumped, splashing hot tea on her hand and deck. "Ouch. Hot."

Releasing her, Deena stepped back. "Oh, I'm sorry. Are you okay?"

Leila balanced the mug on the edge of the deck rail and turned. "I'm fine. Why are you up so early?"

"I've behaved badly. I'm sorry." Deena grabbed Leila's hand and dragged her to a chair. "I know I've been distant, but I had a lot of thinking to do. Our pasts might be similar but not identical. I don't want you to lose out on a chance to reunite with your family if that is what you want. I won't lie. I'm terrified for you and Mia."

Relief swept through Leila. Deena heard the sirens warning a storm was on the way and panicked. Maybe now—together—they could prepare for the storm surge and hurricane force wind. Perhaps, Leila wasn't alone after all. "Oh, Deena, I am so grateful I have…"

"Just listen, please." Deena exhaled a long breath. "Promise me you'll consider what I say before you act."

Leila nodded.

"You and Mia are my family, and the thought of you getting hurt any more than you already have been makes me sick." Deena swallowed hard. "But I love you, and if you're taking this monumental step, I'll stand by your side. Just remember one thing. You are a mother now. Any decisions you make will impact Mia." She squeezed Leila's hand "When you are certain you are doing the right thing, start with Niveen. She would do anything for you." She stood and left.

Leila closed her eyes and raised her chin, letting

the sun warm her face. Deena wasn't a mother, and although she did her best to support Leila, she couldn't fully understand a mother's duty to her child or a mother's heart. Leila didn't need Deena's warning. Mia served as a daily reminder of what she lost as well as the gift she received. Her baby girl was her reason for living.

She sacrificed much to have Mia. But good mothers sacrificed for their children. What sacrifices did Karima make for her daughter—her *habibtee*?

When she needed her mother the most, she was horrified to watch Karima turn her back. Even if Leila forgave her, she couldn't forget. Karima promised one day Leila would understand her actions. But one day was today, yesterday, and the day before. With each passing day, Karima's actions were more incomprehensible and indefensible. Under no circumstances would Leila exile Mia. Until the day she took her final breath, she would protect her little love. No one would raise their voice or their hand to her daughter.

Standing, Leila glanced one last time at the roaring ocean, breathing in the salty, moisture-filled air. She was not Karima. Daily, she stood strong and proud. She chose a difficult path, but she harbored no regrets about her decision to have Mia.

An hour later, Leila steered her ancient sedan into a parking space in front of the Skyland Medical Arts building and turned off the engine. Although thick clouds eclipsed the sun and rain was imminent, she rolled down the driver's window and stared at the semi-full parking lot.

Despite her deep desire to spend the day hiding in

the car or in bed, she would do what Deena suggested. Niveen was Leila's first cousin on her father's side. The Solomon family was a large, close-knit tribe. But Niveen was the person she was closest to since birth—a sister of the heart.

Yusuf, Leila's father, had two younger brothers—Aziz and Hassan. Hassan was married to Amal, Niveen's mother and Leila's godmother. The three brothers, along with their wives and children, immigrated to the United States. For the last thirty years, they co-owned and operated *Baharat*, a Middle Eastern grocery store and bakery in Jersey City, New Jersey.

Living a mile apart, the nine cousins attended the same public schools, shared toys and clothes, and ate most meals together. Many nights Leila and Niveen refused to be separated and slept tangled around one another. From the moment they babbled, they created their own language, sharing each other's dreams and secrets.

Leila sucked in a deep breath and pulled her cell phone out of her pocket. Her hands shook as her pulse accelerated. Once she called Niveen, the flood gates would open, and her family and all their drama would rush back into her quiet world. The past would engulf her.

Did she want to end her peaceful existence? Was she making the right choice—for Mia, Deena, and herself? Leila's lips quivered, and her eyes burned with unshed tears. She was not a victim. She was a survivor.

History would not repeat itself. This time she was capable and powerful. She must open a door and invite her family to know the woman she now was and the beautiful child who graced her world. If they welcomed her and agreed to live in harmony, fine. If they were entrenched in the past, refusing the peace she offered, she would slam shut the door once and for all.

Placing her phone in her lap, she shook out her hands, gulped in another breath, and picked up the phone. She remembered Niveen's number. Until three years ago, she dialed the number hundreds of times. As the phone rang, Leila's breaths became labored. On the third ring, the line connected.

"Hello?"

Leila squeezed shut her eyes and savored the sound of her cousin's sweet voice. Images of two little girls in matching red-and-white, polka-dotted dresses, chasing each other through Central Park with their ponytails swinging, flashed one by one across her eyelids. She swallowed hard and licked her dry lips. "Nivi," she croaked.

For a few seconds, silence reigned.

Would Niveen refuse to speak to her? After all, Leila was the one who cut off all communication with her cousin a few weeks after she moved to Florida. Perhaps Niveen was too hurt and angry to welcome Leila back into her life…and her heart.

"Lala?" Niveen whispered. "Dear God. Lala, is that you?"

Niveen's voice was a mix of sorrow and excitement. Leila's eyes welled with tears. *Lala*. She hadn't heard that pet-name in so long. As a toddler, Niveen nicknamed her Lala, and the name stuck. Leila cleared her throat and blinked away the tears. "Yes, Nivi. I am so happy to hear your voice."

"Oh, Lala, where have you been? Every night I

search for you in my dreams and pray for your safety." Niveen sobbed. "Three-and-a-half years have passed, Lala. Much has happened. I've missed you, *yah ell-bee*."

Yah ell-bee, my heart. The familiar endearment was a balm to Leila's aching heart. She took a stuttering breath. "And I missed you, too—all of you."

"Where are you?" Niveen sniffed. "Will you tell me? Please promise me you won't disappear again. I can't bear you cutting me off."

Leila hung her head. After arriving in Florida, she had called home, but her father and brother monitored the house phone, and the second they heard her voice, they disconnected the call.

Niveen, however, always answered her calls. She suspected Leila was pregnant and was under the impression she ran away. Niveen did her best to negotiate reconciliation, but after three weeks, she told Leila the situation was hopeless. Karima refused to speak to Leila and asked her to stop calling. Yusuf ruled the entire family with an iron fist, and he made Karima's and Niveen's lives a living hell.

Her family was *everything*. Breaking the gravitational pull was almost impossible—*almost*. Cutting Niveen out of her life almost killed her. But she loved her, and Niveen didn't deserve the treatment she received from Yusuf. Devastated, Leila defied gravity.

Leila took a calming breath. "I'm sorry, Nivi. I never meant to hurt you. One day I'll tell you everything. Perhaps you'll understand and forgive me. I tried to…"

"You have my forgiveness," Niveen blurted. "Promise me you will not disappear again. I've never stopped loving you. You were out of my sight but never out of my mind. You're loved and wanted. Stop running, Lala."

Closing her eyes, Leila allowed Niveen's words to sink in. Every cell in her body greedily absorbed those precious words—*You are loved.* The words wrapped around Leila's heart and squeezed until she barely breathed. Leila rested her head against the steering wheel—her muscles all but jelly. She ached to feel Niveen's arms around her, supporting and guiding her and lending her strength. She longed to see her mother's face, to hear her native tongue, and to smell and taste the food that nourished her from the day she was born until the day she was expelled.

"Lala, are you there?"

"I promise." Leila cleared her throat. "I won't disappear again. I love you, too."

Niveen exhaled a long breath. "Good. We have much to catch up on. Let's begin at the beginning. The baby?"

Smiling, Leila opened her eyes and straightened. For the first time, she could share Mia with a family member. "I have a daughter. Her name is Mia. She's beautiful and sweet. She is my greatest joy. Mia is all the good things in life in one tiny package."

Niveen laughed. "How wonderful. I can't wait to meet her. Will you tell me about your life?"

Hesitating, she flipped down the driver's side visor. Tucked underneath the garage door opener was a picture of Mia playing in the sand, smiling at the camera. Kissing the tips of her fingers, Leila touched her daughter's face. "For you, my love," she mouthed. "Mia and I live in Skyland Beach, Florida. I've been here since I left home. We live with a friend in a beautiful cottage on the beach. I work as a medical assistant, and I am in the process of getting a real estate license. Life was tough for a while, but we're doing well."

"I am glad you and Mia have a good life. But speak the truth. Are you happy?"

Leila's smile faltered. That question was difficult to answer. Despite the hardships and sacrifices of the last three years, Leila *was* blessed. She lived in a beautiful home, and her child was healthy and happy. She didn't have much in the bank, but soon she would have a new career. Guilt flooded Leila. She wasn't happy. A hole existed deep in her heart only her family could fill.

"I am fortunate. I have everything I need to be happy but my family. Nivi, I…" She gripped the steering wheel as beads of sweat sprouted on her upper lip and forehead. "I need to come home," she whispered. "Mia deserves to know her people—her grandparents, aunts, uncles, and cousins. Please, will you help me?"

Chapter Five
Think

Paperwork. God, how he hated it. Aiden shoved away from his desk, stood, and stretched. All morning he fought the urge to peer out his office window, but now he lost the battle and was drawn to the brilliant sun pouring into the room and reflecting off every surface. Calculating how many hours of light were left to catch the setting sun, he grabbed his camera. Shackled to his desk instead of his camera was severe punishment. He should be capturing the sun bouncing on the waves in the horizon where the expansive blue Florida sky melted into the Atlantic.

Florida sunsets were nothing new to Aiden. He, similar to dreamers, nature lovers, and photographers, captured thousands of images of nature flaunting its glory at the end of the day. But each image was unique and few were flawless. Aiden was a perfectionist—some said to a fault. He dreamed of being at the right place at the right time, in harmony with Mother Nature—a rare and miraculous occurrence.

At the age of nine, Aiden snapped his first picture. A few weeks before a family vacation to Disneyland, his father purchased the best camera on the market and indulged Aiden's curiosity, allowing him to occasionally use the complicated device. From the first click, he was hooked and launched a zealous campaign for his own camera.

Just when he thought he won his crusade, disaster struck. His father lost his job, and his mother lost her mind. Aiden's world fractured, and he gave up on his dream. A month after his tenth birthday, however, he received a mysterious package with no return address. Inside laid an expensive camera and a handwritten note. *Happy birthday, Aiden. I hope one day you will forgive me. Love, Mom.* Although he was tempted to hurl the package against the wall, he couldn't make his hands obey his brain.

Aiden glanced out the window once more and shifted the camera from one hand to the other.

"Put down that camera, Aiden. Stop petting it like a puppy."

With a hand on her hip and a scowl on her face, Tyra leaned against the door frame. "You're not going outside until every proposal is reviewed and every email returned." Tyra shook her head. "Come on, man. Get a grip. I force you into the office once every other week, and I must come in and check on you every fifteen minutes."

"You know I hate this shit. Why can't you sign for me?" He dropped into the old leather chair facing the desk and shoved the files and notepad to the edge of the desk. Almost a year passed since the last time he sank fully into his craft—just him and the camera. He looked forward to the Costa Rica trip, and now he was more restless and irritable than ever. Although Aiden loved his work, he loved his son more. He didn't begrudge AJ a second of his time. Taking out his frustration on Tyra was unfair.

Tyra lifted her chin and glared. "My name isn't

Aiden Stone. I've told you a million times, I will not forge your signature unless absolutely necessary. Besides, coming in and viewing the numbers every now and then is good for you."

Since the day the Vero Beach Gallery opened five years ago, Tyra managed every aspect with ease. Similar to his Miami Beach and New York galleries, which his brother Matt managed, the Vero Beach Gallery showed a remarkable profit. Aidan's photos sold in limited-edition for between four and twenty thousand dollars. He built a solid reputation, and he was free of financial worries. "I don't need to see the numbers. That's what my accountant is for," Aiden growled. "And I trust you with my boy. Nothing is more valuable. Why wouldn't I trust you with my signature? Matt signs my name all the time."

"Forcing you to do paperwork is my way of keeping you humble." Tyra smirked. "Besides, Matt's last name is Stone. Mine is not. Must we have this argument again? Anyway, aren't you done yet?"

Aiden ran a hand through his hair and huffed. He wouldn't win this battle. "Yeah, I'm done...for the most part. I have a few emails left then I'm out of here."

Straightening, Tyra turned. "Since you've been good, you can go out and play with your camera all day tomorrow," she called over her shoulder.

Aiden pivoted, reaching for the files and banged his leg against the desk drawer that never fully closed. Cursing, he rubbed his knee. One day he would order a decent desk.

For some odd reason, Tyra loved the rusted hunk of junk she brought when she agreed to give up her job as a social worker and run the gallery. She insisted the desk grounded and reminded her of the important things in life. Aiden spent little time in the office. When he wasn't on a shoot, he worked in his home studio. Once school closed, he spent time with AJ and took him to visit Matt at one of the other galleries.

Matt was three years younger than Aiden, and although he resided in Manhattan, he also owned a condo in Miami. Other than their identical light brown eyes, they didn't resemble each other in the slightest. Aiden was a blend of his parents. He inherited his nose, forehead, and build from his father and his eyes, hair, and complexion from his mother. Matt, however, was short and stocky with olive skin and jet-black hair.

When they were children, their starkly differing appearance wasn't discussed. To his credit, Edward Stone loved his boys and treated them equally. Although he had to have known Matt wasn't his biological child, he never uttered a word—not even after their mother escaped with Matt's lookalike, Jack Harrison, Edward's business partner and best friend.

Closing the computer program, Aiden smiled as AJ's grinning face stretched across the screen. He studied his boy's precious features—cinnamon hair, freckled creamy skin, small nose and ears, and green eyes slanting upward. His heart burst with love for the boy who didn't resemble him.

Aiden and his father shared a common history. The difference was when Gina, AJ's mother, fled, leaving the child behind, Aiden's life didn't stop. He, unlike his father, didn't surrender to anger or grief, relinquishing his responsibilities or drowning his sorrows in a bottle or two daily.

Tyra kicked Aiden in the ass, reminding him of the child laying in the NICU fighting for his life.

Clicking on the email program, Aiden scrolled through the list of unanswered emails. He straightened, blinking as he fixated on a new message received within the last few minutes. Unable to believe his eyes, he leaned in, gaping. At the top of his inbox was a message from Gina Sanderson with the subject line reading, "We need to talk." Aiden broke out into a cold sweat.

Six years had passed since he last spoke to or saw Gina, but six years weren't long enough to wipe out her past sins or soften his heart. After a long and tiring trip to Australia, Aiden had arrived at his apartment dead on his feet. Unable to summon the energy to shower or change, he collapsed on the living room couch and immediately fell into a deep sleep. Incessant banging on the front door woke him. Dazed and bleary-eyed, he stumbled to the door.

Gina stood outside his apartment—blonde hair disheveled and blue eyes dilated. "I can't take care of him anymore. I've tried, but I can't." Her entire body shook, and she licked her lips repeatedly. "He's your responsibility too. Everything you need to know is right here." She slapped the yellow envelope to his chest, and it slid to his feet.

Jet-lagged and still emerging from slumber, Aiden rubbed his eyes. Fog permeated his brain and sludge ran through his veins. He struggled to assimilate what Gina said. "Huh? What?"

"I'm leaving. He deserves better. The time has come for you to take some responsibility." She pointed at the envelope. "The name and number of the social worker handling his case are in the envelope. She's expecting your call."

"What?" Aiden shook his head. "Who's expecting my call?"

"Haven't you heard anything I've said?" Gina yanked her hair with both hands. "I tried to tell you, and you wouldn't listen. Grow the hell up, Aiden. Don't be an irresponsible ass like your father." Gina had turned, run down the steps, and hopped into a pickup truck idling in the parking lot.

Aiden took a deep breath and ran a hand over his face. After all this time, Gina found him. Locating him didn't take genius. He was a well-known photographer with an active social media presence. What did she want to talk about? The only thing they shared was AJ, and he was not a topic Aiden was willing to discuss.

He'd do whatever he had to protect *his* son. Squeezing his eyes, Aiden sighed. Six years ago, Gina wasn't interested in being a decent human being. He doubted she changed. Maybe she was after money? As long as she left him and his boy alone, she could have all the money she wanted. AJ was fragile and incapable of understanding the complexity of the situation. Aiden wouldn't subject him to unnecessary confusion and anxiety.

Clicking on the e-mail, Aiden read Gina's message. His vision blurred then turned crimson. His pulse pounded a wild, rage-filled rhythm. Grabbing the closest item, he hurled the object across the room. The camera smashed into the door and shattered, littering the room with plastic, metal, and glass. Aiden pushed to stand, and the desk chair zinged backward, crashing against the wall. He dug his hands through his hair and scrubbed them over his face. *This nightmare couldn't be happening.*

Tyra threw open the office door. "Aiden? What the hell's going on? Are you okay?" She took a few steps and froze, scanning the room.

Aiden flattened his palms on top of the desk. His muscular arms flexed and strained, shaking with his body weight. He expelled a long breath as he leaned into the stance, hanging his head between his shoulders.

"What's wrong?" Tyra whispered.

Silence reigned.

"A?"

He raised his head. "She's back." He groaned.

"Who's back?" Tyra frowned. "Make some sense," she snapped. "You scared the shit out of me. What the hell's going on?"

"Gina. She's back." Aiden straightened. He ground his teeth and nodded toward the laptop. "She sent an email. After all this time, she wants to…" He closed his eyes and shook his head as he clenched his fists.

Walking to him, Tyra rounded the desk. She dragged the chair toward him and pushed his shoulders. "Sit."

Aiden slumped into the padded chair.

Opening the bottom drawer of the desk, she produced a bottle of Glenlivet and a crystal tumbler. She poured a generous portion and handed him the glass. "Drink. I'll lock up. Be right back, and for the love of God, don't throw anything else." She nodded at the shattered camera. "That burst of temper, my friend, is gonna cost you."

Wincing, Aiden nodded. Destroying his camera was idiotic. He would purchase another device, but like a trusted friend, she was irreplaceable. He ran a hand through his hair and picked up the glass. He had much more pressing problems to fret about.

"Aiden?"

He met her gaze.

"You're not alone." She swallowed hard. "I've always known this day would come. We'll deal."

Aiden took a healthy swig of the drink. The amber liquid hit the back of his throat and burned a path down to his already souring stomach. "AJ," he croaked.

Frowning, Tyra nodded. "We'll do what we must to protect our boy. We'll do what's in AJ's best interest." She glanced away for a brief second and peered back. "Even if what needs to be done is not what she deserves and not what we deserve, but what *he* deserves." Tyra turned and strode out of the room.

He picked up the glass and finished the drink in one long swallow. Slamming the glass onto the desk, he closed his eyes and rested his head on the back of the chair. Since the second he saw AJ and accepted the awesome blessing and responsibility of being his father, he protected him, and he would continue doing so regardless of the cost.

Tyra was AJ's mother, and *he* was his father. Those facts are what his boy understood. AJ might never gain the ability to comprehend otherwise, or he might mature to the point Aiden could discuss his biological mother. He hadn't given the issue much consideration. Neither he nor Tyra planned on having a child—let alone a special needs child. AJ brought them together. They formed an unconventional family for a little boy who was abandoned by his mother three weeks after he was born and who lived the first six weeks of his life in St. Joseph's Hospital NICU, fighting for every breath and heartbeat.

Aiden regretted many aspects of his life but being AJ's father wasn't one of them. Someone needed to care, love, and advocate for him. Straightening, he punched a few buttons on the keyboard, bringing the email back on the screen.

I know a long time has passed since we talked. I'd like to speak with you and see AJ. So much has changed. I've changed. Please give me a chance to explain. I'm staying at the Biltmore Hotel. Call me.

Shaking his head, he balled his hands into fists. Aiden wasn't interested in Gina's explanations. He couldn't understand many things in this world. Most of the time, he gave in and accepted them as mysteries of the hand of God, miracles of Mother Nature, or complexities of human nature. No matter how hard he tried, he couldn't fathom a mother walking away from a child she shared her blood, breath, and heartbeat.

Where was Gina all these years when her boy needed her? She left AJ in the hands of a man who walked out on her a few months earlier, didn't want the responsibility of another human life, and didn't make a secret of saying so every time the subject of children was discussed. If Tyra hadn't forced Aiden to step up, what would've happened to AJ?

Tyra operated beyond the boundaries and tenets of her social work training to champion an orphaned baby boy hooked to so many machines, he was barely visible. Would AJ have survived without Tyra and Aiden advocating with Dr. Klein, dozens of specialists, therapists, and nurses over the years? Doubtful.

Hovering his trembling fingers over the keyboard,

he formulated a reply to Gina's email.

"Don't do anything rash, A. Think carefully."

Aiden glowered at Tyra standing in the doorway. Think? What was he supposed to think about?

Sitting in the chair across from his desk, she crossed her long, mocha legs at the knees.

"I have nothing to think about," he spat. "She made her decision a long time ago, and now I'm making mine."

Tyra shook her head. "But this situation is not just about you. Is it?"

Narrowing his eyes, Aiden stood. "No, this mess isn't all about me. But he's mine. AJ is mine to love and protect. She doesn't exist in his world. I'm making sure she never does." Thinking complete. Decision made. He positioned the cursor over Gina's email and clicked the Delete button.

Chapter Six
Unashamed

"Why is every day such a bitch to get through with Dr. Ash?" Leila straightened from her relaxed position on the beach lounger and faced Deena. "Nothing I do is ever right. He takes joy in seeing me squirm. After enduring his abysmal behavior on Saturday, I thought he enjoyed his fill of histrionics and degradation. I was wrong. Today, I reached my mid-week BS limit." She dug her lime green-colored toenails into the warm sand.

"Go ahead, entertain me. What did Dr. Ass do?" Deena reclined in her beach chair and tilted her face toward the setting sun.

"Oh, the usual amount of berating and demeaning. Saturday was particularly bad, and my self-esteem and confidence didn't recharge before he started in on me Monday." Leila hung her head. "Today, I caught myself before I referred to him as Dr. Ass to our new office manager." She glared at Deena. "I blame you for putting that name in my head. It's been on the tip of my tongue more times than I care to admit."

Deena giggled. "Well, he worked hard to earn that title. He can't accuse you of defamation."

Fighting the wind, Leila gathered her long curls and twisted her hair into a messy bun. "Every morning I tell myself I will stand up to him. But as soon as I see his face turn red, his eyes bug out, and he loses his mind, I placate him. I'm dealing with my father all over again." Rubbing her cheek, Leila recalled the sting of her father's hand. For twenty-five years she tolerated his outbursts and tirades. As a child, she learned to duck and hide, keep her mouth shut, and live on the periphery when Yusuf was in the house.

Six months after Karima, Yusuf, and Gabriel, Leila's brother, immigrated to the United States, Leila was conceived. When Karima discovered she carried a girl, she was overjoyed. Often, she told Leila the story of the night she was born. Karima took one look at her dark-haired baby and named her Leila—dark beauty who was born at night. For Karima, Leila was a blessing. For Yusuf, she was the root of all his failures.

"Do you know, I become physically ill every morning before work?" Leila shook her head. "My head hurts, and I'm nauseous. I will grow a backbone and stand up for myself." She sighed. "I swore when I started a life on my own, I wouldn't be a willing participant in my own abuse. What kind of role model am I?"

Sitting, Deena took Leila's hands and squeezed. "You're a fantastic role model. We both know why you hold your tongue." She nodded toward Mia playing in the sand. "Enduring his despicable behavior has nothing to do with weakness. The strength of Goliath is required to keep your mouth shut, sacrifice, and tolerate an intolerable situation."

Leila stared at the endless ocean—powerful and fierce. She wished she possessed an ounce of its strength. Deena was right, though. Dr. Ash was a means to an end—a paycheck guaranteeing food, clothing, and shelter. Compared to some other jobs she'd held, working for him wasn't all that bad. Few people appeased Dr. Ash. The man lost four medical assistants, two nurses, and three office managers in the last year and a half.

"I'm not sure how much more I can take before I lose my mind. Frankly, his advances were easier to handle than his temper." Leila relaxed into the chair and released a long breath. "Once he understood our relationship must stay professional, he centered all his energy into making me miserable, the smarmy bastard."

"Keep your eye on the ball and his hands off you." Deena lounged in her chair. "Leila, you know what you need to do. Save money, take those classes we talked about, and pass your licensing exam. You don't love working as a medical assistant anyway. Time to pursue what you love."

"I know I complain about my job, but I don't hate every aspect. Working as a medical assistant is better than making gyros." After high school, Leila was interested in interior design, but her father believed spending money on her education was a waste. Karima thought only two honorable careers existed in the United States—law and medicine. Leila detested the thought of either. Thus, she spent her days working at *Baharat*, unloading boxes, cleaning shelves, working the register, and making falafel sandwiches, and hot, mouthwatering gyros—one day blending into the next.

"Freeing you from the *Baharat* kitchen is the one thing you can thank Gabe for."

Leila nodded.

Gabriel convinced Yusuf to invest in Leila's education by uttering the magic words, "I need help." As a first-generation NYU Medical School graduate

Mona Sedrak

and genius US doctor, Gabriel was the golden child. Although a fourteen-year age difference existed, Gabriel spoiled Leila and often battled Yusuf and won on her account.

Gabriel broke Leila's heart when she needed him the most. He joined the rest of the men in her family—a pack of dangerous hyenas with claws and sharp teeth. They relished in pouncing on their prey and shredding them. She raised her face to the setting sun. Gabriel was his father's son.

"Leila, give yourself some grace. Don't let the ass tear you down. He's a miserable creature no one can stand. Moving in with me was a good idea, and soon you'll have a new career. You're a great mom, and you have built a wonderful life for your daughter. See how happy your little girl is?" Deena nodded in Mia's direction.

Peeking at Mia, Leila smiled. Her sweet baby *was* happy and healthy, evidenced by her chubby belly and sun-kissed skin. Leila's heart expanded with love.

"She has adjusted to her new home and loves the beach. I am grateful you're sharing her with me." Deena's voice dropped. "She's everything I'll never have, and I love being an aunty, twenty-four-seven."

Leila's smile receded. God how her heart ached for her friend. No matter the brave face and tough exterior she portrayed, Deena hurt. "Deena, you can't predict the future. You can…"

"Stop." Deena shook her head. "I have you and Mia. You guys are my family and are enough." She swallowed hard. "You did me a favor moving in. I hated living by myself. Even this cottage was too big without…" Deena's eyes welled with tears, and her voice faltered.

"Without Jesse," Leila whispered. She tucked the wisps of hair escaping her bun behind her ear and linked her fingers with Deena. "I've given you time and space. Although you're a fantastic actress, you're hurting. Are you ready to talk?"

Closing her eyes, Deena took a shuddering breath then shook her head. "I know you want to help, but I'm not ready to discuss Jesse." Standing, she adjusted the sarong around her waist. "You relax while I grab some wine and snacks. This day has been hellacious. I'll even take Mia with me."

An impenetrable, self-protective shield surrounded Deena. When she was ready to share, she would. Pushing only fortified the shield. Leila didn't particularly like Jesse, but she respected Deena and Jesse's relationship.

Deena shocked Leila when, a few months ago she appeared on her doorstep, sobbing. She stayed three days with Leila while Jesse moved out. Whatever happened between the couple was momentous because Deena erased all remnants of Jesse from her life.

A month later, Jesse moved to Pensacola.

"Mia," Deena called. "Come, let's grab some snacks. You can also use the potty."

Mia grinned. She dropped her bucket and shovel and stumbled to Deena, linking her tiny hand with hers.

Mia adored her Aunty Dee and did anything she asked, including giving up precious beach time. Since the day Mia was born, they bonded. No one else in the world existed who Leila trusted Mia to. This fact troubled Leila. Where Leila grew up with a huge extended family—a rowdy village of cousins, aunts, and uncles—Mia's village consisted of Leila and Deena. She missed out on the joy of being loved and protected by a tribe. Guilt flooded Leila each time her mind strayed to this sad state of affairs.

In reality, Mia's family consisted of Uncle Gabriel, Aunt Nora, and two first cousins—a five-year-old boy and a three-month-old baby girl Leila never met. She also had grandparents and a great grand-mother. Many more people made up Mia's village. In the Middle Eastern tradition, Leila's cousins were considered to be Mia's uncles and aunts. Even close friends were accepted as family. Sadly, many more people existed on Mia's father's side—none of whom Leila knew.

A gust of wind blew off the Atlantic, and Leila brushed the hair off her face. Perhaps what she needed now was a dose of family love. Reconnecting with Niveen gave her hope. Leila spoke with Niveen a couple of times over the last few days, but their conversations were brief because of work and family obligations.

Grabbing her cell from the beach bag, Leila dialed Niveen's number. Niveen answered immediately and with genuine joy. Leila absorbed the love emanating from her beloved cousin. Nothing took the place of family love. Although they hadn't spoken in years, the women picked up where they left off, laughing and confiding in each other as they used to.

Niveen regaled Leila of all the family comings and goings over the last three-and-a-half years. Teens grew and left for college, babies came into the world, two cousins married, and one was pregnant. Niveen also shared news about Karima. "I don't know if you realize how much your parents suffered when you left, Lala.

Uncle Yusuf, he…"

"Nivi, stop," Leila snapped. "Don't mention *Baba* to me—not ever. Tell me about everyone else, but he doesn't exist for me, as I never existed."

"When you left…"

"I didn't leave. I wasn't given a choice. I…"

"Lala, please calm down. I understand."

"No, I don't think you do and someday, I'll tell you the entire story. But…"

"The past is the past." Niveen cleared her throat. "Listen, *Tante* Karima has changed. You are her heart. Without you, she's lost her reason to live. She goes through the motions of living, but she doesn't smile or laugh. No more family gatherings happen at your house or at *Baharat*—no laughter and no joy fill the air. She doesn't resemble the carefree, loving woman of our childhood."

Leila's gut clenched, and she doubled over. She closed her eyes and deep breathed. She wouldn't cry. She wouldn't feel guilty. Her mother was not the only injured party. "*She* sent me away. She knew where I was. I called and called. I too lost my will to live. Yes, I made a terrible mistake. But *she* was the mother, and *I* her child. I needed my mother. She could have stopped both our suffering."

"Believe me, Lala, she has suffered. I am not surprised she sent you away. I don't think she had any other choice."

Leila opened her eyes and straightened. "Are you kidding?" she spat. "Are you defending her actions? I'm a mother, and I would *never* abandon my child. Time and time again, she chose *Baba* over me." She scoffed. "She put up with his shit night and day."

"Leila, stop right now," Niveen said. "I love you, and I have always been on your side, my sister. But stop talking for a few minutes and listen. Okay?"

Taking a deep breath, Leila exhaled.

"I understand we must confront the past to lay it to rest. But sometimes, we need to put aside all past hurts and deal with something much more pressing in the present." Niveen cleared her throat. "I'm not sure, but I think *Tante* Karima is unwell."

"What do you mean?" Leila widened her eyes.

"I think she's seriously ill. She's lost weight. Often, she is short of breath and has no energy. She rarely leaves the house and has stopped working at the store." Niveen sighed. "I can't remember the last time she attended church. Something is wrong, and everyone is being secretive."

Just as quickly as her anger formed and strengthened, it dissipated. Leila's gut clenched. "Mama's not going to *Baharat*? She doesn't go to church?" she whispered. For as long as she remembered, Karima didn't miss a single day of work—not even when she was sick with the flu. In her mother's rule book, no good reason existed to miss church.

Leila swallowed past the lump in her throat. How could her invincible mama be sick? The past was insignificant when her mother's life might be in jeopardy. She wiped her wet cheeks and remembered the last time she saw Karima's face—tear-streaked and devastated. She was the cause of her mother's agony. Surely, God wouldn't be so cruel as to take her mama before they reconnected and found forgiveness and understanding.

As a sense of foreboding filled her, Leila trembled. Could she and Karima achieve peace before they ran out of time? Leila needed to ask for her forgiveness and her love. She wanted to introduce her to Mia. Their story couldn't end this way. She took a deep breath. "Find out what's wrong. Please, Nivi." Life was unpredictable, and Leila would do whatever was required to end the reign of silence for both their sakes.

After Leila made Niveen promise to gather more information, she ended the call and threw her cell in the bag. Defeated, she slouched back in her chair, laid back her head, and closed her eyes. Adulting was over-rated and reality sucked. Lately, her reality was one concession after another. Gone were her childish plans of returning home with her head held high, successful, happy, dressed up, and driving a fancy car with her husband and children in tow. Reality was nowhere close to the fantasy.

Now, she would run to her mother's bedside in haste, wearing thrift-store clothes, and driving a 1999 beat-up sedan, with a child in tow and no husband in sight. Perhaps if she was married her burdens wouldn't be so heavy. Karima swore the right man wouldn't add to her troubles. Instead, he would carry them and her when needed. He would be her rock and her shelter from any storm, loving her and protecting her from all the evil that walked the Earth. Although married to Yusuf, Mama wore rose-colored glasses and held antiquated beliefs.

Even if her mama was right about this rare breed of man, where did all those knights on white horses reside? In the last three years, only Aiden Stone came close to her mama's description, and he was off-limits.

Over a span of a few days, she crossed paths with Aiden three times. What was the universe telling her?

Leila smiled. Over the last year, Deena pointed out every eligible, good-looking male in the vicinity, insisting Leila should move on with her life and date. On several occasions, Deena suggested blind dates, but Leila refused. None of those men were the least bit tempting. Deena was convinced Leila needed therapy to restart her life.

"It's Leila, right?"

A deep male voice interrupted her thoughts, and she jolted upright as a shadow fell over her chair. She trailed her gaze up a long, lean body in black swim trunks—muscular legs and thighs, a flat abdomen with a few freckles, and a well-defined chest with a smattering of dark-blond hair. Broad shoulders, cognac eyes, and sandy-colored hair blowing every which way in the breeze completed the stunning image. She blinked and focused on Aiden's smiling face.

Searching for a coherent thought, Leila opened and closed her mouth. Exposed and vulnerable, sitting in only a bathing suit in front of a man she barely met, she grabbed a beach towel and wrapped it around her. But she couldn't escape Aiden's comprehensive inspection. Leila cleared her throat. "Ah…hello, Mr. Stone. Uhm…nice to see you again." She flushed under his inquisitive stare.

"Aiden, please." He smiled. "It's a pleasure to see you, as well. I guess we're neighbors, huh?"

"Sort of." Leila nodded, glancing over her shoulder. "We live in Breeze Bay Cottage."

"And we're in Harbor House—as you know." He grinned.

"Harbor House is my favorite house on the beach." As soon as the words left her mouth, heat invaded her cheeks, and she wished she could dig a deep hole in the sand and bury herself.

Aiden quirked an eyebrow.

A child's laughter and screams echoed in the air. "Daddy, Daddy, help."

He peered over his shoulder.

She followed his gaze to AJ and the brown-skinned beauty chasing him across the shoreline. The woman wore the world's skimpiest, emerald string bikini, and she was stunning—tall with miles of toned mocha skin and curves in all the right places. She caught AJ and swung him around, threatening to throw him into the ocean.

Squealing, he clung to her neck, burying his face in her head of wild braids.

She threw back her head and laughed.

God, what did being so bold and audacious feel like? Could Leila ever be as carefree, confident, and unashamed? Could she ever forget the hundreds of rules and admonishments ingrained since childhood, let go, and just be free? *Sit straight. Lower your voice. Uncross your legs. Cover your body. Never attract attention to yourself.*

Leila wished she could close her eyes and become someone entirely different. No one monitored and judged her behavior now. She could be anyone and do anything she desired. Memories of the past and the weight of her own fears, however, shackled her, curtailing her ability to stretch beyond her circumscribed childhood to recreate herself.

Maybe she could start by wearing the bikini Deena

bought for her birthday and bury the black one piece she always wore. Donning a bikini wasn't a huge leap but choosing to wear it could be the start of a new her. Leila blinked and turned to Aiden. Her breath caught.

Aiden focused on her. His eyes were wide, and he appeared flushed. A pulse hammered at his neck. His chest rose and fell with his quickened breaths, and a small smile played at his lips.

Pulse racing, her lips parted, and she blinked. Did Aiden find her as attractive as she found him? She wasn't certain. The emotions and sensations she experienced when his appreciative gaze lingered on her weren't completely unfamiliar, but she hadn't felt desirable in a long time. Warmth flooded every centimeter of her body, and she tingled all over. Lord, she felt *good*. She was *alive*.

Dropping her gaze, Leila sucked in air. Aiden was a married man. She could look, but she couldn't touch. Feeling attraction and desire wasn't illegal or immoral—as long as she didn't act on those feelings. Being a single mother attracted to a handsome man didn't mean she was a whore. Wearing a swimsuit didn't mean she was promiscuous. Leila lifted her chin and once more met Aiden's gaze. With shaking hands, she released the towel she held to her chest and smiled. For the first time she could remember, shame failed to make an appearance.

Chapter Seven
Fixated

Aiden was captivated. Leila captured his interest when they met at the clinic and again when she surprised him on the deck of Oceanfront Manor. She was a rare beauty—smooth olive skin that warmed when she blushed, a heart-shaped face, intelligent hazel eyes with stories to tell, and a shy, tentative smile that did unexpected things to the rhythm of his heart.

At the clinic, she was a confident and competent healthcare provider. Now, she appeared unsure of herself. The look of unabashed reverence, and the variety of other emotions skating across her features as she observed Tyra, intrigued him. Aiden kicked himself for forgetting his camera. Although he rarely took candid photos of anyone but family, he was compelled to photograph Leila. His camera, an extension of his heart and mind, loved her.

On Sunday, he snapped a few pictures while she was lost in contemplation—eyes closed, face tilted, worshipping the sun, and hair flying wild and free. Transfixed, he focused the lens and captured image after image of raw, uninhibited beauty, longing, sadness, and strength—all in a span of seconds.

Leila opened her eyes, and the smile they shared was familiar—intimate even. Her unconcealed yearning was palpable. She stole his breath. For a few seconds, they communicated with their gaze and hearts. His clumsy, out of practice heart skipped a few beats, then like the sun having been dimmed by a prolonged superstorm, mustered its strength, pushed past the clouds of doubt and remnants of past trauma and danced to a new beat until it lit the sky.

"Mommy. Mommy." A child's voice carried across the sand.

Leila stood and turned toward the house.

He had an unobstructed view of her compact body. She dressed in a conservative, one-piece, black bathing suit similar to those athletes wore. The suit accentuated her lean, yet curvy, frame and full breasts.

Turning, she caught his gaze, her cheeks blossomed again, and she bit her lower lip. Grabbing a T-shirt from the beach bag, she pulled it over her head, allowing it to slide down to her knees.

"Mommy. Look."

Dragging a plastic bag, an adorable, blonde-headed pixie in a pink-and-white polka dotted bikini stumbled their way.

A woman with Leila's coloring and curly hair followed her, juggling wine glasses and a wine bottle as she spoke animatedly on her cell.

"I got thnack'th. Grape'th, tom-toe'th, and pig'th."

When the child reached her, Leila's face broke out in a tender smile. Scooping up the girl, Leila brushed the hair out of her eyes and kissed the top of her head. "Hello, my love. Those are delicious snacks. Did you make the pigs?"

"Ye'th." She nodded. "I covered them 'cause they were cold and cooked them."

"I bet they're delicious. We can try them in a bit.

First, I have someone for you to meet." She cleared her throat. "Mr. Stone, this is my daughter, Mia." She glanced at Mia. "Mr. Stone is a new friend. Remember your manners and say hello."

With inquisitive azure blue eyes, the color of tropical waters, Mia studied him. Although she was a beautiful child, she didn't resemble Leila in the slightest. He didn't recall seeing a wedding band on Leila's hand, but the lack of a wedding band meant nothing. She could still be in a relationship. Disappointment shot through him.

Mia wriggled out of her mother's arms. She straightened her back, protruding her rounded belly. Squaring her shoulders, she lifted her chin, and held out her right hand. "Hello, my name is Mia Tholowman."

The child was precious and precocious. Aiden grinned. She enchanted him. He crouched, met her serious gaze, and shook her tiny hand. "I'm delighted to meet you Mia Solomon. My name is Aiden Stone. How old are you?"

"Three," she replied with a wide toothy grin, holding up four fingers.

"Ahh, I see." He chuckled. Touching each of her fingers with the tip of his index, he counted. "One, two, three." When he reached the fourth finger, he glanced at Mia.

"Uh-oh." Using her free hand, Mia forced down her fourth finger and peeked at Aiden. "Three." She grinned.

Mia Solomon stole Aiden Stone's heart. He bet her father was wound around her tiny baby-girl fingers, and he couldn't blame the poor sucker. She was intelligent and irresistible. He ruffled her hair and grinned. "Yup, you're correct. Three fingers. Well done, Mia." He pointed at AJ. "That boy is my son, AJ. He's shy, but I bet he would love to be your friend. If your mommy agrees, you can go say hi."

Pivoting, Mia stared in AJ's direction. With furrowed brows, she regarded Aiden. "A-J? What's him name?"

He frowned and tilted his head. Then he nodded and smiled. "His name is Aiden James Stone, but he likes to be called AJ."

"'Kay." She giggled. "I like AJ." Hopping up and down, she tugged on Leila's hand. "Mommy, AJ's my friend. Plea'th, Plea'th. I go play."

Leila gripped Mia's hand. "Okay, but don't go in the water. Understand?"

Staring in AJ's direction, Mia nodded.

Crouching, Leila tugged on Mia's hand. "Please look at Mommy."

She shifted her gaze to her mother.

"Don't go into the water, my love. The waves are too high. Use your words, and tell me you understand."

"Ye'th, Mommy. No waves. Water is big."

Smiling, Leila kissed Mia's forehead. "Good job." She released her hand. "Go have fun."

Mia skipped across the sand.

"She's a beautiful little girl." Aiden smiled, admiring the gold flecks in Leila's unusual hazel eyes—his new favorite color. "Just like her mother."

Leila's smile vanished. She focused on the shoreline where Tyra chased AJ then met Aiden's gaze.

Her eyes darkened and transformed into cold, hard jade. What the hell happened? Small talk wasn't Aiden's strong suit, but if his memory served him, telling a woman she was beautiful was a compliment. Wasn't it? How did he mess up?

"Thank you," she snapped, turning her attention to the bag.

He was dismissed. He frowned and ran a hand through his hair. Shit. She probably was in a relationship and thought he was a dick for flirting. He couldn't help himself because she was lovely. Giving himself a mental slap, he opened his mouth to apologize. Before he uttered a word, the woman who was trailing Mia approached with a welcoming smile and a confident strut, reminding him of Tyra. Tall and lean with toned legs and arms browned by the sun, she wore a tiny, red, halter-top bikini and a don't-screw-with-me attitude.

"Well, hi there." She surveyed him from head to toe. "Where did you come from? I thought we were alone on the beach this evening." The woman thrust the wine glasses at Leila, set the wine bottle on the chair, and extended a hand. "I'm Deena Hanna. And you are?"

He shook her hand. "Aiden Stone. Nice to meet you. Sorry to interrupt your evening." He smiled. "I was surprised to see Leila on the beach. Thought I'd say hello."

Glancing from Leila to Aiden, Deena grinned. "You're a welcome interruption. We're just relaxing. How do you two know each other?"

Aiden waited for Leila to speak, but her lips pressed tight. He cleared his throat. "We met at the clinic the other day when my son saw Dr. Ash." Aiden pointed toward AJ. "Leila swept in and stopped AJ from spiraling into a colossal meltdown. Quite a magical feat

I never thanked her for."

Focusing on Leila, he smiled, hoping to find his way back into her good graces and lure her into easy conversation. "You did a nice job. Normally, once AJ's anxiety kicks in, little helps. Over the last year, he's formed a fear of healthcare providers, making visits with anyone other than Dr. Klein difficult. Your gentle touch made a huge difference. Thank you."

Leila considered him for a few seconds. Her shoulders relaxed, and a small smile played at her lips. She licked her lips. "You're welcome. AJ's a sweet boy, and Dr. Ass is a good doctor. You can trust him."

Deena snorted and burst out laughing.

Aiden's lips twitched. Deena's laughter, which was more like a cackle, was infectious. He threw his head back and laughed.

Frowning, Leila glanced at Deena. "What's funny? He *is* a good doc…" She gasped and widened her eyes. "Oh my God." She covered her reddened cheeks with her hands. "I said *ass*, didn't I?" She glared at Deena. "I know I'll screw up in front of him and lose my job. Don't blame me if I'm penniless, and you must feed, clothe, and shelter me and my daughter."

Deena continued laughing, tears sliding down her cheeks. "You're the best medical assistant that ever worked for that pompous prick. He'll never fire you, and if he does, you'll be fine. I've got you covered."

Leila dropped her head in her hands. "No one has me covered." She raised her head, squared her shoulders, and focused on Aiden. "I was unprofessional. I'm sorry for my runaway mouth. Dr. *Ash* is a great doctor. He's tough on the staff, but he's one of the best pediatricians in the area. I take my daughter to see him when she's sick." She shook her head. "My day sucked, and I…"

"Don't worry." Aiden shrugged. "The man most definitely *is* an ass. I heard him berate you when you left the examining room and bark at you on our way out. He might be a good doctor, but he lacks social skills. Your secret is safe with me. I promise." He drew a cross over his heart with a finger.

"Thanks, but I shouldn't have spoken in that disrespectful manner. I'm not usually so…" She dropped her head.

"Hey, stop apologizing." He closed his large hand over her much smaller, more delicate hand. "We all have bad days."

She gasped and ripped her hand out of his.

Aiden widened his eyes. His gesture was automatic and innocent. He only meant to comfort her. "I'm sorry," he mumbled and took a step back. Shaking his head, he reviewed the few facts he gleaned about Leila over the last few minutes. She was a mother, lived with Deena, and worked for an ass. He also remembered seeing Deena's face on for-sale signs all over Indian River County. She was a well-known and respected realtor in the area—Hanna Realty. But where was Mia's father?

An air of innocence and vulnerability surrounded Leila. She was beautiful, intelligent, soft spoken, and gentle. If he allowed his raging hormones and vivid imagination to run amuck, they would shove aside logic and govern his actions and emotions. The woman was in a relationship, and he was a grown man, not a hormone-ruled teenager. Friends, that's all they could be.

Deena cleared her throat. "I think I'll go meet Mia's new friends. Why don't you two have some wine?" she said over her shoulder as she sauntered away with a smirk.

Leila's gaze trailed after Deena.

For a few seconds, silence reigned.

She sighed and glanced at him. "Sorry. My nerves are a bit fried today."

"No, if I overstepped, I apologize." He ran a hand through his hair. "My day was long, too." He nodded toward the bottle of wine. "What are my chances of getting a glass of that vino?"

She chewed on her lower lip, peering back and forth from the shoreline.

Leila reminded him of the many wild birds on Florida's coast—fragile, yet fierce creatures. They begged for treats, but when beachgoers offered them morsels, they took two steps forward and four steps back, dancing for their supper. If the humans moved too fast, they spooked the untrusting birds, causing them to take off or snatch the offering, nipping fingers, and drawing blood.

"Okay. Sure." She searched through the bag and plucked out a bottle opener.

"Let me do the honors. Why don't you sit and relax?" He opened the bottle and filled the glasses she held. Sitting on the sand, he raised his glass. "To new friends."

She tucked a few wayward curls behind her ear. A tentative smile touched her lips. "To new friends." She touched her glass to his before taking a sip and licking her lips.

Aiden drank the wine and admired the setting sun.

Years passed since a woman captured his interest. Now, he was drawn to a woman with a child and possibly a husband. He shook his head in self-disgust.

Since Gina, all his relationships were trivial—no-strings-attached encounters with both parties understanding the terms of engagement. Those arrangements did not include access to his home, heart, or more importantly, his son. He and Tyra understood the importance of maintaining a stable family environment for AJ. While their circle of friends was large, casual hook-ups were strictly forbidden from the household. Aiden and Tyra's relationship was unique, and their history complicated. Few understood their relationship. They didn't care what society thought.

Leila was unlike any woman he knew. He couldn't understand why she impacted him so strongly, but he trusted his gut. He built a successful career by relying on his instincts and his unerring ability to see beyond what was obvious. In his mind's eye, he recognized raw beauty where no one else could. Aiden could be extraordinarily focused, holding still for minutes extending into hours. With exceptional talent, tenacity, and an unwavering commitment to detail, he captured unique images for the whole world to enjoy.

Now, he fixated on the intriguing Leila Solomon. Thinking back on their brief interactions, he bet his career much more existed to Leila than met the eye. She was an injured bird. Someone clipped her wings—grounding her. Gravity weighed her down. He cleared his throat. "How long have you and Mia lived here? I don't recall seeing you guys on the beach before."

"We moved in with Deena a month ago." Leila gazed at the shoreline.

His heart did a little backflip. Was she single? One way to find out existed, but he must approach with caution, or she would flee. "Just you and Mia?"

She skated her gaze across his features then connected with his. She chewed on her lower lip and nodded. "Mia's father lives on the East Coast. How about you guys? How long have you lived in Harbor House?"

Peeking at Leila's left hand, Aiden's smile grew. His imagination hadn't played tricks. She wasn't wearing a ring, and Mia's father wasn't living with them. Could he possibly be this lucky? Was Leila free? The little bird took a tiny nibble from his hand, but she wouldn't come any closer than she had to.

Perhaps if he shared more about himself and AJ, she would reciprocate. "I bought the place shortly after AJ was born. He has a congenital heart defect and respiratory problems, and he needed as much fresh air as possible." Aiden shook his head and smiled. "You should've seen the place when we bought it. The house was a wreck—a true health hazard."

Widening her eyes, she shifted her body toward him. "Really? Harbor House is stunning."

Happy he found a safe topic that interested her, he relaxed. Would she approve of the work he'd done to the inside? "Glad you like the house. Over the years, the place was ravaged in a series of storms, and the previous owners abandoned it. The house was a sad-looking heap and was losing the fight to stay upright. The paint was non-existent, the roof leaked and sagged, and the floors and deck cracked and splintered. The water damage was extensive, and mold ruled. The neighbors insisted the house be demolished."

She fully faced him, pulled up her legs on the chair, bent her knees, and wrapped her arms around them. "How did you see beyond the mess? Wouldn't buying a new place have been easier?"

"Easy isn't always best," he murmured, unable to shift his gaze from her exquisite face. "See, underneath all of the damage and havoc existed great bones, a strong foundation, and most importantly, a will to live and thrive."

"You took a great risk," Leila whispered. "Was the house worth the energy and expense?"

"Absolutely." He grinned. "Harbor House needed someone to believe in it so the house could believe in itself again. I simply looked and saw, listened and heard, felt and was touched. I took the risk, because in my heart, I knew what was underneath the surface."

"What was that?" Leila swallowed.

Aiden's pulse rate accelerated, but he kept his voice steady, and his gaze never wavered from hers. "You see, Leila, the house was neglected and bruised, but it wasn't broken. I was convinced, if I was patient and bid my time, heard what the house said, and examined what it revealed, underneath the rubble, I would discover rare and precious gifts others didn't fully understand and foolishly discarded."

Chapter Eight
Bruises

As May rolled closer to June, warm muggy air and climbing temperatures took permanent residence in Florida's Treasure Coast. While Mia and Deena slumbered, Leila stood on the deck of Breeze Bay Cottage leaning against the railing—eyes closed and body faced toward the ocean. Complements of Mother Nature, the wind, accompanied by sand, salt, and sea spray, administered her daily facial and exfoliating treatment.

Since moving in with Deena, Leila rose before the sun did. Even on weekends when she didn't work for Dr. Ash, she started her mornings at five a.m. with either a strong cup of tea and her journal or a run on the beach, depending on how many problems she needed to untangle.

Today was a rare Saturday in which she had nothing planned except a leisurely cup of tea followed by a run. She wouldn't allow herself the gift of taking flight on a long run, however, until she grew a backbone and called Gabe. Sleep eluded Leila since Thursday when she received Niveen's email.

I think I've figured out what's going on with Tante Karima. I hate to tell you this news, but I'm certain you'd never forgive me if I didn't. Over the last year, she developed high blood pressure and heart disease.

Apparently, several months ago, she suffered a mild heart attack and needs bypass surgery. She has refused all treatment. I don't know her prognosis, but without surgery, it can't be good.

Mama and all the old women have circled the wagons. They're not giving me much more data. For the best information, you know who you need to call. Nothing about Gabe has changed. I doubt he has softened where you're concerned. Although I'm still not his favorite person, you know I love you and will gladly run interference. You are stronger now, and I am confident you can stand up to the men of this family.

Since receiving the email, Leila played phone tag with Niveen. In her last voicemail, she begged Niveen not to approach Gabriel. She must confront Gabe and all her family members herself.

Dread took root in Leila's belly, and no matter how many times she tried to oust it, she failed. Although time was of the essence, she must tread carefully. Yusuf was still the patriarch. She was no longer a scared young woman in shock and in crisis. Partnered with Gabriel, Hassan, and Aziz, however, Yusuf wielded enough power to close ranks and deny her access to her mother.

Leila tilted her head and studied the hazy sky and shifting clouds. She believed God had a plan. Unfortunately, he wasn't too forthcoming with the details. Deep down, she understood what she must do. No matter her parents' actions or words, family was family. Their blood gave her life, ran through her veins, and ran through Mia's. Although they were hypocrites, they taught her to be a good person. *She* understood the value of family.

Gabriel, however, was a different story. His betrayal surprised her most and cut deepest. Leila placed a hand over her sternum and rubbed. Pain shot through her chest whenever she thought of him. At one time, she adored him and worked her ass off to help him succeed, asking nothing in return but his love and respect.

Due to low insurance reimbursement and stiff competition, Gabriel couldn't sustain a traditional medical practice in New Jersey. Taking every penny he saved, he partnered with Eric Dixon, a friend from medical school, to open Patient Centered Care, a concierge internal medicine practice for the elite of New York City. Gabe was the brains behind the operation, and Eric bankrolled the practice. He was charismatic and lured the rich and powerful.

From the second Gabriel and Eric launched their practice, Leila worked tirelessly by their side. She took extra online practice management courses and proved herself as a competent office manager. As the practice turned a profit, Gabriel sang her praises. Yusuf even threw a compliment or two her way. Under her brother's appraising eye, she blossomed. She never imagined Gabe could hurt her in the manner he had.

She opened her eyes, took a fortifying gulp of her cooling tea, and stared at the phone. With shaking hands, she dialed Gabriel's number. Most people slumbered at five a.m., but Gabriel would be driving to the hospital for morning rounds. Like her, his routine never wavered. After all this time, would he recognize her voice? Would he hang up, or had time gifted him with a forgiving heart?

"Hello, this is Dr. Solomon."

Gabriel's deep baritone voice filled her ears. Leila's breath hitched as her heart rate accelerated, and she trembled from head to toe. As memories, tender and ugly, accompanied by a variety of emotions—pain, love, longing, anger, and fear—bombarded her, she gripped the deck railing.

Time hadn't dimmed her memory of her brother. She closed her eyes and pictured him clearly—curly, black hair slicked back, olive skin, tall, and thin with a serious demeanor. At this hour, he would be clean shaven and dressed in a three-piece suit, drinking a travel cup size of Turkish coffee with cardamom, which he ground and prepared. Gabriel, like her father, uncles, and grandfather, was addicted to the potent brew.

Leila had observed Karima prepare the vile concoction many times. Using a *kanaka,* a small copper coffee pot with a long wooden handle, she mixed two teaspoons of finely ground coffee, just the right amount of water, and sugar. Over a low flame, she stirred the brew clockwise until a foamy top referred to as a *wish,* meaning face, formed. But the pièce de résistance was skillfully pouring the finished product into dainty china cups so the *wish* layered evenly over the coffee.

According to her mother, preparing Turkish coffee correctly was essential to securing a good husband and the approval of Leila's future mother-in-law. To Karima's disappointment, as well as Yusuf and Gabriel's disgust, Leila served hundreds of cups of burned bitter coffee, all lacking the essential foamy face.

"Hello, is anyone there?" Gabriel repeated.

Shaking her head, Leila forced a word passed her lips. "Gabe."

Gabriel gasped. "Who is this?"

"It's me, Gabe…" She swallowed hard. "Leila." With quivering legs resembling over-cooked noodles, she sank to the deck floor. How could he not know her? Surely he recognized her voice.

"I no longer know a Leila. She died three and a half years ago."

Gasping, she doubled over. His voice lacked any hint of emotion. She thought she was prepared for his rejection, but she was wrong. His voice was arctic while her entire body was aflame. She sucked in air and sat straighter. She would harden her heart to match his. Later, she would allow the pain to reverberate through her. Now was not the time to show weakness. She cleared her throat. "Gabe, do *not* hang up."

She needed information, and he wouldn't answer her calls again. "I don't care if you don't want to speak with me," she lied—her voice wavering and her heart breaking. "Tell me…" She blinked furiously, refusing to allow the tears to fall. "How is Mama?"

"You don't have a mother here," he snapped. "Don't call this number again. You no longer exist for us. Do you understand me?"

Did she understand? Leila ground her teeth and pushed the hair from her face. She longed to let loose and scream, "No, I don't understand you pompous, judgmental prick. How does hate replace love in a split second?" But she would lose even more ground with Gabe if she gave into hysterics. He despised emotional women.

Leila removed the pleading from her voice. Bullies responded to strength. Now was the time to stand strong and proud. "Gabriel, stop this childish behavior. I have a right to know what's happening with our mother. Hate me. I don't seek your love or approval. But don't keep me from her. I know she is ill. Tell me how she is, or…"

"Or what, Leila?" He laughed. "You're nothing to us now. I will not allow you to disrupt our lives with your soap opera lifestyle."

Filling her lungs, she gripped the deck rail and hauled up her wilted body. "Listen to me, dear brother. You no longer control me. If you don't give me the information I'm asking for, I promise I will come to Jersey tonight. You and *Baba* will no longer keep your dirty little secret hidden in the shadows of the family tree. I will even attend church and make sure everyone knows I have a child out of wedlock. *Tell me* what is wrong with Mama."

"Don't threaten me, you little tramp. You have no right to ask for anything," he bellowed. "Getting over you has taken her years. Show up at our door, and we will spit in your face, kick you, and wipe our feet on you."

Agony ripped through Leila's belly. How could he be so cruel? Where was the sweet boy who teased and tickled her when she was a child? Did no part of the loving man who spoiled her with little gifts and played backgammon for hours exist? "Gabe…"

"Don't say another word," he barked. "You almost killed her. She cries for you every holiday and birthday. I won't have you raining down more pain and shame at the end of her days. Leave us alone, and go back to your own life—the world you gave up your family for." He took a deep breath. "Is life on the outside without your morals and beliefs worth everyone and everything you lost?"

Before she answered, silence filled her ears. If he waited a second more, he'd have heard her answer because he asked the one question she could definitively answer. Yes. God, yes. Mia was worth every second of agony, shame, groveling, and tongue-lashing. If she lived the rest of her life without her family, on her deathbed, she would answer in the same way.

Long after Gabriel hung up, Leila huddled on a deck chair—knees to chest and arms wound around them. Eventually, anger kicked in. What did she expect? Nothing changed—not for Gabriel and most likely not for her father. Unbelievable. Leila's family and extended family lived in the United States for decades and were proud naturalized Americans. While they gained an understanding and an appreciation for the culture and assimilated well, they maintained their cultural heritage.

Yusuf was a difficult man. Everyone in the family accepted this fact. He flew the American flag and was proud of his citizenship status. However, he wasn't just the patriarch, he was a bully. His beliefs were the only ones that mattered, and he possessed opinions on every topic—politics, religion, marriage, child-rearing, etc. His name could have been Bob, Larry, or Henry—his heritage had nothing to do with his unsavory personality.

Often, he flew into rages lasting hours. Occasionally, a priest from their parish arrived to calm him. For the most part, the Solomons rode out the storm behind closed doors because what happened behind those doors was no one else's business. Family was family. Outsiders weren't welcome.

Sighing, Leila stood. Now, more than ever, she was determined to penetrate the Solomon stronghold and break the silence once and for all. She needed a plan.

Ten minutes later, dressed in running gear, Leila stretched on the beach. She took deep cleansing breaths, sweeping her arms from her sides to above her head in a long stretch. She gazed at the blue Atlantic and cleared her mind, focusing on her breathing, the crashing of the waves against the shoreline, and the cries of the seagulls as they rode the wind then swooped to catch their breakfast. She envied their freedom and longed to join them—defy gravity and live wild and free.

Her fascination with flight began when she was in middle school. One time, she dreamed she awoke in the middle of the night. Her family was deep in slumber. Rising, she slid on her slippers and robe and threw open her bedroom window. She glanced at the full moon and swore it smiled and winked. Taking a deep breath, she held it and was immediately weightless.

Like in the children's story, *Peter Pan*, she floated above her bed, out her bedroom window, and into the dark night—her every action illuminated by her new friend, the moon. Without fear, she glided over her house. She glanced below to the dilapidated homes peppering her Jersey City neighborhood. Except for the sounds of the night creatures and the wind rustling through the trees, silence reigned.

For the first time in her life, Leila was free. No one held her down, told her what to do, how to act, or what to wear. In the darkness, with the moon and the stars as her companions, she was accepted, safe, and deliriously happy. She glided over the city, visiting new and exciting places. Under the veil of darkness, she danced, performed cartwheels, and back flips then threw back her head and laughed. This freeing dream recurred often and continued well into adulthood.

When she was in high school, she wrote a paper about dreams. After hours of research, she discovered her dream signified her deep desire to be free—escape from the reality and the pressures of daily life. Flying dreams and the ability of the dreamer to control the flight represented a personal sense of power.

She understood how different she was from her family members. Although she loved her people and their traditions, she felt suffocated and marginalized. They, however, were contented and fulfilled within the strict confines of the Middle Eastern culture. A middle ground must exist. To thrive, she would break free from the chains holding her down without losing her family's love. Her dreams were her only escape, helping her tolerate the oppression of the life she had been born into.

The screeching of the seagulls overhead startled Leila. Time to take flight the only way she could. She set a pace and allowed her muscles, bones, and nerves to take over as her brain negotiated the intricate twists and turns of her life. As she ran, she took in steady breaths and exhaled, focusing on her form, stride length, and pace. While her heart urged her to buy a ticket on the next plane to Jersey, her brain advocated for sensibility. She didn't have money to waste. She must strategize.

Leila clenched her jaw. Gabriel left her no choice but to contact her aunts. She hated involving the entire family again in what was sure to be the new family drama starring her and Mia. *Tante* Amal was most approachable. She shook out her fists.

Deep in thought, she looked down and noted a shadow of a jogger keeping pace beside her. Gasping, she whipped her head to the side, and found Aiden Stone—grinning. Losing her rhythm, she tripped over her feet. Before she face-planted, she was grabbed by strong arms that wrapped around her waist and pulled her firmly against a hard, sweaty chest.

Aiden stumbled and swayed but managed to keep upright, laughing as he did so.

Flustered and panting, Leila pivoted in his arms. Laying her palms against his muscular chest, she looked into his eyes. "Oh God, I'm sorry. I didn't notice you jogging next to me. Thanks for catching me. That would've been a nasty fall."

Smiling, Aiden swept a sweaty curl off her cheek, tucking it behind her ear. "Don't worry, beautiful. I've got you. Rest assured, I'd *never* let you fall."

Leila froze, and her breath hitched as she registered the promise in his words and the sincerity in his eyes. Her brain, however, shunned what her heart longed to feel. In her head, a self-authored mantra played on repeat.

Men should not be trusted. Scornful words and empty promises that woo a woman into believing she was special came from their mouths. Clasped around her wrists, their hands would be shackles, weighing her down, and forcing her into submission. Without reason or warning, those unyielding hands would lash out, leaving a permanent mark on a woman's heart, long after the bruise faded.

Chapter Nine
Rapunzel

Flustered, sweaty, and dressed in black running shorts and an oversized T-shirt, Leila Solomon was breath-taking. But as usual, Aiden somehow embarrassed her. She turned a lovely shade of rose. Tendrils of hair loosened from her ponytail, and curls stuck to her neck and face.

As Aiden stretched, readying to start his daily run, he spotted Leila jogging past Harbor House, and for the last ten minutes, he trailed her. He was surprised when she didn't notice him. She was lost in her own world.

"Uhm, I'm good now. You can let go." Leila pushed against his chest.

He couldn't take his gaze off her. Enjoying the feel of her soft body, he was tempted to hold her a little longer, but she was uncomfortable in his presence. Since their conversation on the beach a few days ago, he often thought of her. He wanted to know her better, but she excelled at erecting roadblocks. Aiden wasn't thwarted easily.

Normally, Aiden was confident around women, but in Leila's presence, he was uncertain. He second-guessed himself, measuring every step and reconsidering every word. On the beach, she was comfortable with Tyra and AJ, sliding easily in and out of conversation, laughing, and joking. Yet, when she was on her own, she rarely held his gaze and tripped over her words. Was she uncomfortable with all men or just him? He wouldn't be surprised if he was the problem.

The Stone men were cursed where women were concerned. The curse went as far back as his great-great-grandfather. The usual stories of separated soulmates and broken hearts littered his family history. Ridiculous tales of men who lost their fortunes and their minds when their beloveds ran off with the grocer, mailman, or, in the case of his mother, his father's best friend and business partner also existed.

Leila cleared her throat and pushed once again against his chest.

Blinking, Aiden steadied her then stepped back. "I'm sorry I startled you. I've jogged behind you since you passed Harbor House."

Peering over his shoulder, Leila raised an eyebrow. "Wow, I didn't realize I ran so far. I didn't hear you behind me." She smoothed hair off her cheeks and forehead then gathered her ponytail. Attempting to release her thick, tangled curls, she struggled with the hair-tie. "I get a little caught up in my thoughts when I run. I guess zoning out isn't safe, but I can't help myself."

Leila's hair hung half-way down her back. Those thick, curly ropes reminded him of black licorice—his favorite candy. Her big hazel eyes, combined with her petite stature and all that gorgeous hair, painted a picture of a vulnerable young woman. However, she radiated strength, especially when Mia was near. Hidden beneath her delicate beauty was the courage and fortitude of a mama bear. She adored her baby girl, and he was certain she would single-handedly battle an army of hungry lions, tigers, and bears to protect her.

Why was every woman in his life so damn complicated? Aiden smiled.

As she worked to unknot her hair, the wind picked up, and her curls took flight in every possible direction. "Nothing like being attacked by your own hair," Leila muttered, as she grabbed handfuls of glorious runaway strands. "One day, I'll cut off all this mess. I hear bald is beautiful."

"Cutting all that glory would be a shame." He chuckled. "Do you need help?"

She shook her head. "No, I'm used to this disaster. I should've braided my hair before I started my run. The wind is fierce today." She gathered her hair, combed her fingers through it, and split it into three sections.

Fascinated, he shook his head. "That's quite a skill you have. I don't think I've ever seen fingers move so quickly. Very impressive, Rapunzel."

"Rapunzel?" Leila knitted her brows.

"You must have read the fairy tale when you were a kid?" He smirked. " 'Rapunzel, Rapunzel, let down your hair.' "

She shook her head. "Hmm, I'm afraid I've never read that fairy tale. When I was a child, my parents regaled me with stories about the Pharaohs and the secrets of the pyramids and sphinx. Although I was born in the United States shortly after my family immigrated from Egypt, I led a pretty sheltered life. My parents were more familiar with Egyptian folklore than American fairy tales. But Mia loves fairy tales." She shrugged. "Guess we haven't come across that one yet."

"Well, one day we will remedy that problem. Where did you learn to braid?"

"Braiding isn't complicated." She shrugged. "I've been braiding since I was a child. My mother taught me out of necessity, and I grew up with a zillion cousins. We used to hold competitions for the fastest braider or the most intricate design. You should see my French braiding skills. I'm a master."

Leila's smile lit her entire face. Aiden's heart tripped over itself, and his brain stuttered. Her smile was exquisite. Unlike the previous imposters, this smile originated in her heart, traveled to her face and eyes, curved up her bow-shaped lips, and radiated from her entire being—outshining the dazzling Florida sun.

Now was his chance to find out more about her. Speaking about her family made her happy. He cleared his throat. "A zillion cousins, huh. Does your family live close?"

Her smile faded, and her shoulders sagged. "No, that life was a long time ago—different time and place." She hung her head and stepped back. "Well, nice to see you again, but I should head back."

Aiden ran a hand through his sweaty hair. Leila was a sophisticated labyrinth built on thin ice. He was in constant danger of slipping into frigid waters. But he loved puzzles of every kind, and wasn't ready to let her go.

Why did her sudden sadness tug at his heartstrings? He was determined to reproduce her rarely sighted but captivating smile. He needed to tempt his little bird with an irresistible morsel before she flew off to higher, unreachable ground. "I'm ready to head back, too. Stop by Harbor House, and I'll give you a tour."

"A tour?" She frowned and cocked her head to the side.

"You're interested in the house, and you'll pass right by." He shrugged. "Stop in for a cup of coffee and a donut unless you have to get back to Mia right away."

"Um. Well, I…" Shifting from foot to foot, she glanced everywhere but at him. "Mia and Deena are probably asleep, but…"

"But?" He tilted his head and smiled. She wavered too much and left him no choice but to pull out the big guns. Few resisted what he offered next.

"Maybe another time would be better." She chewed on her lower lip. "I hate to walk in on Tyra without warning. Won't she be asleep?"

"Tyra? Asleep? At this hour?" Aiden shook his head and chuckled. "No way. She and AJ were up before I left. By now, they're probably on their way back with a couple dozen Good God Donuts. You've heard of Good God, haven't you?"

"Are you kidding?" Leila grinned. "Of course, I've heard of them. I'm not dead. Their donuts are like crack. I'm addicted to their Creamy Goodness donut, as is everyone else. Mia and I rarely arrive at the shop early enough to find the good stuff. People around here are crazy. Adoring fans form a mile-long line in front of the shop every Saturday morning."

"Well, Ms. Solomon. Today is your lucky donut day." He rubbed his hands together. "I can provide your next fix—no lines, no hassle. Silas, the owner, loves AJ. His son, Miles, also has Down syndrome and attends the same school. Silas keeps a special stash of the good stuff for us."

Leila played with the ends of her braid and licked

her lips.

"Give in, Rapunzel." Aiden smirked, pleased he discovered her weakness. "You know you want to. I'll even send you home with sweet treats for my friend, Mia."

"You're sure Tyra won't mind?" She glanced in the direction of the house then back.

"Not at all." He shook his head. "She and AJ will be happy to see you. I promise."

"Uhm…well, okay." She nodded. "Just for a little while."

Aiden performed a silent cheer. He won round one at Wimbledon. Using herculean efforts, he schooled his features, aiming for a casual tone. "Great. Let's go. The donuts wait for no one." He turned in the direction of the house.

"Ah, Aiden?"

He dug his heals in the sand, took a deep breath, and pivoted, raising an eyebrow.

She scrunched her nose. "No coffee. That stuff is vile, and I demand a Creamy Goodness *and* a Strawberry Sunshine donut."

He relaxed his shoulders, and a smile stretched across his face. Rapunzel liked to play. "No Death by Chocolate?"

"Ick." Leila shuddered. "No chocolate donut. No chocolate anything…ever. But I must be guaranteed the others before I move."

"I don't think I've ever met anyone who didn't like chocolate." Grinning, he shrugged. "Fine, more for me and AJ. You're weird."

"Whatever." Leila held up two fingers. "Promise me the Goodness and the Sunshine, and we have a deal."

"A Creamy Goodness *and* a Strawberry Sunshine, huh?" He rubbed his chin and frowned. "You understand those donuts are highly coveted. If you insist on both, you should earn them."

Leila huffed and stomped her foot.

She resembled her daughter, and Aiden burst out laughing.

"Earn them. Uh-uh." She shook her head. "You're the one who invited me, promising endless donuts and a Goodness goody bag to take home." She placed her hands on her hips and glared. "Are you reneging?"

"Rapunzel, Rapunzel." He smirked. "I think you're afraid of a little competition. I thought I sensed an inner warrior, but perhaps I was mistaken. Stop pouting and buck up, woman. Whoever gets to the house first gets the Goodness." He took off in the direction of home. "Don't let all that hair hold you back. You might be cute, but I'm not cutting you any slack. The stakes are high," he called over his shoulder.

By the time they arrived at Harbor House, Aiden and Leila laughed and were out of breath. Leila did well keeping up. But to keep the triumphant smile on her face, at the end, he let her run a few steps ahead.

Panting, she collapsed at the bottom of the steps leading to the deck.

He sat next to her and removed his running shoes.

Wheezing, Leila glanced up the stairs. "I can't climb those stairs." She groaned. "Toss down my winnings."

"Come on, lazy bones." He pulled her to stand. "Only fifty-three steps lead to the deck and pool. I go up and down these stairs ten times a day for a little cardio." He smirked. "Ty, AJ, and almost everyone else we know love my castle in the sky but hate my beloved stairs. Surely, you're not a hater, too?"

Leila scowled as she slowly followed him, grumbling all the way until she reached the deck.

The patio door opened, and AJ raced out. "Daddy. We gots do…" He froze, focusing on Leila. His smile widened. "Hi, Lala." He peered around her. "Mia?"

"Hello, Brave Boy." Leila crouched. "You know, someone very special also calls me Lala. I love that name."

AJ shrugged. "Want Mia. Where's she?"

"I'm sorry I couldn't bring her. Mia's sleeping. Can I have a hug, though? I've missed your beautiful smile." She opened her arms.

Leaping into her embrace, he wrapped his arms around her neck and legs around her waist. AJ laid his head on her shoulder, closed his eyes, and sighed.

Leila kissed the top of his head and stood. For a few seconds, she swayed back and forth, whispering in his ear.

Right then, Aiden Stone lost a small piece of his heart to Leila Solomon. If she promised to continue holding his baby boy in that tender manner, he would gladly give her the rest of his heart. Shocked at his ludicrous thoughts, he broke out in a sweat once again. AJ might have fallen for the dark-haired fairy who appeared out of nowhere, but Aiden wasn't as gullible. He gave himself a mental slap. At most, he was infatuated or maybe in lust with Leila. But he wasn't a romantic—not any more.

For a brief period of time, he believed he loved Gina. Now, he wasn't sure he believed in love or marriage. People who entered the institution of marriage should be institutionalized. Most couples grew apart and ran from their commitments and promises, leaving a trail of misery in their wake.

AJ tugged on Leila's braid, and they giggled.

The ocean breeze cooled Aiden's flushed skin. His breath stuttered. Perhaps he should reconsider everything he understood about affairs of the heart. Could an old, wounded dog learn a new trick or two?

Leila was a beauty on the outside. Despite his lack of objective evidence, he was also one hundred percent certain she was exquisite on the inside. He didn't need evidence, because his gut was a finely tuned instrument. Every fiber of his being surged to be near her. The problem was, she was anything but easy. Did he really need more challenges in his life?

AJ wiggled in her arms until she put him down. He grinned and grabbed her hand. "Want donuts?"

"Sure do. Do you have any Creamy Goodness? Those are my favorite."

"Yup. Four." AJ held up two fingers on each hand. "You can have one." He dragged her toward the deck door, pointing out the hot tub and the pool, explaining he was a good swimmer, but he wasn't allowed on the deck without his daddy or Mama Ty. At the door, AJ released her hand and ran inside, shouting for Tyra.

Leila paused and turned toward Aiden, biting her lower lip. "Are you certain Tyra won't mind me barging into her home on a Saturday morning?"

"Relax." He shook his head. "She's probably dressing for work." He glanced at his watch. "Soon, you'll witness Tyra in action. It's a sight you shouldn't miss. She'll fly down the stairs wearing some outrageous outfit, grab two donuts, and a disgusting, slimy green shake from the fridge. She'll shove each donut in her mouth in two bites, wash them down with the putrid drink, and run out the door—her braids flying behind her."

"But…"

Smiling, Aiden grabbed her hand. "Come on, Lala. No buts. I promised you donuts, and I always keep my promises."

Leila tugged at their joined hands. "No…wait." She swallowed hard. "I shouldn't be here," she whispered. "You're, well. You're…" She regarded their joined hands, frowned, and yanked her hand from his.

Confused, Aiden held up his hands and stepped back. Leila chewed on her lip so much, it was seconds from bleeding. Her eyes darkened to a deep olive. He shook his head. What set her off this time? He rubbed his forehead. "Leila, look…"

"No, I'm sorry. I have to go. Say hi to Tyra for me." She shuffled past him.

Enough was enough. He ran a hand through his hair. If she insisted on leaving, he wouldn't stop her. He treaded carefully, kept conversation light, and did everything he could to make her comfortable. He wouldn't run after someone who was hot then cold and struggled with some elusive obstacle. Frustrated and more than a little embarrassed for chasing a woman who wasn't interested, he turned and followed AJ. Perhaps his gut was screwed up, and he needed one of Tyra's slime smoothies.

One foot in the house, he peered over his shoulder. Leila descended the first few steps and sat—head down and shoulders sagging. The defeated picture her tiny,

Mona Sedrak

huddled form portrayed against the backdrop of the churning sea and the rising sun in the distance froze him in his tracks. Waves crashed, and seagulls cried out to one another across the deserted white sandy beach—their missive plaintive and chiding.

Aiden rubbed the back of his neck. Damn it. He couldn't abandon his skittish, incredibly infuriating little bird. He wanted to bang his head against the deck door. Why was he so drawn to her—pulled into her atmosphere against his will and his better judgment? Expelling a low growl, he stalked across the deck and dropped to the top step.

Straightening her spine, she squared her shoulders.

"Don't run. Talk to me. What's going on here?"

Slowly, she turned.

Her eyes were dark and stormy—filled with confusion.

"I'm sorry if I gave you the wrong impression. I didn't mean to flirt, and I need you to stop flirting, as well. You're married, and I…"

Eyes wide, he gasped. "I'm what?" He lifted his left hand to eye level and stared. Nope. He wasn't insane. No wedding band wrapped around his ring finger, and no suspicious tan line existed either. "Married? I'm not married," he sputtered.

"Whatever. In a relationship then." She glared.

Aiden leapt to his feet. "Tyra is…"

"Tyra is a lovely woman, and I'm not a home-wrecker." Leila stood, gripped the wooden banister with one hand, and placed her other hand on her hip. "And God, you have a beautiful family. Are you crazy? Why would you jeopardize your family? I would give anything to have all that beauty."

"Leila…"

"No." She raised a hand. "Stop. Go find someone else if you insist on screwing up your life. Family is everything. You'd be a fool to throw away all that happy. But if you insist on destroying your life, count me out."

Not all, but much of her behavior now made sense. He clenched his jaw. Looking back at all their interactions he understood, her assumption he was married or in a relationship was plausible. Glancing at his feet, he took deep, fortifying breaths. The fact Leila assumed he was a cheater and thought little of him stung. But she didn't know him, and she jumped to logical conclusions. Perhaps events in her past influenced her thinking. Did Mia's father cheat on Leila? Perhaps Leila's father cheated on her mother? If Aiden planned to have an affair, why on earth would he bring her to his home where his supposed wife resided?

He didn't know if he should invest time and energy in a relationship with Leila and prove not all men were cheating bastards or let her walk away. If he pursued a relationship, he would be forced to clean up the mess someone else left behind. Her experience with men was tainted. He had attempted to fix one damaged woman and failed. In the end, he was the one left bruised and broken. Was she worth the work and the risk to his own beat-up organ?

When Leila entered Aiden's life, the part of his heart that withered from a lack of blood supply suddenly sprouted new tributaries. Energized, his heart beat stronger and at an alarming pace each time he was in her presence. His wayward heart demanded he stop his neglect and take notice.

Leila swallowed hard and met his gaze. "I'm not worth the risk, Aiden. Actually, no one is worth throwing away your precious family. Don't be foolish."

Studying her, he sighed. He wasn't afraid of hard work. In fact, he reveled in it. But over the years, he learned a thing or two. Some miracles couldn't be forced or rushed to the surface. If you wished to experience heaven on Earth, you had to do the work— pack for a long-assed trip, travel to where you first sighted that wonder, unpack, set up camp, and sit your ass down. Get comfortable, but stay vigilant because the wait for beauty to reveal itself was unpredictable.

Few things in the world were worth the sacrifice and the toll the wait took on the heart and spirit. Now, as he scrutinized the earnest woman before him pleading for him to be a good and faithful man, he was fairly certain Leila was worthy. Aiden wouldn't force his way into her world. After he cleared up some pretty insulting assumptions, he'd go about his tried-and-true routine. He'd unload, grab a beer, and sit his ass down, praying his actions, if not his words, convinced her of his character.

"Are you done?" He cleared his throat. "Are you ready to listen, or will you continue building a protective wall of assumptions and accusations that will tumble the second you allow me to speak? I'm willing to scale the castle walls, Rapunzel. But are you brave enough to meet me halfway? Will you let down your hair?"

Chapter Ten
Revelations

Open-mouthed, Leila stared. Castle walls? Assumptions? Accusations? Rapunzel? What the hell was he talking about? Why was she still standing on Aiden's deck, entertaining what was sure to be a well-crafted story?

Closing her eyes, she shook her head. She must get a grip and go home before she made a bigger fool of herself, falling for a sob story as millions of women did each year. Once, she was stupid and didn't stop to consider the ramifications of her actions. Now, she was older, wiser, and much more cautious.

Deena believed Leila was too cautious for her own good. After Deena met Tyra and Aiden on the beach, she was adamant they weren't romantically involved. But Leila wasn't convinced. After all, Aiden and Tyra lived under the same roof, were affectionate, and AJ called Tyra, *Mama*.

A healthy dose of reality and a tsunami of guilt and shame crashed into Leila. Karima's voice echoed in her ears—a warning. *Decent women don't flirt, throw themselves at men, or pursue other women's men. Never cheapen yourself, Leila. Once you do, you will be untouchable.* Swaying, Leila opened her eyes and tightened her grip on the wooden banister.

"Are you okay?" Aiden grasped her elbow,

steadying her.

She gulped. His usually playful liquid gold eyes darkened to the color of the cognac Deena enjoyed on occasion. Leila wished she was more experienced with men. What was the man thinking? She was nothing special—short with too many curves in the wrong places, crazy hair with a mind of its own, and a ridiculous amount of baggage.

Aiden confused and threw her off balance. Since the second she witnessed him swaying with his son on this deck two weeks ago, she was captivated. Perhaps she was drawn to the picture of the doting father and family? God, how he tempted her to throw caution to the wind.

"Come on." Aiden squeezed her elbow. "Sit with me for a few minutes, and give me a chance to explain."

Unmoving, Leila studied him.

"Be brave, Leila." Aiden smiled. "You don't know me. Don't make assumptions. *You* wouldn't wish to be treated in a judgmental manner. Would you?" He quirked an eyebrow.

She widened her eyes. How did he discover her every weakness? First, the donuts and now, the concept of judgment. Her past was filled with intolerance and castigation. Had she learned nothing? She nodded and followed him to the deck chairs. She sat across from him with her arms wrapped around herself, preparing to listen then leave.

Even if she was wrong about him and Tyra, she wasn't ready to be in a relationship. She and Aiden led complicated lives, and their children depended on them to make good choices. She couldn't afford to screw up again.

One day, Leila would explain to Mia why her daddy wasn't in her life. Every time she thought of the conversation, a wave of nausea hit her. Soon, she would devise an age-appropriate answer based in reality but as far from the truth as possible. If she allowed Aiden in her life, she would need to explain him, as well.

"Look at me, Leila," he commanded.

She focused on him, fascinated by the variety of emotions skating across his features. She expected to see anger or cunning but was surprised to find frustration but also understanding.

"I'm not married, nor have I ever been." Aiden drew in a deep breath and released it. "Tyra is obviously not AJ's mother. She and I are not a couple. How we came to live with each other is a long story for another day."

Relief washed over Leila, and her shoulders sagged. Questions raced through her mind. She pursed her lips. Aiden didn't have to explain. Although he could have let her walk away, he made the effort to right the assumptions she made. The sincerity etched in every inch of his face, and his straightforward, no bullshit manner, left her with one conclusion. Nausea roiled in her belly. She was a judgmental idiot.

Leila wore an ancient set of eyeglasses she owned since childhood. Ill-fitting and scratched, they skewed her vision. Still, she utilized those defective lenses to gather facts, catalog evidence, make assumptions, jump to conclusions, and launch accusations. She despised people who behaved in this manner, and now she acted the same.

In her defense, in the Middle Eastern culture,

single men and women didn't live under the same roof, playing house and being just good friends. Those types of living arrangements and relationships were unorthodox and unacceptable. Families came in differing combinations of shapes, sizes, and colors. She needed to widen and refocus her lens, stretching beyond her cultural teachings. Leila swallowed hard. "I'm sor—"

"Uh-uh." He shook his head. "I let you talk, and now you'll hear me out. You don't know me, but if you did, you would know two things. Although I've made my share of mistakes, and I'm sure I'll make plenty more, I don't lie or cheat. Now, you can either believe me or not. The choice is yours."

Hurt was evident in Aiden's voice. Leila winced. A knot formed in her belly, and she pressed a hand to her midsection. She wanted to explain and apologize, but where did she begin? He thought his story with Tyra was long? Well, her life story spanning her twenty-nine years would fill an encyclopedia. Once she read him the first few pages, no apologies would be necessary. If he was sane, and she was certain he was, he'd take his sweet boy and flee. "I'm sorry, Aiden."

"I like you, and I think you feel the same about me." Aiden ran hand through his hair. "I'd like to know you and Mia better, but I won't apologize for the way I choose to live. But you would have to take a tiny risk, drop your guard, and trust me a little." Smiling, he stood. "Now, I'm going in before my boy takes a bite out of each donut. If you decide to come inside, you are most welcome. If not, I'll be disappointed."

Leila licked her lips and nodded.

He stepped toward the patio door.

"Aiden?"

Twisting, he raised an eyebrow.

"You said I needed to know two things." She tilted her head. "What's the second?"

He smiled, took a step back, and met her gaze. "I'm a fairly easygoing guy, but I have my quirks. One of them is my persistence. When I see something I desire, I go after it with relentless tunnel vision and focus. I chase the elusive. Often, others can't see what I do, or they're simply not brave enough to take risks, defy gravity, and uncover and unleash what's hidden. But do you know what I find each and every time I trust my gut, put in the time, and do the work?"

"What?" she whispered, entranced by his voice and his molten eyes.

"Heart stopping, raw, wild, and unimaginable beauty." Aiden grinned. "I'm a landscape photographer. Photography is not only what I do. Photography is also who I am. Through the lens of my camera, I see what others think only exists in dreams and movies. I believe. I commit. If you decide to come inside, I'll show you what I'm talking about." He spun and strode toward the door.

Aiden said his piece and issued a challenge. Leila could walk away or cross the threshold and take a chance, praying this time her heart wasn't trampled. She chewed on her lower lip. Even if she walked away, Aiden wouldn't. The man would track her down.

Standing, Leila paced. She was out of her element—stuck between two worlds. Too Americanized, she didn't fit into the Egyptian culture. Yet, she wasn't American enough. Leila spoke Arabic with an American accent and spoke English with an

Arabic accent. She rarely felt comfortable in her own skin. But the more she denied her heritage, the more lost she was.

She searched her heart and mind, drawing on any past experiences to guide her through this new endeavor with Aiden. She had led a sheltered life. As a teen, she never dated and possessed few male friends. Even as a young adult, she was closely guarded and spent every moment not at school or at work with family.

Her parents did her a huge disservice. When Mia's father set his sight on her, he didn't need an intricate trap. Leila was ripe for a disaster of the heart. She lacked experience with men and wasn't prepared for a wolf in sheep's clothing. She fell for the first handsome man who didn't fear Yusuf and showered her with attention.

Most of Leila's Middle Eastern girlfriends were dating or engaged in their early twenties. But no man in her close-knit community dared to speak to her. Yusuf's reputation was well-known, and no one wished to deal with his explosive temper. Leila recalled the sheer joy of tumbling down the rabbit hole of love. She floated through the day, believing every word he said and glowing under his appraising gaze. Butterflies danced in her belly when he brushed by, and for the first time in her life, she experienced desire, lust…infatuation.

Leila's people didn't believe experience led to knowledge, and knowledge was empowering. The justifications for their actions were flawed and lacked logic. Teaching a young person about condoms and safe sex condoned sexual activity. Allowing girls to wear bikinis, shorts, or mini-skirts led to promiscuous behaviors and encouraged unwelcome male attention.

Allowing a young woman to use tampons meant she was no longer a virgin and ruined her chances for a good marriage.

Shaking her head, Leila turned toward the patio door and took a hesitant step. She and Aiden were raised in different worlds. What would he think if she opened up and let him into her muddled world? He admitted he was quirky, but the extent of *her* quirks would shock him. Would Aiden run once she confided in him? Could she take the chance with her and Mia's hearts?

She tilted her head to the now-dazzling blue sky and closed her eyes. "What should I do, Mama? I know he's not Middle Eastern, and he will have difficulty understanding our ways, but I sense he is a good man. I've been on my own for a long time. Help me. Speak to me."

Follow your heart. Be brave. Those words played on repeat in Leila's mind. She said a prayer for strength and opened her eyes. A strange, yet wonderful, peace washed over her. Her pulse accelerated, sending a dose of unfettered excitement and joy whooshing through her arteries and veins. Today was the first day of a new and exciting life. She took a deep breath, and on wobbly legs, she strode across the deck, opened the patio door, and stepped across the threshold.

Aiden stood at the kitchen sink. He peered over his shoulder, and for a few seconds, his gaze held hers.

At first, Leila's smile was hesitant, then it grew until she grinned.

His answering smile stretched wide. "Ready for a donut?"

Nodding, she closed the patio door. Red oak

hardwood floors, gleaming white cabinets, aqua marble countertops, and an enormous kitchen island made up the massive kitchen. Two boxes of Good God Donuts sat on the kitchen island.

"What would you like to drink? Juice or milk?" Aiden opened a massive, stainless-steel refrigerator door. "I can also offer you a slimy green shake. I have no idea what Tyra puts into the concoction, but in all honesty, the sludge is the most disgusting stuff I've ever smelled or tasted. Drink at your own risk." He looked over his shoulder and grinned.

His beautiful smile complete with dimples caused her heart to flutter. She shook her head and scrunched her nose. "The green goo sounds tempting, but I'll pass. Do you have hot tea?"

"That, I can handle. Grab a donut and make yourself at home. Look around. AJ's watching TV in the family room, and Tyra should be down in about ten minutes."

Grabbing a donut, she surveyed her surroundings. The kitchen with its small, eat-in nook opened onto a large dining and family room. Hypnotized by Saturday morning cartoons, AJ sprawled on the floor munching on a donut. He briefly glanced up when she passed. Chocolate covered his face. He flashed an adorable toothy grin then turned back to his show.

Leila wandered from room to room. Coffered ceilings and stacked crown molding provided a sense of elegance. A neutral palette with pops of blues and greens, accentuated the ocean view, making the rooms comfortable and inviting. Photographs covered the walls.

Spellbound, she strolled from photo to photo,

studying landscapes from all over the world. Oceans, volcanoes, jungles, forests, and waterfalls surrounded her. All were stunning masterpieces with magnificent displays of vivid colors—bold and provocative. She was ensnared and entranced.

Meandering back to the family room, she stopped in front of a floor-to-ceiling bookshelf dedicated to family photos. AJ was in almost every shot—laying in Tyra's arms or lap as an infant and playing ball or fishing with Aiden. In several photos, AJ played with a man who shared Aiden's eye color and dimpled cheeks. A few pictures included all three members of the Stone family—Aiden, AJ, and Tyra.

"There you are."

Leila jumped, banging her elbow against the bookshelf. "Owh." She clutched her elbow and rubbed it.

"Easy, Rapunzel." Aiden placed her mug of tea on a nearby table and chuckled. Holding her elbow, he rubbed it with his thumb. "I didn't mean to startle you. I seem to have a knack for catching you off guard. I have to discover a better way of transporting you back to the present when you're lost in thought that doesn't cause either of us bodily harm." He bent and gently kissed her elbow.

Leila ceased breathing. Her face flushed and pulse raced.

"All better?" Aiden released her.

She nodded. Flustered, Leila picked up a small photograph. Baby AJ lay in a hospital bassinet. His tiny, delicate fingers clutched one of Aiden's. Father and son stared into each other's eyes. The expression of adoration and protectiveness on Aiden's face brought tears to Leila's eyes. *Baby Stone* was written in block letters at the foot of the bassinet.

"Did you take these pictures?" she asked in a husky voice.

Aiden took the photograph from her hand. "All but this one. Tyra snapped this photo on the day we brought AJ home from the hospital, six weeks after he was born."

"Um, can I ask you something?" She bit her lower lip.

"You can ask me anything." He smiled. "I'll always answer you truthfully."

Leila peered at AJ who lay on the carpet mesmerized by his show then she met Aiden's gaze. "Okay, but don't feel pressured to answer if the question is too personal."

He nodded.

"Where's AJ's mother?" She shifted from foot to foot. "I don't see her in any of these pictures."

Aiden's smile fell, and his jaw hardened. For a few seconds, he broke eye contact then focused on her once more. "Let's sit in the kitchen while you drink your tea, and we can chat." He grabbed her hand and towed her behind him. When he was seated, he concentrated on his coffee mug. "All the people that matter to me in the world are in those pictures." He lifted his chin toward the family room. "My brother, Matt, Tyra, and AJ. Gina, AJ's biological mother, has never been a part of his life. She walked out when he was three weeks old and never returned."

She couldn't conceive of a mother abandoning her sick, possibly dying, child. Leila's heart ached for AJ and Aiden. What kind of person was Gina? "I'm so sorry." She laid a hand on Aiden's forearm and squeezed.

"Thanks, but don't be." He shrugged. "She did us a favor." After a few seconds of silence, he took a deep breath and raised his gaze. "My turn?" he asked, tilting his head to the side.

Aiden answered her questions, and she would answer his. She wasn't ready to tell him everything, but she would share a morsel of her past. Would he think poorly of her when he learned she was a single mother who never married? She didn't think so, but the butterflies in her stomach taking flight made her queasy. She swallowed past the nausea and pushed out the words. "I'm not married and never was. I'm also not in a relationship. Mia's father is not and has never been in her life."

"And your family?" He frowned.

She hesitated, glancing away for a few seconds as she chose her words carefully. "For several years, I've been lost to them and they to me. Where once my village was large, loud, and colorful, now, all the people who I can depend on and who love Mia and me can be counted on one hand."

Mona Sedrak

Chapter Eleven
Blessings

"Aiden, I've left you several messages and emails. I understand I'm not your favorite person, and you might not want to deal with me, but I won't give up. Call me. We need to talk."

Without a second's hesitation, Aiden erased the message on the Gallery's answering machine and fought the urge to launch the device across the office as he had his camera. Each time Gina's voice penetrated his brain or he read her emails, he froze, his pulse accelerating and pressure built in his head. A stroke was imminent. He fought to control his physical response, but he failed miserably. Why couldn't this woman take a hint?

Regularly, he deleted Gina's emails, voicemails, and ignored the messages she left with his assistant. Tyra claimed his behavior was childish. But what did he and Gina have to talk about? For some twisted reason, she insisted on seeing AJ and disrupting his carefully ordered world. No way in hell would Aiden allow her to do so. Gina wasn't AJ's mother. She'd been the incubator giving him life, keeping him safe and warm, and she did a shitty job of that task.

Festive music filled the room, jolting back Aiden to the present before he slipped further into anger and despair. With growing anticipation, he looked forward to this day for the last week, and he wouldn't allow Gina to dampen his excitement. If she persisted, he would be forced to deal with her, but he was determined to enjoy the day.

The Saturday of Memorial Day weekend was always busy with tourists and locals flooding the Vero Beach Art District. Strolling along the dock straddling the mighty Atlantic, people stopped to have lunch at one of the many delectable eateries while listening to live music as band after band played on the makeshift stage at one end of the dock.

The Vero Beach street party was a much-awaited kickoff to the summer season. The event was always celebratory, especially when the weather cooperated, and Leila and Mia would arrive by lunchtime. Aiden rarely gave personal tours of any of his galleries. He was an introvert, enjoying life hiding behind the camera. But Leila and Mia were special guests. Even Tyra was excited about their visit.

Last Saturday as Aiden and Leila shared donuts and chatted, as predicted Tyra raced down the stairs, grabbed her green slime from the fridge, and snatched two donuts from the box, shoving one in her mouth. With powdered sugar all over her face, she grinned and hugged Leila. After chatting for a few minutes, she invited herself to dinner. "Deena said you'd make us some Middle Eastern food 'cause she can't cook worth a shit. I gotta run, but I'll be in touch."

Turning, Tyra strode to the deck door calling out behind her, "A, don't let our boy eat more than two donuts, no more fish, and don't forget I'm out with Jayden tonight. Might or might not make it home." She paused, peered over her shoulder, and grinned. "Don't worry. I'll definitely do something you wouldn't."

Although Aiden could kill Tyra for embarrassing him, he recognized she went out of her way to make sure Leila understood she and Aiden weren't a couple. After Tyra left, Aiden and Leila had spent the rest of the morning discussing their mutual love of beaches and lighthouses, his rescheduled trip to Costa Rica, her ambition to work fulltime in real-estate, and their children.

Aiden ran a hand over his face and glanced at his watch. Leila and Mia would arrive in fifteen minutes.

"Daddy, I want chips." AJ tugged on Aiden's trousers. "Chips!"

Normally, AJ preferred to spend busy gallery days with Miles. Today, however, for no apparent reason, he woke up clingy and continuously on the brink of tears. Fragile art filled the Stone Gallery, and patrons were surprised to find a child running about, but Aiden didn't care. He owned the joint, and if they hoped to purchase his art, they would respect his son.

Tyra's office served as a makeshift playroom. But even with shelves of toys, a six-foot teepee where AJ often hid, napped, played, and watched movies, the boy rarely lasted more than a few hours before he was bored. Then Aiden initiated Plan B. Either he or Tyra took AJ on an adventure, leaving the gallery short-staffed on an incredibly busy day.

"Daddy, chips."

"AJ, you're not having chips for lunch today. Give me a few minutes, and I'll order something. How about a hamburger or chicken nuggets?"

"No, I want my fish." AJ stomped his foot. "I want chips. I want to go home."

Taking a deep breath, Aiden prepared for an AJ meltdown and crouched. "Peanut, your fish are at home. After you eat lunch, if you're still hungry, you can have chips. We can go home later, but right now Daddy and Mama Ty have to work."

AJ burst into tears.

Hauling him into his embrace, he stood and strode to the window facing the ocean. Holding his sobbing son, he swayed, waiting for the storm to pass. At times, he wished Gina stayed and was the mother his boy deserved. He and Tyra made a good team. Sooner or later, Tyra must build a life of her own. She would never stop being an important person in AJ's life. For her sake, however, he hoped one day she'd have children of her own. But where would that inevitably leave him and AJ?

Aiden wondered how he and AJ's life would be different if Gina hadn't taken off. Perhaps they would have formed the family AJ needed. He shook his head. What the hell was he thinking? With drugs and alcohol in the picture topped off by infidelity, staying together wasn't an option. AJ's mopey attitude was affecting him, leading him to consider the ridiculous. He was grateful Gina left when she had. His only regret was she hadn't stayed gone.

Kissing the top of his boy's head, Aiden continued swaying. If he and Gina stayed together for AJ, their lives would have been hell. They came from broken families with no good role models, and they used each other—each having their own agenda, and differing needs and expectations. They were too immature, damaged, and selfish to be parents.

Aiden ran a hand over his boy's rust-colored hair.

Thank God for Tyra. Raising AJ wasn't easy. She taught him how to be a good parent, and daily, AJ taught him to be a better human.

"Lala. Mia." AJ wiggled.

Tears suddenly dry, the child almost leaped out of Aiden's arms. He put down AJ and watched his son transform. Gone was the sullen, sobbing boy he held a minute earlier.

A huge smile decorated AJ's face as he ran into Leila's open arms.

"Hello, Brave Boy." Leila held the child away from her body and wiped his wet face with her thumbs. "Oh-oh, are those tears? Have you been crying?"

AJ nodded. "Daddy's mean."

"Really? Leila arched her brows. "Why?"

"Daddy said no chips." AJ stuck out his lower lip.

"I see." Leila stood from her crouched position, straightening the skirt of her dress. "Have you eaten lunch yet?"

AJ shook his head. "I'm hungry."

"Oh, I understand now." Leila's lips twitched. "You're hungry, and your daddy won't feed you." She glanced up and met Aiden's gaze. "Want me and Mia to help you?"

AJ grinned and grabbed Leila's hand, weaving his tiny fingers with hers.

Smiling, Aiden leaned against the wall, folded his arms across his chest, and waited for Leila's verdict.

Turning to Mia, who hid behind her legs, Leila tugged her daughter forward.

The child was adorable in a white sundress with a huge, smiling sun painted on the front—its rays wrapping around to her back. With a matching yellow bow holding her wispy blonde hair in a ponytail and white sandals, she was as bright and beautiful as the sun.

"Mia, be a big girl, and say hello to Mr. Stone and AJ."

"Hi," she whispered.

"Hello, Sunshine," Aiden said with a broad smile.

Frowning, Mia placed a hand on her chest. "Mia."

He crouched and poked her belly directly over the sun on the dress. "Yes, I know your name is Mia, but you are as pretty as the sun. May I have a hug?"

Mia smiled but shook her head. She raised her chin. "No, thank-um."

He burst out laughing and stood. "Okay, Sunshine. Maybe later?"

Facing AJ, she gave him a huge grin. "Hi, AJ." She held out her hand.

AJ giggled and released Leila's hand then threaded his fingers in Mia's.

The children smiled at each other, sharing a private, nonverbal conversation.

AJ wrapped his arms around Mia's neck.

Opening his mouth to warn him Mia might not want to be hugged, Aiden froze.

Mia circled AJ's waist with her tiny arms and laid her head against his chest.

Chest aching, Aiden closed his mouth. He was mesmerized. The kids were as enchanting and wondrous as the woman standing behind them. As she watched the children, her eyes were glossy, and a soft smile graced her mouth.

Although he longed to reach for his camera, he didn't want to break the spell. Instead, he took mental pictures of the children. As long as he lived, this moment would be etched on his brain and in his heart. Even if he and Leila's relationship never progressed beyond friendship, Aiden was one hundred percent sure that little ball of sunshine, who unquestionably and unconditionally accepted his son, and her big-hearted mother with her sad, soulful eyes, *would* be in his and AJ's world.

Aiden's heart expanded, making room for new tenants. Unknown to Mia and Leila, Aiden moved them in—permanently. Like it or not, Mia and Leila Solomon joined the small, yet tight, Stone tribe.

Sliding her gaze to Aiden then back to the children, Leila cleared her throat. "Mia, do I let you have chips when you haven't eaten your lunch or dinner?"

The children separated but continued holding hands.

Mia tilted up her head. "Uh-uh."

"Am I mean?"

Mia scrunched her forehead and wrinkled her tiny nose. She glanced at AJ and shrugged.

Both kids dissolved into giggles.

Leila laughed and shook her head. "I see how life will be when you two are together. Why don't you guys play for a few minutes while I look around? Then if it's okay with Aiden, I'll take you both to lunch at the Flying Fish."

Widening his eyes, AJ stepped back, pulling Mia with him. "I don't eats fish."

"I don't eats fish." Mia mimicked.

"Okay, okay." Leila held up her hands. "No one has to eat fish. We'll go somewhere else. Go play."

Although Aiden enjoyed watching the kids

maneuver Leila, he longed to spend time with her alone. "AJ, take Mia to see your tent while I show Leila the gallery. If you two behave, I may allow you to go to lunch together. Okay?"

The kids nodded and ran off to the far side of the room, disappearing into AJ's teepee.

Aiden focused on Leila. She was dressed in a simple, collared, denim dress embroidered with tiny, white flowers scattered throughout. The top hugged her ample chest and tiny waist then flared into a full skirt skimming her knees. Her flat white sandals revealed tiny toes with bright fuchsia toenails. Each time he met her, he noted her toenails were a different color. The colors were always bold—contradictory to the conservative aura she presented.

As a landscape photographer, Aiden specialized in capturing and manipulating nature's vivid color pallet until the vibrant colors leaped off the walls and hypnotized his patrons. Using that tiny splash of color on her toenails, Leila unwittingly enthralled him. "Hi," he whispered, stepping toward her.

"Hi." She blushed, shifting the inky curls off her shoulders. "I hope you don't mind us coming back here unannounced. Tyra was busy and directed us."

"Not at all." Aiden shook his head. "You always arrive at the right time. AJ was crabby all morning and was spiraling into a full-fledged meltdown. You saved me."

"He's a sweet boy, but you know we're in trouble, right?" She raised an eyebrow.

"Hmm?" He frowned.

Raising her chin toward the teepee, she laughed. "Those two might look innocent, but now they've tag-teamed, we don't stand a chance. Mia has never bonded with another child as easily. Until a few weeks ago when she started daycare, she stayed with an elderly neighbor and didn't have many friends her own age."

Aiden nodded. "They appear to have a special connection. Since they're occupied, I'll show you around."

The gallery was designed as a series of rooms, each with a different theme. As they strolled from room to room across gleaming Brazilian ebony floors, patrons enjoyed various sounds of nature. Vivid landscapes grabbed people's attention, transporting them to the most beautiful places on Earth. The main attraction, however, was a powerful series of photographs titled, Paradise—a tribute to the Florida coast.

"Let's start at the Paradise exhibition." Aiden led the way.

Just as they arrived at the exhibition, Tyra motioned to Aiden.

He nodded and glanced at Leila. "I'm sorry, but Memorial Day weekend is crazy busy." He grimaced and ran a hand through his hair. He hated to leave her, but now he was spotted, it was impossible to hide. "Wander about, and I'll catch up as soon as I can. Promise."

"Don't worry." Leila smiled. "I'm fine on my own. Go take care of your admirers."

Forty-five minutes later, Aiden extracted himself from an avid collector. Normally, he exercised patience with this particular patron, but today, he couldn't escape fast enough. As he strode from room to room searching for Leila, he noted the growing crowd. He was proud of all of his galleries, but The Stone Gallery at Vero Beach held a special place in his heart. He thought of the gallery as AJ's.

Aiden searched every room of the gallery, including the office. The kids were still playing in the teepee. Leila was nowhere in sight. One room was left, but it wasn't open to the public. Shrugging, he strolled back to the corner of the gallery and found the door slightly ajar.

Sitting on a swivel chair in the middle, Leila spun slowly. Eyes wide, lips parted in an angelic smile, she studied the photographs of his boy's face from birth on.

When Aiden beheld his child's face, he didn't see the face of a child with Down syndrome—slanted, almond-shaped eyes, flattened nose bridge, low-set, small ears, and short neck. All he observed was unerring beauty. God didn't make mistakes. Through his lens, Aiden documented each month of his child's life and the magnificence of God's creation—Aiden James Stone.

Although he took the photos, this project was Tyra's. She'd begged and badgered him to display the images until he finally relented. Most of the time, she kept the room locked and didn't allow him or anyone else to view how she arranged the photographs. Now, through Leila's eyes, Aiden witnessed how the beauty of his boy's face impacted the human spirit.

"Aiden?" Leila whispered.

Blinking, he focused on her.

She stood and stepped toward him. Tilting her head, she met his gaze. "You're amazing. The entire gallery is extraordinary, but this room…" She wiped her cheeks. Laying a hand on his forearm, she squeezed. "You…" She swallowed hard and took a deep breath, letting it out slowly. "AJ might never understand how lucky he is to be loved by you. Not every child has the privilege of unconditional love and acceptance. But everyone who sees these pictures will understand the *true* definition of love. Where others see deficiency, you reveal perfection. AJ is your biggest blessing and your finest accomplishment."

Emotion tightened his chest, and his breath hitched. He didn't deserve Leila Solomon. Who was the fool who let her out of his sight? How hard would he need to work to keep this little bird from flying away? She broke through the barriers to his tightly locked, well-guarded heart. She shook him out of a deep slumber. Now, he was fully awake. Yes, AJ was his biggest blessing—the finest gift he received to date. Although Aiden was entirely undeserving, perhaps, God wasn't through bestowing blessings on him yet.

Chapter Twelve
Backbone

Tilting her head to the sun, Leila sighed. The day was perfect. She glanced at the children and smiled. Hand in hand, AJ and Mia jumped over tiny waves hitting the shore. They were wet, sandy, and content.

Aiden had acquiesced to the lunch and a visit to the beach only after Leila agreed to have dinner with him on Monday. Although he warned her AJ was moody all morning, the child wasn't the least bit difficult.

Before leaving the gallery, without drama, AJ hugged Aiden and ran back to hold Mia's hand.

Leila opened the gallery door, letting the children walk in front of her as a tall, attractive blonde with blue eyes approached.

The woman stared at AJ as he and Mia skipped down the dock.

For a few seconds, Leila froze, and a shiver of awareness ran through her.

"Are those your children? Is that AJ Stone?" the woman asked.

Pausing, Leila regarded the woman. A protective instinct surged through her, and she had hurried after the children. All afternoon, Leila kept a close watch over the kids. She didn't recognize the woman, but since the incident, she was unsettled. The world was not a safe place for innocents.

Now Mia and AJ chased one another across the beach, occasionally falling to their knees, laughing, or laying on the warm sand—heads close, whispering. Every now and then, she called to them, and they ran to where she sat with their half-eaten burgers and fries on the wooden steps leading to the beach. One bite of their sandwich followed by a gulp of juice, and french fry in hand, they ran off to feed the seagulls.

Leila longed for the days she and Niveen used to chase one another on the beach on a rare day Karima and Amal liberated them from the stifling heat of the *Baharat* kitchen to the Jersey shore. AJ's and Mia's friendship reminded her of the bond she and Niveen shared. When Leila told Mia they must leave the gallery, she watched as Mia clung to AJ just as Leila and Nivi used to do.

Finishing her sandwich, she yelled for the kids to come for another bite, but they ignored her. She took a gulp of iced tea. After gathering their trash, she threw it in a nearby, overflowing trash can—keeping the fries for the kids to munch on. As she settled on the steps again, she felt her cell vibrate. She pulled the phone from her pocket, and without checking to see who the caller was, she answered. "Hello?"

"Leila?"

Gasping, she almost dropped the phone.

"Leila? Are you there?" a soft female voice asked.

"Mama?" she whispered. "Mama, is that you?" Tears burned behind her eyelids, and she fought to hold them at bay. Her vision blurred as she searched the beach for the children and focused on them running toward her. She couldn't move, breathe, or hear the crashing of the waves. Spots appeared before her eyes.

"Mommy, Mommy fries, plea'th." Mia's sandy hands tugged on Leila's arm.

Leila gulped in air, her lungs inflating with much-needed oxygen. Gripping the telephone, she straightened. She blinked, and her vision cleared, landing on the two children bouncing in front of her. She must get her act together and hold her emotions in check.

"Lala, fries," AJ demanded.

She held out the bag of fries.

Giggling, Mia snatched the bag, and ran off with AJ trailing.

Leila commanded her lungs to do their job and her heart to slow the hell down before she passed out. "Mama?" She forced the word past her trembling lips. Soft weeping filled Leila's ear.

"It's *Tante* Amal, *habibtee*, not Karima," her aunt said in Arabic.

Disappointment crashed into Leila. Her gut clenched. How had she mistaken Amal's voice for her mother's? Their voices were similar, but she never erred before. She hadn't heard Amal's voice in three-and-a-half years. Despite her deep disappointment, she celebrated the win. Was this the first chink in the Solomon fortress?

For the last week, Leila spoke to Niveen daily. She informed her of her disastrous conversation with Gabe, and Niveen agreed Amal was their best bet.

"Leila, I am so happy to hear your voice. I'm sorry I surprised you. Nivi said she would tell you I would be calling."

"I-I missed her call this morning," Leila said slowly. She wished she returned Niveen's call. But nothing would have prepared her for the sound of her beautiful native language coming from her beloved aunt's mouth. In all the time they lived together, neither Leila nor Deena spoke a single word of Arabic. They preferred not to be reminded of the world they left behind.

Swallowing hard, Leila swiped the hair off her face and forced the Arabic words past her lips. At first, she struggled with the words, but she quickly remembered the roll and glide necessary to form each syllable. "Hello, *Tante* Amal."

She rehearsed speaking to her mother or aunt for the first time, but now she couldn't remember a single sentence of her speech. She was undeniably happy to hear her aunt's voice. But anger quickly leeched in. Amal was her godmother. They used to enjoy a close relationship. Had Amal ever wondered what happened to Leila? Did she search for her? She should have loved Leila unconditionally, but she too betrayed her.

Leila clenched her free hand—her fingernails biting into her palm. The past wasn't important. She must shove aside the past and deal with the present and future. Gaining a better understanding of Karima's health was what mattered now. She refused to give in to the sobs clawing up her throat. Tonight, when everyone was asleep, she'd *feel* the pain of rejection and loss, and she would grieve.

Clearing her throat, she forced an indifferent tone. "Thank you for calling, *Tante* Amal. How's Mama? Nivi said she was sick, and Gabe isn't helpful."

"*Habibtee*, first tell me how you are. Was that your daughter calling you *mommy*? Nivi will not give me any information about you—where you are and how you are living. She said I must ask you." Amal sighed. "Please tell your *Tante* all about your life."

Leila focused on the rolling waves in the distance. Did her aunt believe ignoring the past was possible? Chatting like long-lost girlfriends without addressing the years of silence and the hurtful words exchanged wasn't possible. Nerves frayed, she paused, her chest rising and falling with effort as her gaze drifted to the children. For a few seconds, she observed their antics until she once again harnessed her emotions. "Why is that information important now?" Reverting to English, she continued. "Please, tell me how my mother is, and then I will not trouble you further."

"We have hurt you deeply, my girl." Amal sniffled. "But the time has come for all of us to find peace. We have been foolish, and we *must* learn forgiveness and understanding."

Grinding her teeth, Leila wanted to count to ten but only reached five. "Peace? Forgiveness? Understanding? Where were you and all those lovely sentiments when I needed you?"

"You don't understand. None of us knew where you were. Karima said you left in the night—so great was your shame."

Leila leaped to her feet and paced. "I am not ashamed of my child. Since you are so interested in me and Mia, I'll tell you exactly why I left." Bile rose in her throat. She was certain she would lose her lunch. She stopped pacing, faced the sea and children, and took a deep breath. Opening the vault where all her memories resided, she sifted through the good and bad scenes, focusing on the last day she was in her family home.

After a day filled with arguments and name calling, a heavy cloak of silence had enveloped the Solomon house as all its inhabitants retreated to their designated corners. Some plotted their next steps while others hung their heads in shame and hid.

Unable to sleep, Leila paced her room and was surprised when at one a.m. Karima tiptoed in carrying a large suitcase.

"You must leave. Now. Tonight," she whispered. She heaved the bag onto Leila's bed, ran to Leila's closet, and yanked dresses, shirts, and pants off their hangers.

"Mama?" Leila widened her eyes. "It's the middle of the night. What are you talking about? What do you mean, I have to leave?" A week ago, Karima appeared years younger than her fifty-seven years. Now, her dark curls were dull and lay lifeless on her slumped shoulders. No longer did she stand straight and strong. But what terrified Leila the most was the defeated look in her mother's bloodshot eyes.

Opening drawers, Karima snatched underwear, socks, and pajamas and shoved them in the suitcase with the rest of Leila's belongings. She threw a dress in Leila's direction. "Dress as quietly as you can. You need to leave before your *baba* wakes."

Leila's pulse leapt, and her heart pounded a ferocious beat. "Mama, stop. Please." She wrung her hands. "Where am I going? You're not making any sense. You're throwing me out? Don't you love me?"

Karima froze. She dropped the clothes on to the bed and straightened. Stalking to Leila, she snatched her hand and dragged her to the dresser mirror.

Emotionally drained and physically exhausted,

Leila didn't resist.

Gripping Leila's chin, Karima met her gaze in the mirror. "Look. What do you see?"

Leila studied her reflection. People often said she and Karima looked like sisters, but the trauma and stress of the last week took its toll. Now, the only feature they shared was an almost-identical handprint on their heart-shaped faces—Leila's on the left cheek and Karima's on the right.

"What do you see? Do you see your future? Your child's future? Is this the life you wish for the child you are willing to give up everything for?"

Karima's tone was as hard and hollow as a steel pipe. Swallowing hard, Leila shook her head. "Of course not, but life shouldn't be this way. Mama, please. I know I made a mistake, but nothing can be done now."

Glaring, Karima squeezed her chin until Leila winced. "A mistake?" She scoffed. "You stupid child. A mistake is a small misstep not a life-changing event with long term ramifications. Leila, you ruined your future and brought shame to this family. How did you expect us to react? How did you expect *him* to react? Hmm?"

"Mama, stop." Leila jerked away her face from Karima's grasp and swiveled around. Her breath stuttered, and her hands shook as she reached for her mother. "Please. Listen…"

"No," Karima spit out and backed away from Leila. She pointed a finger. "You listen, you foolish child. You waited until no decision was left to be made—until we couldn't correct this disaster."

"I waited because the choice was *mine*"—she

slammed a splayed hand against her chest—"not yours and not his." She took in a ragged breath. "Please, forgive me."

"You ask for my help and my protection, but I cannot give you either. You *must* leave." She dug into the pocket of her robe, pulled out an envelope, and threw it on her bed. "This money is all I can do for you." Karima had sighed and ran a hand over her face. "Leila, you know nothing of this world, and you understand even less. My actions have nothing to do with forgiveness. One day, you will understand. May God have mercy on you and your child."

When she heard her aunt's soft weeping, Leila stopped talking. The rest of the story was details of escape and survival. She'd said enough. Leila took a deep breath. The sea air filled her lungs and oxygenated her brain. Sagging on the steps once more, she scanned the shoreline for the children. Thank God they were safe and unaware of the trip to memory hell she just completed. Leila ran a hand through her hair and released a ragged breath. She was wrung out.

"I am sorry," Amal whispered then blew her nose.

"I needed you." Leila sniffled. "I needed my family, but you shunned me. That last night, you sat and listened as Mama, *Tante* Hoda, and the men, plotted my child's demise as if her life meant nothing. She was a cancer that needed to be excised. We were an infestation requiring extermination."

"I'm sorry for the pain I've caused you—the pain we all inflicted." Amal released a long, shaky breath. "I understand you hurt. We all do. We made some terrible mistakes. *All* of us. After all these years, I did not call for us to scream at one another. The past is the past. We cannot change it, but we can do better in the future, or we will live a life full of regrets. Regret is a bitter pill to swallow, especially if you have to swallow it daily. Regret will lodge in your throat and strangle you." She sighed. "Are you ready to listen?"

Amal's words sank in. Leila's shoulders slumped. She could run and hide, but she could never siphon out the Sahara Desert sand running through her blood. That sand, according to her mother, was the secret ingredient strengthening her bones. Right at this moment, she felt defeated and bereft. She ached to feel her mother's arms surrounding her.

Glancing at her watch, Leila stood and dusted the sand off her dress. Her family problems were a heavy burden. "Where do we go from here, *Tante* Amal?"

"You must come see your mama. She is sick and has refused treatment." Amal clucked her tongue. "I know you do not understand, but she stopped living the day she lost her *habibtee*. As much as you might hope to forget your heritage, you know how our culture works. Daughters are the result of a mother's teaching and guidance as sons are the result of the father."

"Karima's heart doesn't work well. The doctors say she eats the wrong foods and doesn't exercise. What do they know? We eat what we have always eaten, and she stands on her feet from dawn until past dusk. She suffers from a broken heart neither food nor exercise will fix. Gabe says she needs surgery, but she refuses to discuss the procedure. She has given up." Amal sobbed.

Agony sliced through Leila. She took a shuddering breath. No matter how angry or how hurt she was, until the day she stopped breathing, Karima Solomon would always be her mother. She couldn't understand

Karima's actions, but Amal was right about one thing—she couldn't waste time rehashing the past.

Leila was raised to honor her father and mother. That commandment did not come with a waiver or with small print letting her off the hook if her parents treated her unjustly. She wasn't a saint, though. She would do what was necessary to help Karima. If nothing else, Karima gave her life and for twenty-five years loved her. Yusuf was a different story all together. Leila didn't care what the Good Book's opinion was on that subject.

If Amal was to be believed, her mother, in her own twisted fashion, sacrificed herself to save her daughter. Now was the time to follow Karima's example. Returning and facing each of her family members would be excruciating. Seeing Mia's father would be dangerous, but she was Karima Solomon's daughter. She was a survivor, and over the last three years, she grew a bionic backbone. She'd stand strong and straight—for both of them. "Tell me what to do *Tante* Amal. How do I help my mama?"

Chapter Thirteen
More

Leila peered at her bedside clock and hauled her body from bed. Yesterday, after she finished speaking with Amal, she dropped AJ at the gallery and returned home to an empty house. Deena was out with friends. Worn out, Mia fell asleep earlier than usual. Leila wasn't as lucky.

When she was certain Mia was asleep, she called Niveen. They spoke for several hours. Leila spent several more hours distracting herself by watching a documentary about sharks and killer whales. Perhaps the show wasn't the best choice for a restful night.

Rubbing her eyes, Leila shuffled to the bathroom and then to the kitchen. She ran directly into Deena.

Deena scanned Leila's face. "What the…"

"Shh." Leila closed her eyes and put up a hand. "Need caffeine first. Dying. Zero sleep."

Raising an eyebrow, Deena clamped shut her mouth and nodded.

Over a mug of hot tea, Leila tracked the sun as it rose. She told Deena of the previous day's events and her conversation with Amal and Niveen.

"What will you do? I agree you should see your mother, but you have no idea what you're walking into. How will you handle your father, the uncles, and Gabe? And what about…"

"Deena, take a breath, will you?" Leila sat up, placing her mug on the side table. "Give me some credit. No matter how tempted I am, I will not fly to Newark, bang on the front door, and demand to see Mama. I'm not a complete idiot."

"I'm sorry." Deena released a long breath and ran a hand down her face. "Of course you're not an idiot, but I remember how broken you were when you first arrived. You and Mia are doing great now. She's thriving, and you have just stumbled on a great guy who, if given a chance, might show you how good life can be with the right person."

"I know you're worried." Leila patted Deena's knee. "I too remember those dark times. But fear can no longer rule me. Although they haven't been involved in my life since I arrived here, my family impacted me in many ways. I have to take back the reins. I'll do my best to keep your name and location private."

Staring at the ocean, Deena took a long drink of her tea and nodded. "Okay. When will you go?"

Leila, too, studied the turbulent water. Far in the Atlantic, a storm brewed, and the wind carried an uncharacteristic coolness. She was in the mood for a rowdy storm complete with thunder, lightning, and wind—cathartic to the soul. She chewed on her lower lip. "*Tante* Amal said *Baba*, Uncle Hassan, and Uncle Aziz leave for Egypt in early July. My grandmother is turning ninety-five, and she is not in good health. They are surprising her. They'll be gone for a couple of weeks. I'm asking Dr. Ash for the time off. Nivi and *Tante* Amal will arrange for me to see Mama."

"And Mia? Will you take her?" Deena raised an eyebrow.

Leila hung her head. "I can't," she murmured. "I can barely afford one ticket. But even if I possessed the money, you know I can't take her. The second anyone sees her, they'll know who…" She swallowed hard and held Deena's hand. "Can she stay with you for the duration? I know I'm asking a lot, but I can't take her. Not yet."

Deena squeezed Leila's hand. "Of course, she can stay with me, but sooner or later you must deal with her father and with the family. You can't hide her forever. She's a beautiful little girl, but with her creamy skin, blonde hair, and blue eyes, she's an exact copy of her father."

Although they talked for several hours, running through every possible scenario she might face in Jersey, Leila was still troubled. Deena insisted a shopping trip was in order. Reluctantly, Leila agreed.

By the end of the day, all Leila purchased was a dress for Mia. Although she tried on a number of dresses that were perfect for her date with Aiden, she refused to spend the money.

While Leila accompanied Mia to the restroom, Deena purchased a dress Leila had tried on and loved. The dress was a sleeveless coral print with an empire waist that barely skimmed Leila's knees and was shorter than anything she owned. Deena refused to return the dress or accept any money for it. She insisted Leila stop dressing and acting like a nun.

After dinner at Mia's favorite eatery, they returned home. They'd shopped all afternoon and took a long walk on the beach. Everyone was exhausted but Leila. Deena offered her a sleeping pill. Leila refused and suffered through another sleepless night.

Leila rolled out of bed Monday morning exhausted but determined to be productive. Moping would not change the facts or finish the laundry or housework. By lunch time, she completed many items on her to-do list. She made Mia lunch and started a movie, and then she collapsed next to Deena on the deck, enjoying a glass of spiked lemonade. Her thoughts turned to her date that evening. She wasn't convinced going out with him was a good choice, but she couldn't back out now.

"Oh for the love of God, woman." Deena glared. "Aiden asked you to dinner not for your hand in marriage. Allow yourself to live in the moment and be happy. Not every relationship leads to a lifetime commitment. Some relationships only lead to friendship, and that is perfectly acceptable. You and Mia need more friends. Hell, we all need more friends."

"He's a lovely man. Although I don't have a lot of experience, I understand he wants more than friendship." Leila looked away and wrung her hands. "How am I supposed to give him what he needs when I know so little about men?" Her face flamed. "I-I've been with one man, and we all know how that mis-adventure ended. Obviously, I wasn't good enough. Every time I think about being with someone intimately, all those words the family called me come flying at me like poison darts."

"Look at me." Deena took Leila's hands in hers.

Leila met Deena's gaze. "You were young, innocent, and trusting. He was a bastard. Don't let your past color your future. You aren't sinful, shameful, or a whore. You're good, kind, gentle, and loving. Being intimate with someone you love is beautiful and doesn't always end in heartbreak."

"I'll probably make a fool of myself." She closed her eyes and shook her head.

"Aiden is just a man—a human. Be honest and open. Do only what is right for you, and when the time is right, talk to him. Give him a chance. Tell him your past, and if he is the right person, he'll understand your fears. Together, you'll find your way. If you find spending time with him is painful rather than joyful, don't say yes again."

Leila stood and paced. "What if he's changed his mind? He hasn't called me."

"Today is Memorial Day," Deena chided. "You and I chose not to work on this holiday, but I'm sure as a gallery owner he's ridiculously busy. Now, stop making excuses."

Exhausted but unable to sit still, Leila tackled her task list. By five-thirty, she was wiped out and collapsed on her bed. Setting the alarm, she closed her eyes. She would rest for a half-hour before making herself presentable for dinner. Tomorrow, she would go back to her regularly scheduled programming. Memorial Day weekend was all but done, and she did everything but rest.

When her alarm blared, Leila jolted from a deep dreamless sleep. She stood under the hot water, fighting to wake up. Although she worried about her decision to go out, she was excited. She'd never been on a *real* date. Aiden wasn't *any* man; he was *the man* she fantasized about since the first time she spotted him swaying on the deck of Harbor House. Perhaps Deena was right. She must learn to let go and be happy.

A few minutes later, Leila slid the silky, coral dress over her head and down her body. She studied her reflection in the mirror and smiled. The color was perfect against her tanned olive skin and dark hair. Running her fingers through her curls, she stared at the warming flat iron. One glance at the clock, and her decision was made. She needed much more than a half hour to straighten her hair. If Aiden wanted her, he would accept her curly mess. Leila shrugged. Even if she took the time to straighten her curls, in Florida's oppressive humid weather, she would resemble Shirley Temple in no time.

Unlike Yusuf, Aiden always complimented her long curls. Americans were fascinated by her head full of tight ringlets. Her *baba*, however, had despised her hair, insisting she straighten it whenever they attended church or any family functions. Straightening her thick hair was an arduous task, and many times she begged her mother to allow her to cut it.

"*Baba* can be difficult," Karima had said. "Please him now, and you will have his blessing for being an obedient daughter. One day, you will find a man who loves you and all those curls God took the time to create one by one. This man will not require you to change a single hair on your head. In his eyes, you will be perfect."

Leila glanced at her image again then rummaged through her makeup bag for concealer and foundation to cover the ravages of sleepless nights and nonstop worry. She wasn't sure what Aiden saw in her. Her nose was too small, her upper lip too thin, and her lower lip overly plump. Her eyes were her saving grace—wide and uniquely colored with thick, dark lashes, and perfectly arched eyebrows.

Each time Leila viewed herself in the mirror, she

was surprised. She appeared older than her twenty-nine years, and she had developed frown lines between her eyebrows and on her forehead. She didn't resemble the innocent girl that bloomed under Eric's appraising gaze and fell in love.

Eric Dixon was Gabe's study partner through medical school. Although he joined the family for dinner on many occasions, he rarely interacted with her. Not wanting to attract her father's ire, Leila never attempted eye contact with Eric. But when she started working at the clinic, their relationship changed.

Handsome, charming, and sophisticated, Eric was every girl's dream. At first, their relationship was innocent. He sent her emails complimenting her work. He thanked her for completing trivial tasks and asked her opinion on cases.

Gabe was frequently away from the office making home visits. During those times, Eric became more attentive. He left small gifts at her desk and took her to expensive restaurants for lunch. He talked about his family and friends. In turn, she confided in him. Eric was the first man to flirt with her, pay her a compliment, and kiss her. He was her first everything.

Pursing her lips, Leila pushed away the memories. She ran late and needed to focus. Finished applying her eye-shadow, she grabbed her lipstick.

Mia ran into the room. "Pretty, Mommy." She tugged on the hem of Leila's dress.

Smiling, Leila glanced at her daughter. She didn't hear the garage door open, heralding Mia and Deena's return from dinner. Deena insisted on taking out Mia to dinner while Leila showered and dressed for the evening. Leila bent and lifted Mia. "Thank-you, *habibtee.* Mommy is going out with a friend. *Tante* Dee will give you a bath, read you a book, and tuck you in. Okay?"

"*Hab-bi?*" Mia frowned and studied her mother.

Leila gasped and snapped shut her mouth. She'd spoken in Arabic. She closed her eyes and settled her forehead against Mia's. Two paths lay before her. She could ignore Mia's confusion and go back to her vow of Arabic silence or use the opportunity to introduce Mia to her rich heritage.

Two days ago, Leila uttered Arabic for the first time since she left Jersey. Although the conversation was agonizing, pieces of herself she believed were lost forever returned and did so with every Arabic word she spoke. She could no longer deny her heritage. Even if she never reunited with her family, to survive and thrive, she would resurrect and embrace her culture. She *was* an Egyptian woman with a beautiful, rich culture. Three and a half years ago, she foolishly and purposefully amputated a limb but experienced phantom limb pain. Leila swallowed hard.

Mia wiggled. "Mommy. Down."

Taking a deep breath, she opened her eyes and put down Mia. "Okay, *habibtee,*" she said, studying Mia's reaction. "*Habibtee*, means *my love*. Say *hah-bib-tee.*" Leila enunciated each syllable slowly and waited for Mia to imitate her.

Mia repeated each syllable. She twisted her mouth, lips, and tongue to achieve a close rendition of the unusual word.

"Well done, Mia," Deena said from the door of Leila's room. "Run and pick out some PJs to wear after your bath, and I will be right there." Deena sat on

144

Leila's bed. "Arabic?"

Nodding, Leila licked her lips and spoke in Arabic. "Do you think I'm making a mistake?"

"What I think doesn't matter," Deena answered in English. "You must be comfortable with the decisions you make. If you're diving back in, you might as well go deep. Mia is a sponge. She'll pick up the language fast."

"And you?" Leila raised an eyebrow.

"I already know how to speak Arabic." Deena smirked.

"Very funny. How do you feel about me speaking Arabic and bringing back some of our culture—a little at a time?"

Shrugging, Deena handed Leila her shawl and clutch. "Look, I have no problem with the language, and I definitely don't have a problem with the food. The people—our people and their judgmental ways—are the problem." Deena's smile faded. "I'll support you in whatever you do. Proceed with caution and give me time to adjust. To be honest, I've missed hearing our language." She looked away. "I'm not ready to utter the words myself. But maybe in time…"

Deena rose and followed Leila to the family room. "Anyway, I can't complain 'cause I kind of invited Tyra for a nice Middle Eastern meal, and you know the extent of my skills in the kitchen."

"I heard about a dinner. I didn't realize I was the chef." Leila peeked at her watch and frowned.

"What's wrong?"

Walking to the bay window facing the front yard, Leila glanced at the driveway. Aiden was late. Maybe he had texted? She strolled to the kitchen and grabbed

145

her cell from the counter. No missed texts or calls. Sighing, she shrugged. "Aiden was supposed to pick me up a half hour ago. I lost track of time getting ready. He hasn't called or texted."

Deena frowned. "Maybe he said eight and you heard seven. I'm sure he'll be here soon."

She was certain Aiden said seven. Her gut clenched. Something wasn't right. Was AJ ill? She chewed on her lower lip and stared at her cell. Should she call or text Aiden? If Aiden had some other emergency, she didn't wish to impose.

In her younger years, Leila wasn't a great judge of character, but she matured over the years. She didn't know Aiden well, but he didn't strike her as the kind of man who stood up a date. At least she hoped he wasn't.

Mia ran into the room with a PJ in one hand and a bathing suit in the other. "K, ready."

Deena laughed. "Give Mommy a goodnight kiss. She'll be leaving soon."

Crouching, Leila caught her daughter in a big hug. She kissed her head. "May the angels of heaven watch over your head as you sleep through the night, my angel," she whispered in Mia's ear.

"Night, Mommy. Love you." Mia gave her mother a wet kiss on the neck.

"Love you too, *habibtee*."

Mia grinned and ran ahead of Deena.

"I'm sure he'll be here soon. Let loose and have a great time. You deserve a night off." Deena waved a hand and sauntered away. "Forget your troubles for a few hours. Be young and happy," she called over her shoulder.

Leila sat on the couch. Tilting her head against the

cushions, she closed her eyes. Aiden wasn't coming. He didn't call or text to confirm the date and time since she left the gallery with the kids.

Her track record with men frankly sucked. Every single man in her life disappointed her. She often wondered if life without a man would be easier. But dreams of a loving husband by her side invaded her nights and even days at the most inopportune of times.

Looking back, Leila sensed something was wrong when she dropped off AJ at the gallery. After she ended the call with Amal, she gathered her composure and rounded up the children. The kids were engrossed in their collection of shells and didn't notice her red-rimmed eyes and blotchy face.

In the car, she did her best to repair her makeup before arriving at the gallery. But she needn't have worried. Aiden was nowhere in sight. Although Tyra wasn't busy with a client, she was distracted and barely thanked Leila before she ushered AJ to the back.

Leila listened to the sounds of the bathtub filling, her daughter's happy little girl giggles, and the silly songs Deena sang. She sighed. This was her life—a little girl who depended on her and was generous with her wet kisses and a devoted best friend. Having more would be nice, but more might come in the form of a better job, an improved relationship with her family, financial security, and a home of her own. More would not come in the form of Aiden and AJ Stone.

For whatever reason, Aiden chose wisely this evening. Leila's life appeared simple on the surface but looks were deceiving. Soon, she would return to Jersey, voluntarily walking into traffic and hoping she wasn't run over by uncaring and distracted drivers. While dodging the swerving cars with their enraged drivers and blaring horns, she'd shield Mia and Deena. She didn't have the time or the energy to begin a new relationship with an American man who she would have to explain her crazy family and culture to.

Aiden was a kind man with a sweet, special needs child. He and AJ's life was not easy. They deserved more—better. But more and better were not Leila Solomon.

Opening her eyes, she stood and scooped up her sandals, clutch, and shawl. She tip-toed to her room, stripped, and hung the dress on the hanger—hoping she could return it the next day. Slipping beneath the covers, she laid her head on the pillow. Leila closed her eyes and willed the tears not to fall. She would not cry over something as frivolous as wanting more. After all, right at this moment, her plate was piled pretty high. Good or bad, more was simply…more.

Chapter Fourteen
We

Aiden ran a hand over his soaked hair and face. Rain poured down in sheets, and his efforts to remove the wet from his eyes were fruitless. Running on a deserted beach at the crack of dawn during a rainstorm was reckless. Yet, Aiden was incapable of battling the forces—his brain and heart—propelling him in Leila's direction this Wednesday morning.

For twenty minutes, he stood under the deck awning, watching the storm gather—beginning as a light mist and progressing to a pummeling downpour. He dressed in running gear, sprinted down the fifty-three steps, and launched himself into the sand. Without stretching or warming up, he jogged then ran to Breeze Bay Cottage.

The weather fit Aiden's mood. Rising out of hell, his ex-girlfriend appeared at his gallery and threw his carefully constructed world into a whirlwind. Now he dealt with a silent and hurt Leila, a not so silent and pissed off Tyra, and a loathsome and unrelenting bitch called Gina.

Aiden had spent most of Sunday, Monday, and Tuesday finding an attorney who handled child custody cases. Due to the holiday weekend, he couldn't reach anyone until Tuesday, and by the end of the day, he was in a foul mood and retreated to the deck to clear his head.

A few minutes later, Tyra followed. She slammed shut the deck door and strode toward Aiden who reclined in a chair nursing a glass of scotch. "You insensitive idiot. You had a date with Leila, and you stood her up?"

Waves of hostility rolled off her and slammed into him. Aiden blinked. "What?" Since Saturday, he hadn't slept a full night or eaten much. The alcohol dulled his senses and slowed his thought processes.

"Aiden," Tyra barked. "Sit up and put down that drink. What the hell do you think you're doing? You had a date with Leila—*yesterday*. You stood her up, you moron. You're a better man." She threw up her hands. "Why didn't you call and cancel?"

Gina's appearance turned his life upside down, and his world had narrowed to his son. Tyra was right. He was a better man than his behavior implied.

As he ran, Aiden opened his clenched hands and shook them out. Since he endured Tyra's tongue-lashing, he tried to make amends. Texting Leila was fruitless. Calls went straight to voicemail. He would beg for forgiveness in person.

Winded, Aiden stopped at the edge of the shore— letting the tumultuous waves break against his running shoes and legs. Panting, he studied the churning sea. The rain eased to a gentle mist once more, but the sky was gray, and the clouds were heavy with moisture. He turned and trudged up the beach and studied Breeze Bay Cottage. The lights were off, and he couldn't detect any movement. The inhabitants appeared deep in slumber. Turning, he faced the sea and dropped to the sand.

Upon opening the first email from Gina, he was paralyzed by anger and fear and made a mess of the situation. Instead of taking charge and dealing with the issue, he behaved like a toddler. Now, Gina gripped him by the balls.

When he had watched Leila and the kids step out of the gallery and run into Gina, he gasped, and a sharp pain sliced through his chest. For a few seconds, noise in the gallery ceased. His boy—in slow motion—passed the woman who gave birth to him.

Gina's shiny blonde hair swished around her shoulders, and a small smile formed on her glossy lips. Tall, thin, and meticulously dressed in a white off the shoulder dress hugging her body from breasts to mid-thigh, she sauntered toward him with runway model precision on black five-inch sandals, holding a matching clutch and catching the eye of every human.

She was always beautiful—in a trashy type of way. Now, she was polished. Someone financed her expertly cut hair, manicured nails, and high-end clothing because Gina barely earned a high school diploma, and she was averse to hard work beyond earning enough to finance her drug and alcohol habit.

Their reunion was not a loving one, and the forty-five-minute exchange that followed was ugly. The past was rehashed—accusations flew, and ultimatums were given. She wanted access to his boy, and she wasn't giving up. Gina gave him a week's reprieve to, "Act like an adult and come to terms with the past."

Dropping his head, Aiden closed his eyes and prayed for wisdom. He scheduled an appointment with a highly recommended attorney on Thursday. AJ deserved the best. How could a woman who abused alcohol and drugs while pregnant, and then abandoned her premature, critically ill baby be the best? Although he understood people changed, he was certain Gina didn't. Why was she suddenly interested in AJ? He ran his hands through his hair.

"Aiden?"

Aiden startled. He raised his head and stared into Leila's stormy eyes. Barefoot, in black running shorts and matching tank, her hair was braided down her back. She appeared young, vulnerable, and beautiful. His pulse accelerated, and his breathing stuttered. He silently thanked God for bringing her to him.

Kneeling beside him, she folded her legs to the side.

He twisted toward her—relief sweeping through him. The elephant resting on his chest shifted, and he filled his lungs to capacity then breathed out. Only a few days passed since he last saw her, but he starved for the sight of her. He knew her a short time, yet each time he gazed into her expressive eyes, he discovered what he was missing his entire life—his other half.

Aiden grasped her hand, and although she resisted, he held on tighter. He kissed her fingers.

Leila gasped.

"Forgive me," he whispered. "I'm so damn sorry. I never meant to hurt you. If you're willing to listen, I'll tell you what happened. Give me a chance—just one chance." Aiden heard the similarity in his plea to the words Gina uttered. But he forgot a date. Gina forgot her son. Aiden closed his eyes, kissed Leila's hand once more, and then glanced up.

She didn't respond, but she also didn't pull away.

Gently, he tugged her closer. He released her hand

and wrapped an arm around her—holding her close to his side.

She stiffened.

"I'm sorry, Rapunzel," he whispered in her ear. "I swear you can trust me. I screwed up, but I have an explanation."

Trembling, she looked away and nodded.

He almost tasted her fear. Was she scared of him? He didn't think so. She was untrusting and skittish. He knew he should handle her with care. Yet, he had been thoughtless. Aiden was damned lucky his little bird didn't fly away forever.

A small smile formed on his lips. Despite her fear, she came to him on her own. Rapunzel let down her hair. He wouldn't betray her trust again because he was fairly certain, next time, he wouldn't be as lucky. "I know you've been hurt in the past, and God knows I never meant to add to your pain. My actions were not malicious or intentional. I looked forward to our date, and I was a happy man you trusted me to give me a chance. But, Leila, after you and the kids left the gallery, my world exploded, and I lost my mind and focus."

Gasping, Leila shifted and focused on him. "Aiden…"

He shook his head and tucked her back to his side, shielding her from the wind. "Shh…I'm okay now you are by my side. My story is long and ugly, but I want to tell you the entire tale—from the beginning."

She nodded.

He kissed the top of her head.

Burrowing into his chest, she relaxed her weight into him.

Aiden smiled. He woke up this morning overwhelmed and tormented. Although Tyra slept in a room above him across from AJ's, he felt completely alone. Now, with Leila in his arms, all the jigsaw pieces of his life fit together—every curve and jagged edge blended seamlessly into the next. He closed his eyes and imagined the landscape of his life as it should have been right from the beginning and as it would be in the future. He was meant to be with Leila, and she belonged in his arms.

The breath-taking image of AJ, Mia, Leila, and him holding hands, walking on the beach was so clear—sheer perfection. Aiden lost his breath, and tears filled his eyes. He wasn't sure where Tyra, Deena, or Gina fit into this picture, but he was convinced, if he and Leila held on with all their might and weathered the storm to come, one day, they would be a family. His job was to protect his family. Protecting his family started with giving Leila his truth and praying one day she would give him the same.

He took a deep breath and blinked away the tears. "I met Gina when I was twenty-five. She was twenty-seven—a bartender at my favorite watering hole. At first, our relationship was based on sex and alcohol." Aiden shrugged. "I was a naïve kid making a name for myself. For several years, we lived together. She worked long hours, and I traveled and took pictures around the world. All I was interested in was refining my craft and making money. I needed to pay my way across the globe, take care of Matt, and fund his education."

"Your brother?" Leila twisted in his arms and glanced up.

Aiden nodded. "Since I was ten years old, I was Matt's caretaker in every way. My mother took off with her boyfriend, and dear old dad decided booze was more important than his kids. One day, I'll tell you the entire sordid mess. In essence, before I understood how babies were made, I traded my childhood for parenthood. I was the only parent my seven-year-old brother counted on."

She placed her hand on his cheek.

Turning his head, he kissed her palm. Aiden threaded his fingers through hers. He held on tight and prayed when he revealed the rest of his messed-up life she wouldn't bolt. "Each time I returned from my trips, I found Gina was by my side—easy and available. She was wild. A hunger raged inside her I couldn't satisfy. I fell for her and tried to make her happy. From the beginning, I warned her I wasn't interested in marriage or kids. I wanted to live a little, and I'd already raised a child."

When he recalled his prior actions, he wished he could tell his younger self to be careful—think before you act. But time travel wasn't an option. "I made a name for myself and so did Gina. I traveled more and more, and while I worked, she slept around, used drugs, and drank more booze than she served. Eventually, I broke up with her. A month later she claimed she was pregnant, and I…" Aiden pulled away and sat forward—head down, shoulders slumped.

"Aiden? What happened?" Leila laid a hand on his shoulder.

Grinding his teeth, he wished he didn't have to utter the next two words because he didn't know the damage they'd do. Leila shared Mia's father wasn't in her life. Did the man abandon his child? He turned his head, and he looked into her eyes. "I left."

"I don't understand?" Leila frowned.

"I packed my clothes and disappeared." Aiden swallowed hard. "I was certain the child wasn't mine, and to be totally honest, I didn't care if he was or wasn't. Two weeks prior, I was informed my father drank himself to death, and I was relieved. I was no longer forced to pay for his booze to keep him away from Matt. Mom was in the wind—living a life that didn't include her kids." Aiden looked away certain her kind, trusting eyes would soon fill with disappointment and disgust. "I was finally free. I behaved like an irresponsible ass. I ran away."

For a few minutes, silence reigned.

Leila cleared her throat. "How did you end up with AJ?"

"Several months later, I returned to my apartment after a long trip. Gina showed up, strung out, and out of her mind." Aiden straightened and met her gaze. "She told me about AJ and gave me an envelope with Tyra's information and AJ's birth certificate and medical records. She took off. She didn't want to be a mother any more than I desired to be a father."

Drawing her knees to her chest, she hugged them. "I'm not following how Tyra fits into this story."

"Tyra was the social worker assigned to AJ's case. After I read the contents of the envelope detailing how sick AJ was, I contacted Tyra with the full intention of relinquishing my parental rights. She insisted I come to the hospital and meet the child. When I saw him…" He swallowed past the boulder in his throat. "When I saw him—tiny and helpless, hooked to so many tubes and monitors, and hovering on the brink of death—fear gripped me."

Aiden blinked, holding the tears at bay. He would never forget the first time he saw his boy and felt AJ's tiny fingers wrap around his. When AJ opened his paper-thin eyelids to reveal luminous sea green eyes, he pierced Aiden's heart with a plea not to abandon him.

Delicate fingers closed over Aiden's large hand and squeezed. "Tell me," she said in a husky voice. She scooted closer and fitted herself to his side once more.

He cleared his throat. "I fell in love with a broken little boy with cinnamon hair and green eyes." He studied their joined fingers. "The birth certificate named me as the father. Although AJ didn't resemble me, and he wasn't really mine, in every way that truly mattered, he *was* mine. He deserved better. I didn't deserve him, but I was all he had."

"AJ's mother—she's back, isn't she?"

Aiden gaped. "How…?"

"She was the lady who passed us as we left the gallery on Saturday. Right?" Leila frowned. "She looked familiar. She asked me about AJ, but I didn't answer her. Something about her unsettled me."

"I haven't heard from her since the day she left until she started emailing me a couple of weeks ago. I thought she'd go away if I didn't answer." Aiden shook his head. "When she showed up, I don't know why, but she surprised me. I chose to hide my head in the sand. I'm sorry, but once I saw Gina, my world narrowed to one thing. I needed to protect AJ."

"I understand more than you know. What does she want?" Leila squeezed his fingers.

"She says she's changed and wants to be a part of

his life." He shrugged. "But Gina's never been a part of AJ's life and doesn't understand his challenges and struggles. Tyra did what his mother was supposed to do. She gave up everything—her career and her freedom. AJ won't understand Gina is his mother, and I have a feeling Gina won't appreciate that one bit."

"I'm not walking away—not from you and not from AJ." Leila continued holding his hand, and with her free hand, she brushed the hair off his face then laid her palm on his cheek. Her gaze never wavered from his. "I know all about sacrificing and fighting for what's important. I'm an experienced warrior and have the battle wounds to prove it." Her lips curved in a small smile. "While I'm certain you and Mama Ty can handle the battle, when the time comes for an all-out war, having a battalion of seasoned warriors gives you the upper hand. You're not alone, Aiden, and neither is AJ. What's the game plan? What are *we* doing?"

We. Aiden closed his eyes and savored that one word. Rapunzel joined the fight. Aiden and AJ were blessed with Tyra and Matt, but now they also had more. He turned his head and kissed the center of her palm. Aiden opened his eyes and stared into hers. "First, we will hire the best damn attorney we can find, and we will join hands and build around AJ the strongest, most impenetrable wall."

Chapter Fifteen
Fierce

For the fifth time in the last fifteen minutes, Aiden glanced at his watch. Other than a few vehicles, the Skyland Medical Arts parking lot was almost empty. One car must be Dr. Ash's. If he guessed, the black luxury sedan belonged to the Ass, and the rest were either patients or employees.

Leila's car was not in the lot. After her shift yesterday, she called to cancel their dinner date because the ancient heap refused to start. Despite her adamant refusal of help, she was surprised when he showed up and attempted to resuscitate the old girl. His efforts were fruitless. He called in a favor, and the car was towed to Max's, a local garage, for diagnosis and treatment.

Lowering the car window, he switched off the ignition. He lived his entire life in Florida and wasn't bothered by the heat and humidity. Leila ran late. Although he was anxious to see her and was tempted to go searching, he didn't want to rush her. She warned him she worked late on Thursdays and wouldn't be finished until six forty-five p.m., but she gave in when he insisted on picking her up and taking her to dinner.

Dinner was a simple act he couldn't pull off, and he was determined to make up for his past negligence. Yesterday, Leila's day began with him burdening her with his problems and ended with her car mortally ill. Once he had her hunk of junk hauled off, he drove her home, held her hand, and reassured her Max the Miracle Man, owed him and would do his best. Unfortunately, Max's best wasn't enough. He called an hour ago and reassured Aiden he gave Leila's car last rites before she passed.

Aiden glanced at his watch again—seven-fifteen p.m. He straightened, opened the door, and hopped out. Glancing at the entrance of the building, he willed Leila to hurry. He was anxious to update her on his visit with the attorney. He needed to make some pretty significant decisions—fast.

After his visit with the attorney, he texted Tyra, hoping to meet her for lunch and fill her in. But she was out to lunch with Jayden and was picking up AJ from school after. Aiden wasn't ready to act without consulting all his trusted advisors, and he needed to speak to Tyra and Leila in person. Too much depended on this battle, and one miscalculation could lead to disastrous results. Leila was the voice of calm and reason.

Aiden strode to the front of the building. He waited long enough. Surely, by now she was done. Two cars remained in the parking lot. Shrugging, Aiden took the stairs to the second floor. Just as he arrived at the door to the clinic, he caught the door as it flew open and almost slammed into him. Leila barreled out, and her small frame collided with his.

Rocking back on his heels, Aiden grabbed Leila's waist and steadied her. "Easy, Rapunzel." He chuckled. "You're compact, but you almost took us both…"

Leila raised her head.

Her eyes were wide and filled with fear. Tears filled her eyes. She clutched at his shirt and buried her face into his chest.

Curling his shoulders forward, he gathered her in his arms, forming a protective barrier. His circulatory system suddenly received a large dump of adrenaline, and every cell in his body went on high alert. "Leila? Baby? What's wrong?" He held her trembling body closer—sharing his body heat.

Leila shook her head and burrowed closer.

Fear gripped him, and his gut clenched. He shifted her in his arms and surveyed her from head to toe. Her hair and scrubs were disheveled, but she appeared otherwise unhurt. Then he spotted the reddened fingerprints marking her upper arm, and his breath hitched. Blood pounded through his arteries and veins—fire hose style. His blood pressure and pulse sky-rocketed, and for a few seconds, his vision transformed to a hazy red. He blinked and shifted his gaze from the shivering woman in his arms to the sign on the door, *Skyland Pediatrics—Dr. Steven Ash and Associates.*

Did Ash put his hands on her? The man couldn't be that stupid. Aiden would destroy him. As he attempted to control his growing rage, he took a deep breath and released it. He ran his hand up and down her back. "Leila?" Avoiding the reddened area on her arm, he held her by the shoulders. "Baby, you're safe now. I'm here, and I won't let anyone hurt you, but please tell me what happened."

Leila sniffed, and with shaking hands, she rubbed her face. She tilted up her head. "I-I'm okay. I had a little scare, but I'm fine now. Let's go." She strained to pull out of his arms.

Shaking his head, he tightened his arms and gentled his voice. "Please, baby, just tell me what happened." He didn't want to add to her trauma, but he wouldn't budge until she told him what occurred.

"I'll-I'll tell you but not here. Let's go." She glanced at the door, and then at him.

Aiden studied her scared and stormy eyes. He would do as she asked now, but he'd deal with the unbelievable ass who had the audacity to put his hands on her later. Aiden would teach him a lesson he would remember long after Leila's bruises faded. No real man put his hands on a woman against her will. Ash was a coward and a bully.

Noting her shaking hands and pale features, he held her for a second longer and turned. "Let's go." He maneuvered her down the stairs and to the car. Helping her in, he secured her seatbelt.

She grasped his forearm and cleared her throat. "Thank-you. I-I was…"

"Shh." Aiden cupped her cheek. "I'm here, and you're safe. I'm sorry I didn't come in sooner. Like an idiot, I waited in the parking lot while you were attacked." He closed his eyes, kissed her forehead, and then rested his head against hers. If Leila had been raped… Every time he allowed his thoughts to drift in that direction, his gut rolled. Sliding his fingers into her hair, he breathed in her jasmine scent. He memorized the feel and smell of her, reassuring his adrenaline-filled brain she was safe. "Let's get you home. Okay?"

Opening her eyes, Leila shook her head. "Not yet. Mia, Deena…I need some time to pull myself together and figure out what to do." She ran her hands over her face.

"Let's go back to my place. AJ spent the night at Miles, and Tyra is out with Jayden."

She nodded.

Although her hands were less shaky, she was still dazed. The bruises on both upper arms shown clearly and would discolor more by morning. He touched one arm and kissed over the bruise. "Do your arms hurt?"

She shrugged. "I've had worse. I'll be fine. Can we go?"

"What?" His entire body locked and heat suffused his face as pressure once again built in his head. "He's hurt you before?"

Widening her eyes, she gasped. "No, Dr. Ash has never done anything like this." She glanced away, and her shoulders sagged. "Tonight was traumatic and brought back bad memories."

Bad memories? Although Aiden surmised her childhood and family life were difficult, he didn't think she was a victim of abuse. He needed to know much more about her past and present situation. But she was correct. Sitting in a car parked in front of her attacker's office wasn't the place to inspire a heart-to-heart. He kissed her forehead again, and with her hand held tightly in his, he drove to Harbor House in silence.

When he arrived, he positioned her on the deck snuggled under a blanket. Back inside, he grabbed glasses and a bottle of wine and called Silas to check on his boy. Sleepovers were a new milestone for AJ. He confirmed the night was going well.

Returning to the deck, he found her curled up with the blanket. Although her eyes were closed, she wasn't asleep. She might not want to talk, but she had to tell him what happened tonight. His imagination was in overdrive. Opening the wine, he poured each of them a glass and sat beside her. He ran the back of his hand down her cheek.

Her eyelids fluttered open.

"Are you doing okay?"

She licked her lips and shrugged.

"Leila, I'm picking you up and holding you in my arms where you'll be safe. Take your time. We have all night. But I need you to tell me what happened tonight, and then if you have energy, everything else you're holding back. You're not alone anymore. I know you have Deena, but I too care about you and Mia."

She stared at him, and then she uncurled and sat, bringing her knees to her chest—her arms wrapped around her legs. She gazed into his eyes for a minute then glanced away. "Why?" She grabbed the glass of wine and took a big gulp. "The past is in the past."

The woman hadn't heard a word he said. He opened and closed his mouth—searching for a response that reflected his deep desire to care for her and Mia. Obviously, he wasn't expressing himself clearly.

"Don't you have enough on your hands?" She met his gaze. "Nothing can be done about the past. That part of my life is over. As for Dr. Ash, I can handle him. What happened today was my fault anyway…a misunderstanding."

Aiden studied her—not believing what he heard. He took a deep breath and released it. He must tread carefully, or she would shut down. "Whatever happened today made you run out of the office—terrified, pale, trembling, and with bruises." He gently touched the bruise on her arm. "Baby, misunderstandings are not a justification for abuse. No woman deserves to be abused—not under any circumstances. Do you understand?"

"You have no idea what I said or did today." She took another sip of her wine then placed the glass on the table. "Let's just drop this issue, please."

"I'm sorry. I won't drop the subject. I can't." Aiden gritted his teeth. He ran a hand through his hair. He couldn't understand why she excused Ash's behavior, but he had to control his temper and determine what was behind her fear and flawed reasoning. Was she raised to believe abuse was a woman's fault? He swallowed hard and prayed for wisdom. "Leila, Ash crossed a line tonight. He's dangerous."

"You're making too much of this incident. Dr. Ash isn't dangerous. He's an egotistical narcissist who behaves like an over-grown toddler—thinking he should have anything he desires and losing his mind when he doesn't get his way." Gathering her hair, she yanked a hair-tie from her pocket and put her hair in a ponytail.

"That toddler hurt you today. Most likely he's treated other women in the same manner. He *must* be stopped. His behavior is illegal." He rubbed the back of his neck. "I have a friend on the police force. I'll call him. He can take a report from you here. You're not going back to the clinic. We'll find you a new job, and…"

"Stop." She swiped a hand through the air. "Just stop. I appreciate you want to step in and fight my battles, but you can't. I won't let you." She swung her legs to the side and stood facing the ocean. "I need to handle this situation in my own way. I have responsibilities, and I don't have the luxury of acting without thinking. I won't let you run my life—forcing me to do what you think is best. You have no idea what I've been through or how hard I've worked to build the life I have."

He pinched the bridge of his nose and closed his eyes. He wasn't getting through, and he wasn't forcing her to do anything. He was protecting her. Why did she assume he wouldn't understand her life? Each tidbit she offered, he accepted without judgment. He never pushed for more details because he hoped she would give her past to him freely. She was an intelligent woman, but now she behaved irrationally. She thought she could *handle* Ash? No way.

Aiden studied her. She'd pulled away and shut down. Leila stood, her back to him, staring at the sea— her arms wrapped around herself. Whatever lurked in her past couldn't be any worse than what he shared about his life. Why did she believe she had to handle everything on her own? Did she believe sharing her problems made her weak?

Standing, he paced. She was right about one thing. He had enough problems on his hands. But she and Mia were an important part of his life, and their problems were now his. He wished he knew how to earn her trust.

Leila waded into battle for him, but she wouldn't let him do the same. Did any man ever fight for her heart and her trust? Perhaps she's been fighting the world on her own for so long she forgot good people— good men—still existed. Maybe no one told her *she* was worth fighting for.

Hearing footsteps, Aiden glanced up. Leila shuffled toward the steps leading to the beach. Damn it. Where did she think she was going? Why did they play out the same scene over and over again on this deck? He pulled her closer, and she pushed him away. She had no idea what she wanted, and she sent out all kinds of mixed signals. But she wasn't a tease. Leila was terrified of getting hurt. Shoving him away and keeping him at arm's length was a self-protective mechanism.

"Leila, stop."

She froze and peered over her drooping shoulder— her eyes wide, and her hair scattering in the wind.

Jesus, this woman would kill him. He released a long breath. "Come here, Rapunzel."

Leila shook her head.

He raised an arm, palm up toward her. "Baby, stop fighting me and yourself. While walking away might be easier, I can't. I'm falling for you, and I think you're right there with me."

Leila parted her lips.

Smiling, Aiden kept his gaze locked on her. "Give me a chance to understand your world—your past, present, and future. Trust me with that information as I've trusted you. I know I'm asking a lot, but I care about you and Mia as you care about me and AJ. You don't need to fight all your battles on your own. Let me in, and together, we'll be fierce. We'll conquer anything in our path."

Her gaze roamed his face. "I'm scared," she whispered.

"I know, baby. Be brave. I swear to God you can count on me, and I won't hurt you."

Leila glanced at his outstretched arm and hand. She took one step toward him, and then ran the few steps past his outstretched arm and straight into his chest.

Clutching his shirt, she buried her face in his chest.

He gathered her in a tight embrace. When he felt her shudder and heaving sobs wracked her body, he scooped up his little bird and carried her to the closest deck chair.

Placing her arms around his neck, she buried her wet face in his chest.

Finally, a breakthrough. Aiden smiled, glanced to the heavens, and silently mouthed—"Thank you." He settled deep in the chair and kissed the top of her head. When she was ready, she'd come out of hiding. Until then, holding her was as close to heaven as he'd been in a long time. He closed his eyes, savoring the weight of Rapunzel in his lap with her hair surrounding them.

When he felt soft lips touch his neck, his heart filled with love and swelled beyond capacity. Emotion tightened his chest in the sweetest of ways.

Raising her head, Leila laid a palm against his cheek. "Fierce?"

Aiden widened his smile, turned his head, and kissed her palm.

She closed her hand over the area he kissed and pressed her fisted hand into her chest.

"Fierce, baby." Aiden nodded. "Together, we can face anything. Together, we're untouchable."

Chapter Sixteen
Collision

Relishing the warmth his kiss left in the center of her palm, Leila studied Aiden. Warmth spread through her entire body and filled her with hope for the future. She had no choice but to trust him now, because she was incapable of stopping the past from oozing into her present. She straightened in his lap and immediately missed the warmth of his body.

Aiden loosened his arms, but he kept them around her. "Stay, baby. Please stay." She froze. He called her *baby* several times, but she was too distraught to savor the beauty of the word. That precious word glided over her skin—raising goosebumps, sinking into her flesh, and wrapping around every bone, artery, vein, nerve, muscle, and finally her heart. She was never *baby, sweetheart, honey, darling,* or any endearment to a man.

Closing her eyes, she rested her forehead against his. She couldn't walk away. But was she brave enough to stay? Relationships were difficult enough when the individuals involved shared a common language and culture. Leila knew of only a handful of couples who succeeded in mixing cultures. Even if she made peace with her family, she knew they would never accept Aiden. In their eyes, he would be an American—an outsider—who couldn't understand their ways.

She took a deep breath and filled her lungs with his heady masculine scent mixed with the ocean breeze. His intoxicating scent swirled around her brain and quieted her fears—silencing the voices of doom and crumbling the final vestiges of her defenses. Leila sagged against him. She opened her eyes and met Aiden's steady gaze.

"Gravity," she murmured.

"Hmm?" Aiden raised an eyebrow and smiled.

"No matter the barriers my brain conjures, it's useless." She shrugged.

"Baby, I'm not following you. What's useless?" Frowning, he tilted his head.

"I can't stay away." Leila looked away. "We are as different as two people can be. You are the sun and I the moon." She met his gaze. "Gravity has me in its grasp, and I can't defy it."

Aiden kissed her forehead and settled back against the lounger.

She sat between his legs with her back resting against his chest.

"Me neither. From the second I met you, I was drawn in ways I couldn't explain." He circled her with his arms. "Don't fight the gravitational force." He squeezed her. "Stay here safe and secure in the knowledge whatever you share, no matter how big or how small, you won't scare me away. I won't judge or run. You didn't run when I told you about Gina. Remember—*fierce*?"

"My story is long and messy. I don't know where to begin." She glanced at the heavens and relaxed against him.

"We have all night." He shrugged. "Start wherever

you like."

"I grew up differently than you." She licked her lips. "I was blessed with a large Middle Eastern family with many cousins, aunts, and uncles." She smiled. "Plenty of people watched over me, and I always had someone to play and share secrets with. But…"

"But?" Aiden squeezed her.

"I was overly sheltered—stifled actually." She cleared her throat. "My world was filled with rules that must be followed and taboos."

"What kind of rules?" Aiden rested his chin on the top of her head.

"No dating or trips to the mall with my girlfriends." Leila shrugged. "I could only wear very conservative clothing, and playing loud music or dancing was prohibited. The list is long, and new rules were created daily." She swallowed hard. "Don't misunderstand me, I love my culture. But *my* family was different from other Middle Eastern families. *Baba*, my father, created his own rules, and he governed our home with an iron fist."

Aiden's hand closed over her fisted hand. He uncurled her fingers and entwined them with his. "Go on."

"In public, our family put on a good show, but behind closed doors, fear, intolerance, and anger lurked." Leila squeezed his fingers and held on. "*Baba* was the dirty little secret no one dared speak about. My cousins and church friends lived differently. I understood a world existed outside of the one I was trapped in, and I struggled to be free."

As Leila spoke, she discovered a clarity she never experienced. All this time, she and Deena took their personal experiences and generalized them to the entire Middle Eastern culture. They survived traumatic childhoods and chose to deny their heritage. But many loving Middle Eastern families existed where freedom, laughter and joy reigned. She could raise her child with all the wonderful Middle Eastern customs. However, she would spare her the stifling rules and taboos and shield her from the darkness lurking in the shadows of their family.

Leila squeezed Aiden's arm. She would share her entire story. If after hearing her out, he stayed—hand-in-hand with her—he would walk through the darkness to reach the light.

"Did your father hurt you?"

Aiden's voice was solemn, and she noted a tick in his jaw. No simple answer existed. She was hurt in many ways, and *Baba* wasn't the only one to draw blood. "In my father's eyes, I was a mistake and the root of all his failings. My mother and the rest of my family adored me. I tried to please him and failed. Often, I spoke out when I should've shut my mouth. I…"

"Answer the question." He shifted her in his arms to face him. "Did-he-hurt-you?"

"He yelled and screamed." Leila hung her head. "He belittled and intimidated. He shoved and occasionally slapped me. Other than some bruises and one time a broken wrist when he shoved me to the ground, and I landed at a weird angle, I wasn't abused. But every decision was stripped from me until I was powerless. As I grew, I didn't have a voice, and my future was bleak."

"Look at me." Aiden placed two fingers under her

chin and applied pressure. "Before we continue, and I want to hear the entire story, I need you to understand what you described *is* abuse. Your father's behavior was unacceptable." Aiden furrowed his brows. "Where were your mother and the rest of your family while this mistreatment happened? Was your brother also abused?"

Leila pulled away and stood, wrapping her arms around herself. Trembling, she couldn't stop her pulse from beating erratically. Aiden asked the question she asked herself many times. How could the people who claimed to love her witness Yusuf's actions and do nothing?

When the heat of Aiden's body warmed her back, and his arms circled her, Leila closed her eyes and tilted her head against his chest. "They were all present—watching and listening but unwilling or unable to challenge him. *Baba* is the patriarch of the family. What he said was law, and what he did wasn't questioned. He was, and still is, powerful and fearful."

"And your brother?"

"In my parents' eyes, Gabe did no wrong." Leila released a long breath. "He is the only son—a precious commodity to carry on the family name."

"How about your mother? Why didn't she protect you?" Aiden tightened his arms.

That was the million-dollar question. "I can't answer that question. In many ways, Mama was the best of mothers, but she didn't protect me enough. Throughout my childhood she made excuses for *Baba*'s behavior. I was a good and faithful daughter. I tried to make them proud, but…" She took a steadying breath. "I was young and starved for attention, and I made one life-altering mistake."

"Mia?" Aiden murmured.

Opening her eyes, she nodded.

Aiden gently turned her in his arms. "Did they push you to have an abortion?"

She met his gaze. "I waited until I was five months pregnant, and the choice to terminate was no longer an option before I told them. If I ended her life, I couldn't have lived. I also couldn't walk the earth searching the eyes of every child and wondering which one was mine. I knew my family would be furious, but I…"

"Tell me," he whispered and led her to the deck chairs, positioning them as they were before.

Every detail of the last week she was in Jersey stormed back in vivid color. "A few days after I told my parents I was pregnant, I woke up from a mid-afternoon nap to find my parents, brother, aunts, and uncles gathered in the living room, drinking coffee. They were a war tribunal out for blood."

Leila stared into the distance. "My father kept screaming, 'Who did this to you? Who defiled you?' But what good would come from uttering the name they longed to hear? We lived in America. No one could be forced into a shotgun wedding." Swallowing hard, she twisted and gazed into his eyes. The sympathy in his eyes stole her breath.

"I have you, baby. Go on." Aiden held her hand, rubbing his thumb in circles.

"I was treated as a criminal—interrogated for hours." She took a steadying breath. "They called me awful names. When *Baba* became physical, he was dragged away by Gabe. Then Gabe…" She pulled her hand from Aiden's and wiped her wet cheeks. "He spit in my face and said, 'The little whore is not worth your imprisonment, *Baba*. She is no longer worthy of the Solomon name. She is nothing but trash.' "

She wasn't sure she possessed the strength to tell Aiden the rest, and yet she was compelled to. She raised her head. "After four hours of interrogation, my aunts and uncles returned home with promises to return the next day. *Baba* and Gabe retreated to the kitchen with a bottle of scotch while Mama, without a word to anyone, slipped into her bedroom and locked the door. The storm was over as quickly as it began…I thought." Covering her face with both hands, Leila rubbed her cheeks and sagged into Aiden. "Late that night, Mama slipped into my room, packed my bags, and told me to leave."

"What?" Aiden stiffened. "She kicked you out in the middle of the night…pregnant…with nowhere to go?"

"She gave me money and told me to go to Deena." Leila shrugged. "She knew Deena and I kept in touch."

"I don't understand. How could she…"

Leila threaded her fingers with his. Aiden wouldn't understand her complicated mess of a life with the little context she gave him. She took a deep breath and told him about her relationships with her mother, Deena, Niveen, Gabe, and Amal, and the impact they had on her life. She recalled her recent conversations with her family, her mother's illness, and her plans to return home.

Throughout her storytelling, Aiden stayed silent— occasionally squeezing her to him or kissing the top of her head. His steady heartbeat and strong arms surrounding her gave her the fortitude to share her troubles. Cathartically, she regaled him with her colorful family history, and then continued with her survival in Florida, and the challenges of finding a decent job that paid enough.

No matter how much she wished to be rid of Dr. Ash, she couldn't leave at this time. She needed the money. Searching for another job was daunting. Summer was Deena's busiest season, and between taking care of Mia and working for Deena and Dr. Ash, Leila didn't have enough hours in the day to accomplish much else.

Leila paused, straightened, and turned. "Right now, my priority is Mia and seeing my mother. When I return from Jersey, I'll look for another job. You see what a disaster my life is? I'm overwhelmed. While I'm no longer trapped in the Solomon maximum security prison, and I'm making my own decisions, with Dr. Ash, I feel cornered again. I'm out of choices."

"You're never out of choices." Aiden frowned. "Let's deal with the most pressing issue first. Has Ash come on to you before?"

Lying to Aiden wasn't an option. Their relationship must be built on honesty. "A few times but never this aggressively." She looked away. "Today, he denied my request for time off. I asked him to reconsider. He insisted *I* reconsider a few things. I said no, and…"

"Ash's behavior can't continue." Aiden's jaw tightened. "You have to report him."

"This is a small community." Leila met his gaze, narrowing her eyes. "He's well-known and respected. If I report him to the police or the medical board, I'll never find a job as a medical assistant again." She grabbed his hand and squeezed. "Listen and try to understand. Mia depends on me for everything. Like many single parents, my life is a difficult balancing act. Like a house built from cards, one wrong move will bring my world tumbling down."

"But you're wrong. You're not alone." Aiden shook his head. "Deena and I are by your side. But while we are on the topic of support, where's Mia's father in this story? Does he pay support?"

Leila pulled away and shifted to the deck chair across from him. He might as well know about this part of her life too. By the end of the day he would be one of two people walking the earth who knew all her secrets. She took a fortifying breath. "Eric doesn't know he has a child."

"What? You never told him?" Aiden gaped.

"No. Eric is a physician—my brother's business partner." Whenever she thought of her brief relationship with Eric, she felt incredibly stupid. She still harbored some shame, but she was also angry at Eric for using her and squandering her innocence.

Leila fisted her hands until her fingernails bit into her palms. "I was infatuated." She spoke quickly—blurting out the words before she lost her nerve. "I believed he was my dream come true. But I was an easy lay—a one-time hook-up. Afterward, he was clear he wasn't interested in a repeat performance. Two weeks later, he announced his engagement to a wealthy socialite."

"That bastard," he muttered.

Even in the dark with the deck light on, she observed Aiden's flushed face and the hard set of his jaw. "Yes, he was a bastard, but I wasn't a victim. He didn't rape me. I was naïve, but I understood how

177

babies were made." She cleared her throat, and her face heated. "Before we became involved, Eric gave me birth control pills to regulate my periods—samples so my family wouldn't find out."

Frowning, he tilted his head.

She swallowed hard. She bombarded poor Aiden with an avalanche of complicated personal history as well as a crash course on the twisted Solomon culture and belief system. She was so far into this tale of misery and mess, she might as well finish. "In my parent's eyes an unmarried woman taking birth control pills meant she was sexually active and promiscuous. Anyway, I forgot to take the pills for a week when I was sick, and I got pregnant."

Studying Aiden, Leila saw his strained features and knitted brows. Confusion and questions lurked in his eyes. Had she lost him? Did he think all her people were ignorant and backward? Even if she hadn't scared him off, and he decided she was worth the effort, how on Earth would Aiden learn to appreciate her culture when all he heard were stories of one dysfunctional, atypical family?

Leila dropped her head in her hands. She had approached this relationship with Aiden in all the wrong ways. Why hadn't she introduced him to the beauty of the Middle Eastern culture first before overwhelming him with intolerance and insanity? Beauty existed in the sanctity of marriage, the strength of the family unit, the respect for the elderly, the lyrical songs that spoke of love, loyalty, and tradition, and the deep history spanning centuries. But many people lacked the ability to appreciate a culture remarkably different from their own.

As in every region of the world, good and bad existed side by side. Yet, daily the world was treated to horrific news stories of religious and territorial conflict, intolerance, violence, hostility, and unrest in the Middle East. Those powerful images were difficult to forget or see beyond. But Aiden used many different lenses to view the world. Perhaps, where she and her people were concerned, he'd pull out his wide lens.

Aiden touched Leila's shoulder. "Baby, come out of hiding."

She straightened. "I'm sorry. I've thrown a lot at you. You probably want to run, and I…"

"Rapunzel, stop pushing me away." He smiled. "I'm not going anywhere. Your culture is new to me, and I'm trying to understand. Don't hold back any details because you're worried about my reaction. Just keep talking. I still don't understand why you didn't tell Eric you were pregnant. Did you tell anyone in your family?"

Leila released a long breath and shook her head. She threaded her fingers through his. "*Baba* would have killed him for defiling me. Although Eric didn't rape me, my family wouldn't care. My father would have acted irrationally—ending up in prison. I'm not exaggerating." She squeezed his fingers. "All my brother's money was wrapped up in that business, and Eric held all the cards. If I named Eric, my brother would have acted as a matter of honor. He would have lost everything."

Pulling away, she rubbed at her sternum—the tightness in her chest making her breaths shallow. "I know this story sounds crazy. While my story isn't unique, and thousands of other girls become pregnant in a similar manner, those girls don't carry the Solomon name. I already brought shame to my family. I couldn't be the reason for their complete destruction." She swallowed hard. "None of that matters now anyway."

"Why?" Aiden quirked his head to the side.

"The time for hanging my head in shame and hiding in Florida is over. I'm not ashamed of my daughter. In the near future, I hope to introduce her to my family. But my baby girl is the spitting image of her father."

"And Eric? Will you tell him he has a daughter?"

"I have no choice." Leila ran a hand through her hair. "Mia will stay with Deena while I go home and face my demons and slay my dragons. My trip to New Jersey isn't a happy family reunion. It's a trip into the jungle where I must stand strong and ready myself to tame lions and tigers and bears."

Aiden released a long breath. "I've listened to everything you said. I've done my best to keep an open mind, but I have to be honest." He shook his head. "I swear I don't mean to hurt you, but I can't understand why you want anything to do with your family."

Leila held his face in her hands and peered into his beautiful eyes. "For the same reason I can't stay away from you—gravity. They are my people, and their blood runs in my veins. For whatever reason, gravity has its hook in me, drawing me closer and closer. Collision is inevitable."

Chapter Seventeen
Now

At five a.m. the next morning, Aiden rolled out of bed. Operating on little sleep, he stumbled to the coffee-maker and made himself a cup of black magic. Wearing a scowl, Tyra strutted into the kitchen. She was always hot tempered, but over the last few days, she was especially difficult—picking a fight at every opportunity. Aiden blamed her moodiness on Gina's appearance, but his gut warned something more troubled her.

Without a word, he brewed her a cup of coffee and took a seat on the deck—watching the sun rise.

Tyra followed him. In silence, she finished her first cup and made another for both of them.

Midway through the second cup, he filled her in on the previous day's events and his intention to invite Gina for lunch with him and AJ on Saturday.

"I don't understand why you think lunch with that bitch is a good idea. But I'm coming." With her jaw stubbornly set, she glared.

"Ty, you're not coming." He shook his head. "Take Saturday off. The day is supposed to be beautiful. Spend the day with Jay. Lunch will be a quick affair, and I'll call you the second we're done."

"Do *not* tell me what to do, Aiden Stone." She waved a finger in front of his face. "AJ is my boy too, isn't he?"

"Of course he is." Aiden sat back. "Why would you ask such a question?" He studied her with growing annoyance.

"Seriously?" She straightened and squared her shoulders.

"Look, Mike doesn't think your presence at lunch is a good idea. He prefers the meeting be as cordial as possible." Aiden rubbed the back of his neck. He knew she would give him hell.

If she could control her temper and be reasonable where Gina was concerned, she could attend the lunch. But she was a mama bear on the warpath. Initially, she was calm where Gina was concerned—weirdly so. But after she experienced Gina's surprise visit at the gallery, she became unhinged and over-protective. Tyra slammed her mug on the side table spilling coffee everywhere. "Who the hell is Mike, and why does he have a say in what happens with my boy and I don't?"

Aiden placed down his mug and rubbed his temples. He had a monster headache, and her screeching didn't help. "Mike Langston is the attorney I hired. I told you I met with him yesterday. And you know you have a say in every aspect of AJ's life. But will you pipe down and listen? My head is about to explode."

Tyra snapped shut her mouth and pierced him with her gaze.

"You know, legally, Gina is AJ's mother."

She opened her mouth.

"Uh-uh." He held up a hand. "Shut it and listen."

Raising her eyebrows, she pursed her lips.

Aiden fought the forming smile on his lips.

Although the matter they discussed was serious, Tyra's raised eyebrows, laser-like stare, and a God-help-you attitude was funny. "I never legally terminated Gina's parental rights. Supposedly, she's clean now." He took a deep breath. "She could make a play for shared custody. Mike gave me a lot to think about." He shook his head. "I can hear her out—protecting our boy to the best of my ability, or I can drag us all through the court system where she might be granted unsupervised visits."

"And I don't have a say in how you handle this situation?" Tyra pursed her lips.

"Our schedules have been nuts. I tried to catch up with you yesterday, but you were out to lunch. Then Leila…" He threw up his hands.

He picked up his coffee mug and took a long swallow and burned his tongue and throat in the process. "Look, we don't know why Gina is here. You know I don't trust her near AJ, but Mike is the best money can buy. He strongly advised we make this process as uncontentious as possible until he can dig up her entire history. I haven't called her yet."

Nostrils flaring, she crossed her arms and huffed.

"Work with me, Ty." Aiden massaged the back of his neck and shoulders. "Go out with Jay. To be honest, I'd rather have you with me, but I will do what Mike says. Please don't make this situation harder than it needs to be."

"I think you're making a mistake. AJ will sense the strain between you and Gina, and he'll act out. You know he fears strangers. Lunch without me is too much. He needs me."

"He does need you—as do I." Aiden smiled. "Remember what you said when I received that first email from Gina? *We'll do what he deserves—even if it's not what we want."*

"That was before I took a look at her. She is an evil and conniving bitch." She folded her arms over her chest. "I can read people better than you can. Hell, I made a living doing so. I am warning you, she is up to no good. Do you honestly think she is what our boy deserves?"

"No. But putting AJ through a custody battle where he might need an evaluation by healthcare providers and social workers, and where he might be forced to be in her presence by himself, is definitely not in his best interest." He focused on her. "Let's stick together and not lose our minds. Please, Ty. I need your help."

She held his gaze for a minute longer, and then her shoulders drooped. "Fine, A. I'll find something to keep myself busy, but I'm not going out with Jay. He and I are history."

"What?" He stilled. "Why? I thought you two were doing well. What happened?"

Tyra stood and faced the rising sun. "Details don't matter." She shrugged. "He wants something I can't give."

"What?" Aiden stood and narrowed his eyes.

She shrugged again.

"Ty, what does Jay want?"

"More. He's becoming needy. You know I don't do needy. I ended our relationship, and I'm not interested in discussing the matter." She stalked toward him, picked up her mug, and stormed inside—slamming the door behind her.

He followed her. The conversation deteriorated until she stomped up the stairs and slammed her bedroom door. Aiden winced. He rummaged through his medicine cabinet and swallowed a couple of pain relievers. He would have to deal with Tyra later. Now, he must dress and drive Leila to work. A small window of opportunity existed to change her mind about going into work today.

Last night Aiden accompanied Leila home to find Deena sitting on the deck.

Over another glass of wine, Leila replayed the events of the day.

Deena agreed Leila shouldn't return to the practice but focus on earning her real estate license and building a cliental. Until then, Leila could increase her hours working for Deena. Other realtors would also be delighted to work with her. Deena offered to help Leila with daycare expenses and purchase a new car. Leila refused to listen to reason.

Showered and dressed, Aiden brewed himself a travel mug of java and drove to Leila's cottage. He parked the car and texted her to come out. Despite his best efforts and arguments, he failed to make her see reason, and now he led her to the lion's den.

He wondered if she had a self-destructive streak. In some ways, Leila reminded him of Gina. Both grew up in abusive homes and were resistant to accepting help. Gina used alcohol and drugs to dull her pain. Leila refused to admit she was a victim and allowed her family to shackle her and drag her into the past.

Aiden struggled to understand Leila's culture and her loyalty to her family. He was thrilled she opened up the night before, and he did his best to ask intelligent questions without sounding judgmental. Her family's reaction to her pregnancy was beyond his comprehension. They were rightly upset, but the extreme actions they might take if they discovered Eric was Mia's father blew his mind.

Opening the car door, Leila slid in the passenger seat. She smiled, but her eyes were bleak, and her face was pale. "Good morning, baby." He stretched across the seat and kissed her cheek.

"Morning," she murmured.

Threading his fingers through hers, he gazed into her eyes. "Are you sure you…"

"Aiden, please. No more." She shook her head. "I think we've said everything we need to say. I understand you don't agree with my decision, but I'm exhausted, and I don't have the energy to argue. If you can't be supportive, I'll understand. Deena will drive me."

He studied the stubborn set of her jaw. He lost the battle, and if he pushed her much further, he would lose her. His gut clenched, and his frustration level with her, Gina, Tyra, and his life on the whole rose to the point he wanted to punch something or someone. Instead, he pursed his lips, expelled a deep breath, and put the car in drive. Twenty minutes later, he parked in the almost empty parking lot.

For a few seconds, Leila stared out the passenger window. She kissed his cheek. "I'll be fine. Thank you," she whispered, stepped out of the car, and walked to the front of the Skyland Medical Offices. She turned, waved, and disappeared inside.

Although he waved back, he couldn't conjure up a smile. Leila needed to exert her independence. He understood she was an adult who could make decisions on her own without his approval. He was convinced, though, her plan to handle Ash was flawed. Although she was experienced with abusers, she was the victim. She intended on having a heart to heart with Ash—chastising him and threatening him with legal action if he crossed the line again. Her strategy was dangerous. Abusers and bullies don't respond well to threats.

Aiden slammed a palm against the steering wheel. He was helpless to protect her, but he couldn't drive away—leaving her in the hands of a monster. He listened to his gut. Switching off the ignition, he rolled down his windows and took a slug of his coffee. He wasn't sure how long he would sit in the parking lot, baking under the Florida sun. Every few minutes, he peeked at his watch and then the front door of the building.

The time was eight thirty-five a.m., and the clinic opened at nine a.m. Leila, her co-workers, and Ash arrived early to ready for the day. Surely by now, Ash and Leila talked. Should he text Leila and see how the chat went, call Gina and see if she was amenable to lunch tomorrow, or call Tyra and apologize for the way he laid into her?

His life was filled with impossible relationships and resembled a reality television show where the man had multiple wives each with their own unique personality, needs, and problems. Aiden smiled and shook his head. He couldn't manage one relationship. Multiple wives were beyond his skill level.

Closing his eyes, he rested his head against the headrest. Right at this second, he couldn't do anything to help Leila, and he had a game plan for Gina. Tyra's problems weighed heavy on his mind. He wasn't sorry for the hard words he delivered this morning. The time for a deep heart-to-heart was long overdue. Although he predicted the breakup with Jayden, he couldn't sit back and watch Tyra make the biggest mistake of her life. He loved her too much and owed her his life to let her throw away her future happiness.

Over the years, he and Tyra swapped life histories. She regaled him of stories of her traumatic childhood in the foster care system. At fourteen, she met and fell in love with Tyrell Williams, also a foster child. Together the Tys survived until they aged out of the system. While she left behind her troubled beginnings and earned a full ride to Florida State University, Tyrell fell deep into the world of drugs and was in and out of prison.

On the day Tyra discovered she was ten weeks pregnant, she left work early and returned to the apartment they shared to tell him her miraculous news. Drug paraphernalia littered her coffee table. She couldn't keep turning a blind eye to his drug use. An innocent was on the way who deserved better.

Tyra and Tyrell argued.

Stoned and furious, he shoved her out of his way and left the apartment. Her body slammed against the wall—skull colliding with and denting the plaster. She fell to the ground and lost consciousness.

Several hours later, on the first floor of St. Joseph's Hospital in the emergency room, Tyrell lost his fight to live—succumbing to an overdose. On the second floor, Tyra regained consciousness but lost her will to live when she learned her baby died, and on the third floor, in the labor and delivery unit, AJ Stone was born but struggled to live. Three weeks later, Aiden Stone walked into the same hospital, held his boy for the first time, and discovered his reason for living.

Gravity. Aiden and Tyra were drawn together by forces completely out of their hands. A sick infant who didn't belong to either of them brought them together. Aiden believed nothing happened by chance. He, Tyra, and AJ needed one another to survive. Now, though, the time had come to open the door and let others into their protective cocoon.

Jayden was a good man with a strong will and a heart that beat only for Tyra. The man put up with her sassy tongue and her array of shit with a smile. Aiden was fairly certain Jay would bide his time then bounce back for another round. Aiden wouldn't allow Tyra to run away from her chance at happiness. He would harass her and put up with her crap until she came to her senses. After all, she had done just that for him where AJ was concerned.

When a tapping came against his driver's side window, Aiden jumped. He opened his eyes and straightened. He met Leila's stormy hazel eyes. For a few seconds, he froze, surveying her pale features. What the hell was she doing out here? Did Ash hurt her again? Did she quit? Although her eyes were a bit glassy and unfocused, and her shoulders slumped, she appeared calm. Frowning, Aiden slowly opened the car door and stepped out.

"You stayed," she whispered as she sagged against him.

"Of course I stayed, baby." He cupped her cheek—caressing it with his thumb. "I felt uneasy leaving you. Are you okay?"

"I'm all right." She pushed her cheek into his palm.

"What happened?" Leaning against the car, he

looped an arm around her waist and drew her closer.

She plucked out an envelope from her bag.

"What is it?" He frowned.

"See for yourself." She shrugged.

Aiden took the envelope but continued studying her. She was eerily calm. Even her voice was monotone. He opened the envelope, and when he viewed the check, he gaped. "Ten thousand dollars?" His brows furrowed.

Standing with her arms hanging loosely by her side, she nodded. "Yup—six months' salary."

She was in shock. Did the bastard fire her and pay her off? Questions raced in Aiden's head. Shaking his head, he tucked the envelope into her bag and guided her to the passenger side. The parking lot was not the place for this conversation. Without questions or resistance, she allowed him to strap her in.

He hopped into the car and started the engine.

Clutching her handbag to her chest, she stared straight ahead.

As he maneuvered the car out of the lot and onto the main road, Aiden lifted her hand to his lips. He drove to Sal's, a tiny diner located near a deserted warf. The place was a hovel and should be torn down, but everyone knew Sal and supported his crumbling business. Sal brewed the best coffee in town and made greasy but delicious breakfast sandwiches and burgers. The man was at least eighty, and when he passed, the diner would close.

Aiden guided Leila to one of the rickety picnic tables facing the ocean. He left her and returned a few minutes later with well-sugared coffee and sandwiches. Removing the lid, he set the cup in front of her.

"Drink."

Lifting the cup to her mouth, she swallowed. Immediately, she made a face, gagged, and set down the coffee. "Oh my God, what the hell is that?" She grabbed the sandwich and took a bite. She made a face again and put down the sandwich. Glaring at him, she grabbed a napkin and wiped her hands and mouth. Surveying her surroundings, she stared at him. "Where the hell are we? I need to know so I can make sure I never come back. My morning sucked, and now you're trying to poison me."

He forgot her distaste for coffee, but that slip-up worked to his advantage. She snapped out of her trance. Aiden smiled. "This is the best brew in the state."

"If this bitter sludge is the best, I now know what I'm not missing." She scrunched her nose. "Seriously disgusting." She lifted her chin toward the sandwich. "I'm not eating that mess."

"Good. More for me." He smiled through a mouthful. "Now, are you ready to tell me what happened?"

"Not much to tell." Leila shrugged. "When I arrived, Dr. Ash was holed up in his office. Me and Katie, the other medical assistant, and Dawn, the front desk receptionist, prepared charts and stocked rooms, waiting for his highness to open the door. When he emerged, he marched to the front door, locked it, and informed us, effective immediately the practice closed. He handed me and Katie an envelope, told us to leave, and human resources would be in touch." Leila shook her head. "He told Dawn to cancel all appointments and refer patients to the other locations."

"That's all?" Aiden tilted his head.

"Yup. He stomped to his office and slammed the door."

"No apologies or explanations?"

"Nope."

"Any thoughts on what happened?" Aiden frowned, not quite believing she told him the entire story.

"Dawn said someone finally reported the bastard to corporate—someone braver than me." Leila hung her head.

Standing, he rounded the table and sat beside her. He wrapped her in his arms.

She closed her eyes and tilted her head to the sun.

Aiden wasn't sure what to say. He wasn't the least bit upset Ash received what he deserved. The man was a predator. Although he was glad Leila was safe, he hated the defeated slouch of her shoulders. "Well, the good news is you don't have to deal with him anymore."

With a sigh, she opened her eyes and met his gaze. "Yes, but I should have reported him a long time ago. He was verbally abusive long before he started making sexual advances, and I did nothing. I let fear rule me, as I've done my entire life."

He entwined his fingers with hers. "Don't be too tough on yourself. He was in a position of power, and you were vulnerable."

"I did a lot of thinking last night." Leila concentrated on the ocean and the swell and dip of the waves. "Growing up, I recognized *Baba*'s behavior was unacceptable, but Mama and the others always made excuses. The Middle Eastern culture is male dominated. While abuse isn't condoned, it is not uncommon. I think women rarely speak up. Mama, my aunts, and cousins were brainwashed to believe whatever *Baba* said was law." Leila dropped her head in her hands and scrubbed her face. "Dear God, if we'd stayed, what would have happened to me and Mia?

Aiden rubbed her back. He was proud of her. Leila began to see her family clearly. If she sought help and worked through her past, she would end the cycle of abuse, and Mia would have a healthy role model. "Give yourself some time to process what happened. Remember you're not alone. You have me and Deena. What do you want to do now?"

"Now, I learn to live without regret." She took a deep breath and faced him. "I face the past and put it to rest so I can build a happy and healthy life. Now, instead of sitting back and waiting for life to happen, I take charge and take what I want and what I need from life." Leila gathered his face between her trembling palms. Leaning in, she touched her lips to his. Then she kissed him again and again.

Wrapping her tighter in his embrace, he deepened the kiss. *Now* was a great place to be.

Chapter Eighteen
Glowing

Leila rolled to her back, stretched, and yawned. She opened her eyes and immediately scrunched them shut. She was blinded by the bright sun invading her room through her not-so-blackout curtains she purchased from a local discount store. For a single mother who was jobless with serious family problems and a hot boyfriend she had no idea what to do with, she was remarkably cheery. In fact, she glowed.

Yesterday started as a complete and utter shit day. From the second she woke up, two bolder-sized, anxiety-producing objects lodged themselves in her throat and stomach. She could barely function, and she felt powerless to change the trajectory of her life. But losing her job was a gift.

Blinking repeatedly, she opened her eyes and stretched once more. Smiling, she grabbed her cell from the nightstand and glanced at the time—seven-thirty a.m. She slept in later than she did in years, and she was energized and ready to meet any challenges the day brought. No matter what happened, Leila was determined to make the day grand. She would take charge of all aspects of her life. No more whining. Grabbing life by the balls, she would create a satisfying life.

Leila had allowed her *baba*, Gabe, her uncles, Eric,

and now Dr. Ash to mistreat her. She believed she was unworthy of their love and respect, and she gave up on herself. Every man in her life, Aiden excluded, overshadowed her and snuffed out her God-given right to be happy and to shine. Now, she shined so bright, she glowed in the dark, and she would teach her daughter to do the same.

Leila stared at her phone and noted a new text message from Aiden.

—Have a great day. Don't forget to change the car title. See you tonight.—

Grinning, Leila glanced at the window, and through the space between the window and curtain, she glimpsed the forest green of her new-used SUV she and Aiden purchased yesterday. The car was eighteen years old with over one hundred and fifty thousand miles. Aiden and Max declared the vehicle to be in great condition and worthy of the forty-five hundred dollars she paid.

—Morning. Getting up now. Agenda for the day. Change title, finger printing, grocery shopping, and cooking. Have a good day.—

She giggled and waited for his return text.

—Finger-printing? Planning on getting arrested?—

Yesterday her new life began. She lost her job but gained perspective, and then she took the initiative and kissed a man. She also bought a new car and booked a ticket to New Jersey leaving July fifth—all before two p.m. After, she and Aiden picked up Mia from daycare. He took them to lunch then dropped them home.

While she watched Mia playing in the sand, Leila sat on the deck and surfed the Internet. She followed the steps outlined on the Florida Real Estate Commission's website to obtain her Florida License. By the end of the day, she completed the application for licensure and signed up for the pre-licensing course. To be a licensed sales associate, she needed to be finger-printed, complete sixty-three hours of online courses, pass the licensing exam, and complete forty-five hours of post-licensing course work.

—*Nope. Need fingerprints for my FL real estate license. Tell you all the details tonight. Go do whatever photographers do, and come with your appetite 'cause you're in for a treat.*—

—*Can't wait. I'm always in for a treat when I'm with you, beautiful.*—

Pushing off the covers, Leila bounced out of bed and readied for the day. The night before, after Mia fell asleep, she updated Deena on the day's events. She accepted Deena's offer to extend her hours working with her. Rebecca Anderson, a local realtor, also asked to borrow Leila to stage a couple of homes. Deena would spread the word she was willing to share Leila. She assured Leila she was a hot commodity and would soon have more work on her hands than she knew what to do with.

As Leila dressed for the day, she made a mental grocery list of the items she needed to prepare a celebratory dinner—Karima style. She hadn't savored her mother's cooking in so long. She'd memorized each recipe by heart but didn't cook a single dish since she left home. Although Leila was a good cook, nothing she produced tasted as good as a dish prepared by her mother.

Today, she would celebrate life and introduce and

reintroduce all the people she loved to the wonders of Middle Eastern cuisine. Leila froze. Love? Were Aiden and AJ included in the group of people she loved? AJ was a sweet boy who was easy to love, but was she in love with Aiden Stone?

The last time she believed she was in love, she was very wrong. Now, she was older and wiser. Although her relationship with Aiden was new, she realized her heart was well on its way to merging with his—oncoming traffic be damned. Aiden was *the one*.

Inhaling deeply, Leila followed the scent of cinnamon rolls to the kitchen. Deena was up and baked the premade frozen cinnamon rolls she was addicted to. Although Leila easily resisted the gooey, calorie filled sweet, she couldn't resist Aiden's sexy smile, warm eyes, and comforting embrace. She wasted enough time beating up herself for the past, she wouldn't waste time defining her relationship with Aiden. She would live in the moment. Unlike the old women in her culture, Leila didn't believe in forecasting the success of a relationship based on a man's familial background, heritage, religion, job, and bank account.

She grew up listening to her mother, aunts, and all their match-making, busy-bodied friends dissect the qualifications of every eligible male in church—weighing his value as a future suitor for their daughters. They rejected men based on trivial and vain facts—familial baldness, bad table manners, poor attendance in church, or a family scandal, such as a divorce. Sometimes the women contacted relatives in Egypt to investigate a rumor linked to the man's family.

Leila shook her head. No secret formula to happiness existed. If a magical concoction existed, her mother and father, and most of their friends who believed these ridiculous cultural rules would be deliriously happy. Many were not.

"Morning, Deena. I see you warmed up the cinnamon rolls without burning them." Leila strolled into the kitchen.

"Don't be too judgmental, girlfriend." Deena stuck out her tongue. "Let's see what you produce tonight."

"I haven't cooked Middle Eastern food for a while, but you, my friend, are in for a treat." Leila poured boiling water over her tea bag and took her mug to the kitchen table.

"To be honest, I can't wait. What's on the menu other than Aiden?" Licking icing off her fingers and lips, Deena sat across from Leila.

"Deena!" Heat traveled up Leila's neck to her face.

Deena threw back her head and cackled. "Girlfriend, you've been wearing a happy grin since I walked in last night, and your eyes have a new sparkle. You're actually glowing. I think a lot more happened yesterday than you finally removing your head from your ass and moving on with life. Right?"

"I kissed him." Leila grinned.

"Yes." Deena slapped her hand on the table. She glanced up to the ceiling. "Thank you, God. You have way too many nuns, and she would be a total waste of your energy. She sucks at celibacy."

Throwing a dishtowel at Deena, Leila glared. "Shut up. Don't remind God of my sin."

"Let's get back to what's important. You kissed that handsome specimen of a man, and…"

With an elbow on the table, Leila rested her chin in her hand. "He's everything I've longed for, and we're perfectly suited. His life is a bit of a mess, but mine is too." She chuckled "When he smiles, he takes away my breath. He touches me, and he causes my heartrate to jump into overdrive. When I'm with him, every unfounded fear, ridiculous rule, and taboo drilled into me since I was a child becomes insignificant. Deena, he *believes* I'm special. At times, I want to pinch myself just to be sure he is not a figment of every wish I've made."

Deena sniffled and cleared her throat.

Straightening, Leila held Deena's hand. She'd been insensitive. Although Leila was finally happy, she knew Deena struggled to find peace and happiness after Jesse. Deena refused to discuss her relationship with Jesse. The cottage was small, however, and sound echoed from room to room. On more than one occasion, Leila heard Deena crying and detected the evidence of sleepless nights on her face. She'd respected Deena's privacy long enough. "I'm sorry, Deena. I didn't mean to make you cry."

"Don't apologize." Deena wiped her face with her hands. "These are happy tears. Don't ever temper your joy. Glow."

"And you?" Leila squeezed Deena's hand. "When will you find happy again? Don't you think the time has come to tell me what happened?"

"I don't have much to tell." Deena pulled her hand from Leila. "Jesse cheated on me. She said I was emotionally detached, and she needed more. I gave up everything for her. I left home when I was a kid and gave up my family and friends. I turned my back on my heritage and changed everything about myself— disavowing who I was. And for the last year, she's been having an affair with a colleague. How cliché."

"I'm sorry." Leila's heart ached for her friend. "I knew she did something awful."

"I'm contemplating what comes next. I loved Jesse, but I too cannot deny who I am. I won't make excuses for my family—their beliefs and their distance." She shrugged. "You know, she was my first and my only relationship?"

"Really?" Leila furrowed her brow. "When did you meet?" She didn't know much about Deena's relationship with Jessica Reynolds. Homosexuality was repugnant in the Middle Eastern culture. Leila didn't believe homosexual relationships were sinful or offensive. People loved who they loved. She wasn't God and wouldn't sit in judgment.

Jesse had been civil to Leila, but in many small ways she was clear Leila and Mia were unwelcome. Leila never discussed Jesse's actions with Deena and moved out as quickly as possible. Then, she kept Jesse at a distance.

"I met Jesse when I was seventeen and Mama finally convinced *Baba* to take us on a real family vacation." Deena smiled. "Remember we vacationed in Cancun for five glorious days?"

Leila nodded.

"Jesse was at the same resort. Mama and *Baba* sat on the beach for hours staring at the waves and gossiping, but I loved the music and the games in the pool. After a few drinks, they relaxed and allowed me out of their sight. Jesse and I met at the pool. Leila, the second I looked into her eyes, I knew…" Deena sighed. "Everything in my life finally made sense. I was seventeen and she was twenty-two. I was inexperienced, unsure, terrified, and confused..." Deena swallowed. "Jesse was none of those things. She knew who she was, and with her, for those five days, *I* finally understood who I was."

Deena stood and wandered to the deck, keeping her back to Leila. "Jesse lived in Melbourne, Florida, and she was convinced, in time, I would forget her. But that was far from the truth. When I returned home, I called several times a day. A few months later, she flew to Jersey for a few days. I snuck out every night to be with her."

Some would say Deena had been a confused and foolish young woman—taking huge risks with a woman she barely knew and giving up everything on a whim. Leila, however, couldn't fault her. Deena was brave. Despite the loss and heartache she experienced, she'd followed her heart, found herself, and discovered love.

Turning, Deena studied Leila. She smiled and wiped away more tears. "As our relationship grew, I became reckless. Mama walked into my room one night and saw Jesse on my laptop. Jesse and I were...ah...having a very private conversation. Mama heard enough. The rest is history." Deena's shoulders slumped. "Must I be more explicit?"

"The walls were thin." Leila shrugged. "Our bedrooms were right next to each other. I had a front row seat to that argument and all the rest to follow. And your mama, well, she spilled her guts to the wrong person. After you left, your secret, wasn't much of a secret. That's why your parents moved. They joined a different church and rarely attended any social gatherings."

"I know." Deena nodded. "Others knew my email

address. I never replied to their vitriol, but I sure read every word and built around me a nice hard shell. You were never like those hateful people. You didn't think I was an aberration of nature. The list of names I was called is pretty extensive." She quirked her head to the side. "But you never expressed surprise. Why was acceptance and love easy for you and impossible for those who created me?"

Standing, Leila walked to her. After all these years, Deena finally shared her story. Deep inside, Leila glowed, knowing she'd earned her trust. Perhaps now she released some of her pent-up pain, Deena could put the past to rest and find some peace. "You are who you are as I am who I am." She gathered Deena into her embrace. "We are all different, but we are all created by the hand of God. God doesn't make mistakes. You, my dear friend, are love, beauty, and grace, and all the good God created tied up in one beautiful body."

She pulled away and held Deena by the shoulders. "You and I have traveled some tough roads, but we've survived, and we've learned about life and ourselves along the way. We can no longer ignore or escape our culture and family. However, we don't have to accept or perpetuate intolerance and hate. We must do our best to forgive—if we cannot forget, and we must pursue happiness with gusto. If we allow all those who judge us to snuff out our light, we will never glow. My life would be darker without your light in the world."

Chapter Nineteen
Peanut Butter

With a silent and sullen Tyra in the passenger seat and an exuberant AJ in the back, Aiden parked the car in front of Breeze Bay Cottage. The forecast called for rain, and they elected to drive rather than walk. Aiden looked forward to dinner and hoped a change in atmosphere brought out Tyra from her funk.

Since her last conversation, she barely said two words. Although they resided in hot and humid Florida, icicles hung from the roof of Harbor House and ice built up on the inside of the windows. Hell, if she kept the deep freeze going, she would cause him to seek treatment for frostbite.

Stepping out of the car, he released AJ from his car seat.

Tyra exited the car and rounded it.

Aiden laid a hand on her forearm.

She glared first at his hand then his face.

Ignoring her taser-like stare, he released his boy's hand. "Peanut, go ring the doorbell. Mama Ty and I will be in soon."

Holding a gift bag with a coloring book and crayons he chose for Mia, AJ grinned and clumsily ran to the door.

"I love you, Ty. I'm sorry I hurt you," Aiden murmured. "You mean the world to me and AJ, and no one can ever take your place. I'm doing my best. As for Jay—I pushed because in my heart, I know he is good for you. I don't think I've overstepped because where you and I are concerned, we don't have those types of boundaries."

Tyra exhaled and relaxed her shoulders.

Warmth entered her gaze. Aiden thanked God a thaw was imminent. "Our lives are changing. New people are entering our tribe, and they are a beautiful blessing. We've been on our own for too long. Let's be brave and add to our family."

"Are you done with your sorry soliloquy 'cause I'm starving? You're forgiven, you idiot. Now can we go inside?" She smirked. "Deena says your girl's the best Middle Eastern cook in this area."

"Yeah, I'm done." Aiden smiled and hauled Tyra in for a hug. "Love you."

Tyra held on for a second, and then released him and walked to the house. "Yeah, I know. Love you too although you're a dumbass where bleached-blonde twit Gina is concerned. What you ever saw in her I do not know." She shook her head. "Must have been thinking with the wrong head. Men. Idiots—the lot of you."

Shutting the car door, he followed her. "Yeah, tell me how you really feel."

As she sauntered toward the house, she looked over her shoulder. "Oh, you know I will, A. Better than that, I'm gonna make sure you don't screw with my boy."

"What does that mean?" Aiden frowned.

She flicked a hand over her shoulder and kept walking.

What was she up to? Although he should be concerned, right at this second, he didn't give a damn.

Spring arrived at the Stone household. He would deal with whatever she plotted. Where Tyra was concerned, anything was possible. He hoped she didn't mess up his plans with Gina.

Aiden took his marching orders from Mike seriously, and he planned to execute them without a single complication. AJ's future was on the line. He glanced up, and his gaze connected with Leila's.

She hugged Tyra then leaned against the doorframe and studied him.

Barefoot, in jean shorts and a white sleeveless top, she was breath-taking.

Leila tilted her head and smiled. "Hi."

Reaching behind her, Aiden dragged the front door almost shut and maneuvered her in his arms. He brought down his lips on hers and devoured her.

Leila melted into his body—enthusiastically participating in the kiss.

He trailed his fingers through her hair and released the clip holding her hair captive. Her thick tresses fell around them. Breaking the kiss, he buried his face in her soft curls and breathed in her jasmine scent. "Hi, Rapunzel," he whispered and kissed her forehead. "Love those curls all around me, baby."

She opened her eyes. "'Kay," she murmured and laid her head on his chest.

"Mommy?"

Leila jumped.

Tightening his arms, Aiden steadied her. He released her but kept her close. Sooner or later, they would deal with Mia and AJ's questions, and now was a good time to start. He glanced at Leila—noting her flushed face and swollen lips. Smiling, he crouched.

"Hello, Sunshine. Can I have a hug today?"

With a shy smile, Mia studied him then glanced at her mother.

Leila smiled and nodded.

"'Kay." Mia shrugged.

Aiden opened his arms. "Come on, Sunshine. I've been waiting for one of your special hugs for a long time."

Giggling, she launched herself at him.

He caught her and felt his heart swell with joy to the point he was certain the organ would burst. Little girl giggles filled his ears as he hoisted her, threw her above his head, and then caught her. "Okay, my little ball of sunshine, tell me when you've had enough."

"'Nough. 'Nough." Mia giggled and squirmed.

Kissing her forehead, he set her down.

Immediately, she grabbed his hand and dragged him into the house. "Come, eat. I made food."

Laughing, Aiden followed. He glanced behind him. Leila's smile was wistful, and her eyes glistened. *Thank you*, she mouthed.

He nodded. AJ had Tyra, but Mia never had a father figure. She was sweet and easy to love. He already adored her. AJ too was lucky to have Leila in his life. Not every woman possessed the patience and compassion to deal with and see past his challenges—loving him for the extraordinary child he was.

As Aiden entered the house, he was overwhelmed by the delicious scents of garlic, onion, cumin, and grilled meat. His stomach growled.

Drinks in hand, Tyra and Deena stood in front of the kitchen table, which was covered with bowls and platters of unrecognizable, mouth-watering delicacies.

"Ready to try something new?" Leila handed him a glass of wine then tucked herself by his side.

Aiden nodded. "Did you make all of this bounty?" Small hands tugged on his pants, and he glanced down.

"No, I cook." Mia stomped her foot and pursed her lips.

"Of course you did, Sunshine." He scooped up the pixie in his arms. "I can't wait to try all this yummy food. Tell me what you made."

"Food." She frowned and shrugged.

He threw back his head and laughed. Kissing the top of her head, he set down the child. "How silly of me. You sure made a lot of food. What a great job you did. Can I try some?"

Grinning, she skipped away.

Deena and Tyra situated the kids with plates in front of the TV. Leila led Aiden around the table. "These are grilled lamb and beef kabobs, stuffed grape leaves with rice and beef, and yogurt, mint, and cucumber salad. The yogurt goes great with the grilled grape leaves and *kofta*." Leila pointed to each beautifully plated dish. "*Kofta* is beef, parsley, onions, and spices all rolled together and grilled. This is Deena's favorite dish—macaroni with beef and béchamel sauce. Finally, this dish is similar to *baklava*, but it's not sweet. This is filo dough with spinach and feta cheese, and this tray is filo dough with beef and pine nuts."

"You made all of this food?" Aiden shook his head.

"I know I went overboard." Leila shrugged. "Once I started, I couldn't stop. I haven't cooked or enjoyed Middle Eastern food in a long time. I couldn't decide what to make, so I made all my favorites and some of

Deena's."

Aiden gathered her into his arms. "Sweetheart, I'm not sure why you denied yourself or poor Deena." He glanced at Deena who shoveled food in her mouth. "But I'm not complaining. Everything smells and looks wonderful."

"Why don't you sit?" Leila blushed. "I'll make you a plate."

"Uh-uh." Aiden shook his head. "You sit, and I'll serve. After all, you cooked."

"You're the guest." She covered his hand. "I'll serve. By custom, guests are served first and by the hostess."

"Okay, but just this time. You'll spoil me, and I'll be intolerable at home. Who'll serve me there?"

Turning, Tyra glared. "Not me, Aiden Stone." She glanced at Leila. "I have him well trained to feed and water himself and everyone else in the house. You break him, you buy him."

"Got it." Leila grinned.

After he consumed two plates, Aiden refused a third.

Leila ignored his protests and began filling his dish.

"Leila, stop," Deena ordered. "The man is about to explode. He doesn't know our customs."

Leila froze. She dropped the spoon in the yogurt and covered her mouth with a hand. "Oh my God. I'm sorry. I channeled my mother. I didn't realize what I was doing."

Deena burst out laughing. "You, my friend, have a lot to learn. In our culture, you will be served, at least three times, unless you insist you can't eat another bite and declare the cook a genius. You could add, you're looking forward to desert." She shrugged. "We were raised in a traditional home where the hostess served and served—hardly eating anything herself until all the guests and her family were filled to bursting. If a hostess accepted your refusal for seconds or thirds without insisting you try more, she would be viewed poorly."

Seeing Leila's horrified expression, Aiden smiled. "Don't worry, I'm a fast learner, and now, you can learn a new tradition." He fixed her a plate and insisted she sit and eat. Keeping her company, he nibbled on the addictive stuffed grape leaves.

After dinner and desert were consumed, Aiden, despite Leila's protests, helped clean the kitchen while Deena and Tyra took the kids for a walk on the beach before the rain started.

As she placed the last dish in the dishwasher, Leila's cell rang. She peered over her shoulder. "Aiden, can you see who's calling?"

He glanced at her cell. "Nivi?"

"Let the call go to voicemail." She smiled. "That's my cousin. I'll call her later tonight."

"How many cousins do you have?"

"A lot, but not all are…" Leila's cell rang again. This time, she dried her hands and picked up the phone. She frowned. "My Aunt Amal, Nivi's mama, is calling. Something must be wrong." She answered the call. "Hello, *Tante* Amal."

He couldn't hear what Leila's aunt said, but he observed Leila's face change from happy and carefree to horrified.

"*Tante* Amal, please calm down. I don't care who

knows I am coming. Honestly, his opinion no longer matters. We live in America. He cannot stop me from coming or seeing my mother. I'm not a scared, young girl anymore. I'm sorry for the trouble this situation caused you." Leila wandered to the family room.

Trailing her, Aiden sank beside her onto a loveseat. The conversation that followed was in Arabic. Although he didn't understand a word, Leila's face and tone told the story.

Suddenly, she straightened, and she glanced at the screen of her cell. "He's calling. I must go. I'll call you later." Leila grabbed Aiden's hand, took a deep breath, and answered the call. "Hello, Gabe. I've been expecting your call."

She spoke in English, and this time, Aiden heard and understood every word. Gabe's voice was loud, and his tone was aggressive as he threatened her with everything under the sun. With every word, Aiden despised him more and more. Throughout Gabe's tirade, Leila gritted her teeth and stayed silent.

"Tell me, Leila, will you bring along your bastard, or will you at least spare us that humiliation?" Gabe spat.

She straightened her spine and squared her shoulders. Her entire body shook.

Aiden snaked his arm around her as he fought the instinct to grab the phone, launch it across the house, through the deck door, across the sand, and into the ocean where the sound of her brother's acidic voice could be drowned.

Leila took a breath then released it. "I once loved you, Gabe, and I was ready to forgive you. But you've crossed a line. This conversation is over because *you* no longer exist for *me*. The only bastard I know is *you*." She disconnected the call and slumped against Aiden.

When he heard her breathing even, and he no longer wanted to hire a hitman to take out a few Solomon men residing in the great state of New Jersey, Aiden glanced at her. "I think I can piece together the story, but tell me what he said."

"My brother overheard my aunt and cousin talking." Leila exhaled. "Unfortunately, Gabe has grown in his father's image. I hoped in time he'd find his voice and become his own man—a good man. But that hope was squashed. If he's completely transformed into *Baba*, I pity his wife and children. The cycle of abuse will continue."

Aiden shook his head and gathered her close. He took a long cleansing breath. He needed his brain to kick in before his mouth worked on its own accord. Everything about her family disturbed him. His family was far from perfect, but what he knew of hers made his family sound like the perfect television family.

"I know he's your brother, and I want you to stand up for yourself. That's why I didn't interfere, but baby…" He kissed the top of her head. "Your brother is…Well, he's an ass. Understand if he, or anyone else, ever speaks to you or Mia in that manner, in my presence, I'll lose my mind. I'm trying to understand your culture and family, but this behavior…" He took her face in his hands. "Baby, this behavior is *not* love, acceptance, forgiveness, or tolerance. Loving families do not behave in this hateful manner."

Leila laid her hands on his and slid them off her face. She squeezed them and intertwined her fingers with his. "I know, Aiden. But don't judge my entire family and all my people by what you've just heard." She regarded their joined hands. "Where good exists, bad does as well. Good and bad American families exist, don't they? By your own account, not all your family members were good people. Right?"

Aiden nodded. He and Matt survived a dysfunctional family, and Tyra endured a hellish childhood. Maybe people of all races were more alike than they thought. People came in all shapes, sizes, and colors, but their similarities outweighed their differences. Families were like peanut butter. They were filled with nuts, but sugar kept them together. Aiden squeezed Leila close. Did a drop of sweetness exist in her jar of peanut butter?

Chapter Twenty
Surrender

At the crack of dawn Sunday morning, once again, AJ woke up whiny and clingy. His attitude didn't bode well for the day's planned activities, and nothing Aiden said or did improved his grumpy boy's mood. Tyra was no help. Normally, she distracted AJ with his favorite snack or extra TV time. Today, however, she drank her green goo, kissed AJ, and escaped stating she was late for an appointment.

Aiden and Tyra hadn't discussed Gina or the planned lunch again. At least Leila was supportive. She, however, was also concerned about AJ and offered to bring Mia and join them for lunch after the open house she and Deena hosted concluded. He declined. Instead, he chose AJ's favorite restaurant and made sure Gina understood lunch would be brief.

Running ten minutes late, Aiden ushered AJ from the house and strapped him into his car seat. The restaurant was five minutes away. Although last night he explained they were going out to lunch today, he knew AJ was distracted playing with Mia and wouldn't remember the details. Aiden cleared his throat. "Hey, Peanut? Do you remember we're eating lunch with a friend?"

"Yes. Mia and Lala."

"Mia and Leila are not coming." He swallowed

hard. "Today, we're having lunch with my friend, Gina."

"Don't want Gina. Want Lala and Mia."

Aiden rubbed the back of his neck. His son was as addicted to Mia and Leila as he. When the kids were together, they were inseparable. They chatted in a language only they understood and giggled continuously. Yesterday, AJ stared at Leila every time Mia called her *mommy*. The children often mimicked each other, and soon AJ would follow Mia's lead and she his—especially if Aiden and Leila continued blending their families.

"I know you like Mia and Leila. I like them too, but you haven't met Gina yet." He forced a smile and pushed out the words. "Gina is a nice lady who is looking forward to meeting you, and guess where we're having lunch?" He peered in his rearview mirror in time to see AJ shrug. "We're going to your favorite restaurant, The Dancing Dolphin. They have a huge aquarium with different colored fish. Remember?"

"Fish." AJ grinned.

Aiden exhaled. Maybe this lunch would go better than Tyra predicted. "Thank-God for the fish," he muttered as he maneuvered the car into the restaurant's parking lot. Switching off the ignition, he said a silent prayer.

A few days ago, he called Gina and suggested lunch. She wasn't happy with the arrangements.

"Let's go to Chatham's instead. We can enjoy a leisurely lunch, and I hear they have one of the best wine cellars in the area. The imperial caviar with Alaskan king crab is to die for. I'm sure AJ would enjoy the lobster."

As Mike directed, Aiden took deep breaths, kept a level head, and explained AJ's challenges. He was firm on the lunch plans but stayed calm and documented everything. But Gina was Gina, and their past reared its ugly head every time they spoke. She insisted he introduce her to AJ as his mother. Aiden couldn't understand why Gina was rushing this reunion. No matter how much he explained AJ's fragile condition, he failed to convince her to tread carefully. Every child with Down syndrome is affected differently. AJ was born with significant medical problems— gastrointestinal, respiratory, and cardiac issues, as well as moderate cognitive delays and problems with motor and speech.

He looked at his watch and opened AJ's door. They were now twenty minutes late. If his memory served him, however, Gina would also be late. The woman lacked the ability to arrive on time for any appointment. When they were a couple that fact used to drive him insane. Today, her chronic tardiness worked in his favor.

The restaurant didn't accept reservations. He knew the owner well, however, and he called ahead asking for a table closest to the fish tanks. Each table was named after a body of water. AJ loved the Red Sea table not only due to its proximity to the fish tanks, but also due to its bright red table and chairs with cartoon depictions of creatures residing in the Red Sea.

As soon as he entered the building, AJ ran to the fish tanks.

Aiden scanned the restaurant and smiled. Gina was nowhere in sight. A few minutes later, Gina hurried in carrying a large gift bag. She was meticulously dressed in a one-piece, off the shoulder white jumpsuit with wide legs and spiked gold sandals. With her large handbag and sunglasses, she appeared long, lean, and glamorous—capturing the eye of every male in the room.

The woman was always easy on the eyes, and when she wasn't drunk or high, she was quick-witted and engaging. She wasn't comfortable in her skin and needed to be the center of attention—gaining validation from the admiration of others. Aiden was the exact opposite.

Earlier that morning, while he drank his morning coffee, Aiden received a call from his attorney. The private detective completed a preliminary report. Three years ago, Gina caught the eye of Charles Stanton, a seventy-two-year-old millionaire. Despite their age difference, they married. A few months ago, Charles was killed in a helicopter crash. Gina was his only heir. This information explained her refined finish. Her sudden appearance in their lives, however, was yet to be explained. Gina was loaded and bored—a dangerous combination.

When Gina spotted Aiden and AJ, she smiled and strutted toward them. Removing her glasses, she focused on Aiden—ignoring the child at his side. "Hi. Sorry I'm late. Traffic was a bitch." Surveying the noisy restaurant, she pursed her lips and frowned. "Honestly, Aiden, we can do better than this daycare atmosphere. The place is wall to wall kids." She wrinkled her nose. "The tables look sticky, and the entire place smells of french fries and fish-sticks. Must we stay?"

He forced a smile. "Yes, we…"

"Daddy? I go home now." Hiding behind Aiden's legs, AJ tugged on his father's pants.

Turning, Aiden crouched in front of AJ. He noted the tremor in his boy's voice and his pale complexion. AJ was minutes from a meltdown. "Peanut, I'd like you to meet my friend then you can go look at the tank with the Redtail sharks." Aiden pointed to a large tank several feet away. "I think the sharks are new. Aren't they super cool? If you look carefully, you'll see they are playing hide and seek. Bet you can't find them all."

AJ looked from his father to the fish tank then to Gina.

"Never mind the fish. See what I have for you? Every kid wants one." Gina thrust the gift bag at AJ.

AJ shrank back—lips trembling, eyes filling with tears and spilling over. "D-Daddy, no. I go home now." His voice rose. "I-want-Mama-Ty." With each word, his voice grew louder.

Aiden's gut clenched. He hauled AJ into his embrace and stood.

The boy wrapped his legs around Aiden's waist and wound his arms around his neck.

"Peanut, calm down. You're safe." He glanced at Gina who stepped back. Mouth open and eyes wide, she scanned the restaurant.

Many eyes focused on them. Clearing his throat, Aiden shoved the bag under the table with his foot and sat with AJ wrapped around him like a baby ape. "Why don't we all sit. Let's open the nice gift Gina brought after we've eaten."

"AJ, you don't need to be afraid." Gina rolled her eyes, sat, and crossed her legs. "You can call me Mama Gina."

Aiden stared and gaped. What the hell did she think she was doing? He explained in minute detail how they'd introduce her. "Gina." He hissed.

Burying his face in his father's chest, AJ curled his fingers in his shirt. "Daddy," he whimpered. "I need Mama Ty. Daddy, please."

At a loss, Aiden rubbed AJ's back. This meeting spiraled out of control, and Gina did her best to mess up things.

"AJ, be a big boy. Enough whining. Sit up and behave this instant." Gina grabbed AJ's shoulders and dragged him toward her. "You're making a scene, young man."

"Daddy, nooo." AJ wailed and clung tighter to Aiden.

"What the hell is going on here?" Tyra's voice boomed over the boisterous lunch crowd.

"Mama Ty." AJ turned his head and held out his arms toward Tyra.

In seconds, Tyra tugged AJ into her embrace.

AJ wrapped around Tyra, laid his head on her shoulder, and sighed. "I go home now."

Tyra glared at Aiden. "Baby boy, Mama Ty isn't leaving you. Not now"—she tasered Gina with her gaze—"not ever. But I have a surprise." She smiled. "Guess who came with me? Look." She pointed to the front of the restaurant.

Aiden peered in the direction she pointed. Deena, Leila, and Mia stood at a distance. Leila held Mia in a death-grip as the child strained to spring free and save her boyfriend. He ran a hand down his face. He needed a do over. This lunch was a complete fiasco. He wasn't sure what the hell Tyra and her posse were doing here, and although he should be furious with their interference, he was grateful.

Leila focused on him as she spoke to Mia who stopped tugging. She eyed Gina, Tyra, and AJ then back to him. Quirking her head to the side, she raised an eyebrow.

He nodded. Whatever plans he made for a quiet, non-eventful introductory lunch was foiled by Gina's outrageous behavior and all the women in his life. Fighting the inevitable was futile. Tyra maneuvered Deena, Leila, and even Mia to come to the rescue. Most likely, they didn't know he and AJ would be at this restaurant, but Tyra sure as hell did.

When AJ spotted Leila, Deena, and Mia strolling to the table, he grinned. "Aunty Dee. Mia. Mommy," he shouted and fidgeted in Tyra's arms. "Down, Mama Ty," he demanded.

"Mommy?" Tyra and Aiden murmured in unison.

"Down, Mama Ty." AJ laid a hand on Tyra's cheek. "Mommy. Mia."

Tyra stood the squirming child on the ground, and as soon as she released him, he launched himself at Leila.

Leila caught him before he collided with her legs.

"Mommy. You stay. See fish," AJ demanded.

Eyes wide, Leila glanced at Aiden.

He opened and closed his mouth then nodded. He said a quick prayer of thanks because his boy, with his big loving heart, unwittingly defined all the women who were important in his life. The village of people who loved AJ and who AJ loved grew—Aunty Dee, Mama Ty, Mommy, and Mia. Unfortunately, Gina was not in the mix, and if the waves of hostility coming off her were any indication, Mount Gina would soon erupt.

Holding hands, Mia and AJ giggled and pointed at the various fish tanks. Like a pack of wolves hovering over their next meal, Deena, Tyra, and Leila glared at Gina. With a hand on her hip and a scowl on her face, Gina stood oblivious or uncaring of the fact she was outnumbered. The silly woman's body language was all wrong. Where was her sense of self-preservation?

Aiden needed to move the kids from the hot-zone before lava spewed, hit the atmosphere, and scorched them. A catfight in the middle of the restaurant was the last thing he wanted. Gina was out of her league. Tyra and Deena alone could neutralize her with their sharp tongues. Leila's mama bear instincts were also awakened, and her reach now extended beyond Mia. One wrong word from Gina, and Leila would tear her to shreds. "Mia. AJ."

The kids glanced at him.

"Tell Mommy and Mama Ty what you want for lunch, and go see the fish." He was surprised at how easily the words *Mommy and Mama Ty* slipped off his tongue. "We'll call you when the food arrives." After he was assured the children were out of hearing distance and lost in the wonders of the colorful fish tanks, Aiden faced the women. "Ladies, call a truce and sit before we are escorted out of this fine establishment."

All eyes focused on him—Deena's chocolate browns, Tyra's dark coals, Gina's sky blues, and Leila's soft hazels that, as always, warmed his heart and stole his breath. Deena sat next to Gina, and Tyra, Leila, and Aiden sat across from them. "Gina, let me introduce…"

"Don't bother. I think AJ beat you to the intros. Mama Ty, right? Then Mommy and finally, Aunty Dee." Gina pointed as she glared at each victim. She speared Aiden with her gaze. "Colorful harem you've amassed. You've been a busy boy." She curled her lip. "*My* child has way too many inappropriate maternal figures in his life. No wonder his development is stunted, and he's confused and unhappy." She shook her head. "You've always been irresponsible, but this little set up has the makings of a *Lifetime* movie—a bad one. And this is *not* an environment I want my child raised in."

Blinking, he couldn't believe the utter nonsense spewing from Gina's lips. She was ruthless, and when cornered, she struck blindly. This attack, however, was a low blow. Screw Mike and his advice to play nice. Before he opened his mouth and set them on a path sure to be bumpy, long, and emotionally draining, he glanced around the table. Deena's face was granite. Tyra's spine was straight, and her shoulders squared. The grim set of her mouth and flaring nostrils warned him of the hell she prepared to unleash. Finally, he focused on Leila, and his breath stuttered.

Leila sat in a relaxed posture with a serene smile on her lips. For a few seconds, he felt as if time stood still. Using her expressive eyes and her fingers entwining with his under the table, Leila communicated.

With her thumb, she caressed the bounding pulse at his wrist.

Her assuring, unfazed gaze warned—*don't rise to the bait*. He was lost in the depths of her eyes—synchronizing his breathing with hers. Like AJ and

Mia, he and Leila were suddenly communicating in their own unique language—deficient of the spoken word, yet rich in meaning. Leila's message was clear. Now was the time to act—not *react*. Although Aiden possessed an entire army of warriors by his side, he must chart a plan for success, set the tone, and lead them into battle. Charging recklessly into a war zone might result in a few successful battles, but they could lose the war. Losing was not an option. A child's life was at stake.

Aiden didn't have the luxury of losing his temper, and he couldn't allow his army to do so. They must harness and conserve all their anger and energy to outwit and out-maneuver the enemy. One sure way of out-smarting the enemy was to act in the most unexpected of ways—surrender to her wishes.

Chapter Twenty-One
Solomon

From her place in the restaurant booth, tucked into Aiden's side, Leila observed Gina. The woman was a beautiful, but deadly creature reminding Leila of a swan. Swans are the epitome of beauty, poise, and grace. They mate for life, and when they curve their necks to nuzzle their mate, their joined necks form a heart. Often swans are depicted as romantic creatures gliding peacefully across tranquil ponds. They are relatively harmless until they're forced to protect their young. While many creatures have this protective instinct, when the odds are against them, they eventually give up. Swans *never* give up. Instead, they attack by chasing and flying at perceived threats at full speed. They bite, pull skin off bones, and hold predators underwater until they drown.

Where AJ was concerned, Gina was no swan, but was she after her long-lost mate? Not once since Leila entered the restaurant did Gina regard her son with love or longing. While Gina was a definite problem AJ and Aiden could do without, she wouldn't be difficult for Leila to handle. Leila was experienced at playing adult games requiring Machiavellian tactics—utilizing strategy and stealth.

Leila was raised in a large community where women excelled at putting on airs and acting nasty-nice. She was an expert at dealing with conniving women. For years, she observed and listened to the ladies in her culture outwit and outmaneuver one another and the unsuspecting men in their lives. They achieved their goals without breaking a sweat or developing a single frown line. These women were experts in the art of verbal combat. If crossed, however, like swans, they could be ruthless.

Although Leila hated the games people played, over the years, she and Niveen, sometimes joined by Deena, observed the *adults* play the game of life. Studying facial expressions and body language, and translating the hidden plots behind covert actions and flowery words, was a spectator sport that kept them entertained for hours.

Now, Leila was in familiar territory. She surveyed Tyra's face then met Deena's gaze. She glared at Deena, willing her to see beyond what was obvious and hear not only what was said, but more importantly, understand what wasn't. Utilizing a juvenile sign she, Deena, and Niveen used in their teens to commence the observation game during dinner or at church, with the tip of her finger Leila touched her nose, her earlobe, and then stared at Gina.

After a few seconds, Deena relaxed in her chair, and she tilted her chin in a miniscule nod. Her lips curved into a small smile.

Leila released the breath she held. Score. Deena was on board. Ignoring the excruciating tension, Gina's nasty comments, and the frowns and scowls resembling war paint decorating everyone's face, Leila smiled at Gina. Deploying some of the tactics she learned in childhood would be enjoyable.

"Harem? That's funny." She forced a laugh and extended a hand. "Hi Gina, I'm Leila. The little thief who stole AJ is my daughter, Mia. Even at three, she's a heartbreaker, and she has AJ wrapped around her finger. They met a few weeks ago, and they have a case of puppy love." Leila shrugged. "I'm sorry for intruding on your lunch. I think the kids cooked up this meeting. Mia insisted on coming here for lunch. Oh, and don't let the *mommy* thing worry you, he's imitating Mia."

Gina stared at Leila's outstretched hand then her gaze traveled to her face. She cleared her throat and accepted Leila's hand. "Ah, hi."

Deena then extended her hand. "Hi Gina, I'm Deena Hanna, the little thief's aunt, and Leila's business partner. You've heard of Hanna Realty, right?" Her smile was more brittle than Leila's, and her voice was overly cheery.

Relieved Deena played her part, Leila forced a relaxed pose. She hoped Deena modulated her uber-happy attitude before Gina caught on to their farce.

Mouth open, Gina shook her head and accepted Deena's outstretched hand.

"No worries." Deena dug in her handbag. "Here's my business card. Leila and I can help with whatever your needs are—short or long term rentals. But if you are in the market to buy, now is the best time 'cause interest rates are at an all-time low." She flashed Gina another fake, but dazzling smile.

Gina accepted the card. "Uhm, okay. I'm not sure of my plans, but…"

"No pressure." Deena shook her head. "I'm not a pushy agent. Leila and I run a no-pressure type of operation." She peeked at Leila. "Isn't that right, Leila?

We're all about the customer." She focused on Gina. "Whatever makes *you* happy. *You* call the shots."

Deena took this little act a bit too far. Business partner? No pressure? Bullshit. Where business was concerned, Deena was a great white shark not a guppy. Leila grinned. If they must deal with Gina, they could have a little fun.

Tyra slammed her hands on the table and glared at Gina. "These two dim bulbs might be all hearts and flowers, but woman, I'm not and never will be. They…" She glanced between Leila and Deena. "They might not know who you are, but I do." She scrutinized her. "Shiny mani's and pedi's, expensive haircuts and highlights, and designer clothes and shoes, do not wipeout the past, they only disguise the heartless bitch you are. That costume won't work on me. *I-know-you.*" She enunciated each word.

Lips curled, Gina's eyes bulged, and her face reddened to the color of a ripe watermelon.

"Now look here you…"

"Uh-uh." Tyra leaned across the table and got into Gina's face. "You look. Your boy is happy and healthy—no thanks to you. That child has been on death's door more times than I care to admit. Every day is a struggle as he learns to assimilate into this crazy, messed up world. He doesn't have you, but he has people who love him in a way you never could."

Sliding out of the booth, Tyra stood. She nodded to Aiden. "He's crazy enough to allow you in our boy's life. I won't stand by and watch you hurt him, though. I know your type, and your type don't change." She put her hands on her hips and using her laser-like gaze, skewered Gina.

"I'll do my best to follow whatever Aiden lays out. If I ever hear or see you mistreat my boy again, Lord help you." She placed her palms on the table and leaned in until she was mere inches from Gina's face. "I grew up in the ghetto. No newly minted rich bitch who finds herself with time on her hands and a guilty conscience will hurt my boy. Understand me?" She hissed.

Tyra straightened and smoothed her hands down her skintight miniskirt. She glared at Aiden. "I'm taking my boy and his girlfriend to the beach. I'm on fire. Tonight, we're having a cookout." She scowled at Deena and Leila. "If you two idiots grow a brain by seven, you're invited. If not, boy genius here," she lifted her chin toward Aiden, "can bring girlfriend home." Turning on her spiky five-inch heels, she threw her braids over her shoulders and sauntered to the children. Lunch was over. Deena and Leila left shortly after Tyra's dramatic exit—leaving Aiden to deal with a fuming Gina.

Dinner that evening was strained. Aiden agreed with Deena and Leila that Gina must be handled carefully until they understood what she was after. Without putting AJ at risk, they would work together to give the illusion they were taking Gina's new claim to motherhood seriously. Waiting her out until she revealed what she really wanted would be less harmful then unleashing her wrath. According to Mike, Gina had a team of attorneys and endless funds to make AJ's life hell.

Tyra argued they were making a mistake by allowing Gina any access to AJ and insisted the best route was for Aiden to file for full custody. By the end of the evening, however, she grudgingly agreed to stay away from Gina while they executed their "idiotic plan."

For the next three weeks, everyone in AJ's village worked hard to keep his world from falling apart. Deena kept Tyra busy by utilizing her flair for the arts and fashion sense to stage homes when Leila was unavailable. Several times a week, Leila and Aiden supervised Gina's visits with AJ.

At first, Aiden supervised all the sessions. Then an important business meeting came up. Leila stepped in— bringing Mia. When AJ had Mia to distract him, he was more agreeable.

Gina's sudden presence in their lives accelerated Aiden and Leila's relationship rather than stalling it. Soon, they fell into a pattern—alternating watching the kids and Gina and working. Although Gina pouted when Aiden was occupied, she learned her attitude didn't sway him. Leila and Aiden ended most days together with dinner at either house—a family.

The stress couples experienced over many years— balancing demanding work schedules, family drama, past lovers, and children—Aiden and Leila encountered within the first month of their tender relationship. Instead of pulling away to fight their battles separately, they combined forces and leaned on one another.

Although Leila was busier than ever—working for several realtors as well as Deena, studying for her real estate exam, and taking care of the kids—she was happier and more fulfilled than she remembered. Their lives magically fused, and their children formed a strong bond. At times, though, she worried her relationship with Aiden moved at the speed of light, and they didn't have a chance to explore everything they needed to know about one another.

Despite being with each other more often than not and ending every day lounging on the deck in each other's arms, Leila and Aiden weren't intimate. The time had come to broach the subject before passion overtook them, and they went too far for Leila's comfort. Would he understand her views about sex? Would he think she was old fashioned?

One balmy night a few weeks before the fourth of July, as the kids slept, and Aiden and Leila cuddled on a lounger listening to the waves.

Aiden held her close and kissed her passionately.

Leila extracted herself and sat up. Breathing hard, she gazed at the ocean.

"Baby, are you okay?" Aiden straightened and touched her arm.

Leila nodded. Licking her lips, she cleared her throat. "I was raised to believe sex outside of marriage is a sin. Although I'm not ashamed of Mia, I regret giving myself to a man who didn't love me. For a long time after, I felt dirty and used." Heat flamed Leila's face. "The next time I give myself completely will be on my wedding night. I know I sound old-fashioned, but I feel strongly about this decision."

"Baby, look at me." Aiden cupped her face in his hands.

Leila met his gaze, and the tenderness and understanding she found in Aiden's eyes stole her breath.

"First, not once have I ever thought of you as dirty or used. You were innocent and were played badly. I'm not a teenager who can't control himself. You never have to apologize to me. You're beautiful, desirable, and sexy as hell, but I respect you and wouldn't do anything to jeopardize what we have. I'm in this relationship for the long haul—wherever that might lead." He gathered her in his arms and kissed her nose and lips. "I'll admit waiting will be a bitch. But think of the fun we'll have until then."

Relief flooded Leila. Although she was inexperienced, she was certain she loved Aiden and AJ and was hopeful Aiden felt the same way about her and Mia. When the time was right, and Gina was no longer threatening AJ's fragile world, she would tell him she loved him. Perhaps, he would beat her to the punch and say those precious words to her. With a smile on her lips, she fell asleep that night—Aiden filling her dreams as he did every night.

When the sun filled her room the next morning, she woke rested and ready to deal with Hurricane Gina. She spent the morning studying, and then while Aiden worked, she and Gina took the kids to the beach. Intent on building a castle, the kids grabbed their toys and began digging. Gina slathered her body in coconut oil and fell asleep. An hour and a half later, the weather turned.

"Mia. AJ. Play-time is done. We must go in. A storm is coming." Leila stood and gazed at the cloud-filled sky. She glanced at the shoreline. The kids still played.

Turning to Gina, Leila nudged the dozing woman's foot. Although she preferred Gina asleep, she needed her help gathering their beach paraphernalia and the kids. The sky darkened at an alarming speed, and thunder and lightning would soon follow. AJ would have a colossal meltdown. She shook Gina's shoulder.

"Gina, wake-up. A storm is coming. We must get the hell off the beach."

Jerking awake, Gina yawned and removed her sunglasses. "Oops, I fell asleep again, didn't I?" She stretched and glanced at the sky. "Sorry." She shrugged.

"Gather the kids, please. We have no time to waste." Leila glared.

Gina stood, stretched her fat-free, tanned and toned body, and strolled toward the children.

Gritting her teeth, she concentrated on gathering towels and beach toys.

"Mommy. Mommy," Mia wailed.

Leila froze and turned in the direction of her child's voice. She gasped. AJ struggled in Gina's arms, and tears ran down Mia's face as she clung to AJ's waist and pulled him from Gina.

Dropping the towels and beach bag, Leila rushed toward the distressed children. She fell to her knees and tugged away Mia. "I'm here now, *habibtee*. You're fine. Everything will be okay. Go wipe your face with a towel, and I'll take care of AJ."

Wiping her nose with the back of her hand, Mia nodded.

Leila turned to Gina who struggled to lasso AJ's floundering body. His arms and legs flailed in all directions. "Give me AJ," she demanded.

Ignoring Leila, Gina spanked AJ's bottom once then again. "Stop this behavior right now. Your father might put up with your nonsense, but I won't."

AJ cried, and his struggles increased.

For a few seconds, Leila's vision blurred. That stupid, stupid bitch hit her boy. No way in hell Leila would stand by while anyone hit a child under her care. She blinked, pulled AJ from Gina's arms, and shoved aside Gina.

"Leila, I'm disciplining AJ. I don't need your help." Gina huffed and reached for AJ.

AJ whimpered, wound his legs around Leila's waist, and his arms around her neck.

Tightening her arms around the child, Leila twisted away from Gina. "Easy, Brave Boy. I'm here, and no one will hurt you." As she stood, Gina's fingernails grazed her shoulder and back. Ignoring the sting, she trudged toward Mia. AJ buried his flushed, tear-streaked face into her neck. "Mommy." He whimpered. "Need Daddy. Need Mama Ty. I go home now," he stuttered between gasping breaths.

Leila swallowed passed the lump in her throat. Every time AJ called her mommy, he caused her chest to ache. The first time she heard the word, she was stunned. Now, she embraced the title.

AJ whimpered and shook.

"You're fine," she murmured as she hoisted him higher on her hip. "Mommy has you. Let's get Mia and go home." Arriving to where Mia stood, she grabbed her daughter's hand. "Come on, *habibtee*. Let's go inside."

Leaving the towels and beach bags on the beach, Leila trudged through the sand toward Harbor House. Arriving at the bottom of the steps leading to the deck, she glanced up the fifty-three steps. The steps were her nemesis, and she despised them. Taking a deep breath, she closed her eyes and wished she could teleport herself and the kids up the deck. A lot of energy and ingenuity was required to carry both kids. Perhaps, she could convince AJ to climb the stairs?

Lightning lit the sky, and a mighty thunder cracked overhead. A strong gust of wind blew sand and Leila's hair in every direction. AJ screamed and gripped her with all his might. Mia shrieked and clung to Leila's leg.

"Holy shit," Gina yelled.

Once again, lightning streaked across the sky.

"Mommy. Mommy," AJ and Mia shrieked in unison.

Normally, Mia wasn't afraid of storms, but she fed off AJ's terror. Leila needed to move faster, and one glance over her shoulder confirmed she was on her own. Instead of helping her with the kids, Gina took her sweet time, shaking out the sand from each towel.

Leila shifted a weeping AJ to her right hip. She shoved her hair off her face. "AJ, please listen," she begged. "I'm not putting you down, but I need to pick up Mia, too. Hold on." Leila bent and hoisted up Mia to her left hip. As she straightened, the muscles in her arms and legs strained, and her back ached. She was in fairly good shape and was used to carrying Mia—with both arms. Eating well and running on the beach several times a week kept her healthy, but she didn't have much upper body strength.

Taking a deep breath, Leila climbed the first step and then another. Gasping for each breath, she paused, her lungs, like all her muscles and back, were on fire. Tomorrow, she vowed, she would join a gym, take vitamins, and drink protein shakes. Why couldn't she carry two munchkins without feeling like she was dying?

"Hold on, Rapunzel, before you hurt yourself. I'm

on my way."

Glancing up, Leila feasted on the sight of her hero rushing down the stairs and released a huge breath. "Aiden," she whispered.

"Daddy." AJ swiftly raised his head—connecting his skull sharply with Leila's chin.

Leila's head shot back, and her teeth rattled. Pain radiated from her chin through her jaw and entire head, and stars filled her vision. Swaying, she struggled to stay upright and tightened her arms around the children. Darkness crept around the edges of her vision, and she blinked, fighting to stay alert until the kids were safe.

In what felt like an eternity but was probably seconds, Aiden stood in front of her and took the children out of her arms. She smiled. "My hero," she murmured as she swayed then plopped down on the steps.

He crouched beside her. "Baby, are you okay?"

"Fine. Fine." Leila blinked. "Get the kids inside. I'll be right up."

"Stay where you are." Aiden frowned. "I'll come back for you. Where's…"

"Beach," Leila muttered. "I'm okay. Go. I need to have a little chat with Gina."

"But…"

She shook her head and winced. Clearing her throat, she met his gaze. "My chin and head ache, but I'm fine. Gina and I will be right in. Now's not the time to argue. The kids are terrified."

He hesitated for a few seconds then stood with ease and climbed the stairs as if he held a couple of fluffy pillows.

Using the banister, she pulled to standing and

waited for the dizziness to abate. When she was steady on her feet, she climbed the stairs.

"You're not waiting for me or helping me with the towels and bags? Seriously?"

Gina's high-pitched, whiny voice irritated Leila's ears. She closed her eyes and counted slowly. But when she reached five, she gave in to her anger. She whirled to face Gina. The ocean and beach tilted. When everything in her vision settled to its natural location, she focused on Gina's too perfect face and wished she was the type of person who struck another human being. That stupid, anemic cow spanked and berated her boy.

"Today, you crossed a line. I've been patient. I hoped, in time, I could help you understand AJ, and you would fall in love with him. But now, the gloves are off. I am done, as are you."

"But he was…" Gina wrinkled her forehead and tightened her jaw.

"Uh-uh, don't attempt an explanation." Leila held up a hand. "You're not here for AJ. We both know that fact. I prayed I was wrong about your intentions, but I'm not. Your problem is AJ and Aiden come as a package. You can't have Aiden without AJ. And here's what you don't understand. Neither want or need you. You're six years too late."

Gina dropped the beach bag and towels, and her hands settled on her hips. Her lips twisted into a sneer. "Do you think I don't know the game *you're* playing? Keep your friends close and your enemies closer." She scoffed. "You're way out of your league. Aiden will choose me. This fact, I am certain of. Know why?" She tilted her head to the side. "He loves that out of control little brat, and *I* come with him—not you. *AJ and I* are the package deal. My suggestion? Move out of my way before you are hurt."

The wind picked up, and the sky overhead opened, pummeling Leila with fat raindrops. At least the truth was out, and they could stop pretending. They both wanted the man, but only one of them wanted the child. How ironic. She prayed for the wisdom of Solomon.

Leila's pulse rate accelerated, and her entire body shook—not due to the wind and rain, but with the conviction of her love for Aiden and AJ. Gina did not come as a package deal with AJ, but she possessed the power to make their lives miserable. Aiden and Leila were adults who could withstand the storm surge and battering winds accompanying Hurricane Gina. AJ could not.

For a few seconds, Leila closed her eyes. She said a silent prayer, hoping her story ended as happily as the one recounted in the *Bible*. She must fight for the people she loved. Opening her eyes, she pierced Gina with her gaze. "We are not at war, and you are not my enemy. But if you want a battle—go for it."

Chapter Twenty-Two
Happy

With the wind and rain pummeling her petite body, Leila climbed the fifty-three steps from the beach to the deck in silence. With each step, the heat of Gina's laser-like glare drilled holes in her back. She longed to turn and shove the tiresome creature down the stairs, but that action was unlady-like…and against the law.

Leila opened the deck door. Aiden was in the family room calming the children. While Leila helped bathe and change the kids, Gina gathered her belongings and left. Later, while the children watched a movie and ate pizza, Leila informed Aiden what happened on the beach.

Redness suffused Aiden's neck and face. He stood, pulled out his cell, and marched toward the kitchen. "I'm putting an end to this farce," he growled. "She'll never lay a hand on my son again. Hell, she'll never see him again."

Trailing him, Leila grabbed his forearm. "Aiden, you must be careful. Consult your attorney before making any grand plays. I agree she shouldn't be left alone with AJ. She truly has no idea how to deal with him. Although I was furious and ached to shove her down your precious steps of torture, I've cooled off. I have an idea what she's after."

Aiden turned, his body vibrating with anger. He

237

took a deep breath. "I'm listening."

"Gina isn't interested in being a mother." She licked her lips. "I'm certain she's after you, and you come with AJ."

Aiden's head recoiled. His upper lip curled. "No way. I'm not interested. Surely by now you know I'm not interested in anyone but you. She knows…"

Smiling, Leila nodded. She was well aware how he felt about her. Aiden wasn't shy and didn't play games. Every chance he found, he held and kissed her and told her she was beautiful. Although she struggled with public displays of affection, Aiden didn't. She wrapped her arms around his waist and tilted her head to meet his gaze. "Sweetheart, I'm not insinuating you're interested in her, I'm simply telling you what I think motivates her sudden burst of maternal affection."

Dropping her head, she gazed at the expanse of his wide chest and swallowed hard. "While you deal with this situation, I'm stepping out of the picture for a few days. You need to make your feelings clear to her." Forcing out the words was painful. Her heart ached, and although Aiden's arms were around her, she missed him already.

Aiden's arms spasmed, and he stiffened. "What? No way. Leila, look at me."

Leila met his gaze.

"You're not the problem. She's not driving you away." He shook his head. "I won't let her mess up my life."

Leila grabbed his hand and towed him to the couch. "Sit," she ordered.

He sat but tugged her on to his lap. One of his hands weaved through her curls.

The man was infatuated with her hair. Every time she contemplated cutting it, she remembered the feel of his fingers running through her hair. Often, Aiden curled one of her long strands around his finger and tugged—just as he did at this second. Her hair was his personal stress reliever, and she didn't mind in the slightest.

"Don't let her ruin us," Aiden murmured and kissed her forehead. "Please." He brushed his lips across hers. "Please don't give up on us. I know we're dealing with so much shit, but hold on. Happy is right around the corner." He squeezed hers. "I love you, Rapunzel. I've been waiting for our lives to settle to tell you, but I need you to know right now. I love you."

Gasping, her heart did a happy dance. Aiden's eyes were molten—earnest and pleading. He said the words she dreamed of hearing since she was a young woman. She cupped his cheek and kissed him softly. "I love you too." How the hell could she walk away, even for a short time, from the only man in her life who loved her?

Until those words left his mouth, she intended to disappear from his and AJ's life, giving Gina and Aiden a chance to figure out their future without her complicating presence. She would walk away and allow gravity to draw them one way or another. But the three words uttered from Aiden's beautiful lips were her undoing.

With the back of her hand, she caressed his cheek. "We can see each other often. I'll watch AJ anytime you want but not with Gina. I don't want to make your life more difficult. The best thing for me to do is step back for a little while. No..." Leila placed a finger on Aiden's lips then kissed him. "I can't leave you." She shook her head. "I'm not strong enough, but Gina needs to think she has your full attention. Talk to her. Find out how she fits into AJ's life. Set boundaries for your relationship. Don't let your anger or your feelings for me overshadow your common sense."

Aiden studied her then nodded. He kissed her forehead, then touched his forehead to hers. "You'll hold on? You won't run while I take care of this mess?"

Leila threw the man she loved into the arms of a viper, hoping he wasn't bitten by her drugging venom and praying he and AJ returned unscathed. She forced a smile. "Nope. The only trip planned is to Jersey and back in a few weeks. Besides, my life's a mess too, and you're not running. Are you?"

"No way, baby. You're not getting rid of me anytime soon. Any other words of great wisdom, Queen Solomon?"

Leaning back, she nodded. "Make an appointment with Dr. Klein. Ask him to educate her on AJ's health. Perhaps the information coming from a physician will sink in. Oh, and for the love of God, don't tell Ty about the spanking. She'll rip out Gina's throat."

Although Aiden was not in complete agreement with Leila's plan, he capitulated. In the ten days that followed he spent time with Gina on his own and with AJ. Often, he called or stopped at Leila's for a brief visit, but he was exhausted and short tempered. Several times he started to tell her about his conversations with Gina and their visit with Dr. Klein, but the kids were always underfoot.

Leila was as frustrated as Aiden, and her imagination was more active than ever. Her dreams were filled with images of Gina and Aiden holding one another. Most nights, she awoke in a cold sweat—anxious and uncertain about the future and where she and Mia fit in Aiden's life. The pressure she was under, as well as her previous painful relationship with a man she thought she loved, influenced her ability to think straight.

At times, she chastised herself, wondering if she should back off completely and give AJ the chance to have a real family with his parents. She didn't doubt Aiden's feelings as much as she doubted her decision-making. Leila wanted the best for AJ and Aiden, even if she must sacrifice her own happiness.

Leila and Aiden operated on survival mode. Two days before her trip to New Jersey, she lay in bed trying to clear her mind when her cell rang.

"Hurricane Gina has turned and headed toward the West Coast," Aiden said.

Leila frowned. "What?" He sounded jubilant.

"Gina left me a voicemail. She said she needed to return to Los Angeles and was unsure when or if she'd return."

She opened and closed her mouth then sat and switched on the light. "What about AJ?"

"I wish I could predict her next moves. I can't, and I thank God AJ hasn't formed an attachment. I'm certain he will not be affected by her sudden departure. For now, we're celebrating."

Relief swept through her leaving her boneless. She sagged against her pillows and smiled. "Oh my God. We're free."

"Yeah, baby." Aiden laughed. "At least for now and tomorrow we're celebrating Independence Day in a big way."

For the first time in days, Leila fell into a deep sleep with a smile on her lips. When sunlight streamed into her room the next morning, she bolted upright with more energy and enthusiasm than she experienced in a while.

By noon though, she looked at her to-do list and panicked. She had two hours to finish packing, prepare the *kofta* and salad, load the food into the car, and drive to Aiden's for their July fourth cook-out. She surveyed the room. An empty, open suitcase was on the bed surrounded by piles of underwear, socks, toiletries, PJs, tanks, shorts, and sweaters. Sweaters in July? What was she thinking?

Leila shoved her clothes to the side and sank to her bed—shoulders slumping. For the last hour, Niveen and Amal tag teamed her via conference call, updating her on the latest happenings in the Solomon Family Saga. She put them on speaker phone, chatting with them as she packed for her trip the next morning, but her multitasking skills were abysmal. She laid out enough clothes for a trip around the world, lasting months and spanning all seasons.

Over the last two weeks, Gabe huffed and puffed and threatened to blow down all their houses if Niveen or Amal harbored the fugitive. Early that morning, Yusuf and his brothers left for Egypt. To the best of the women's knowledge, Gabe didn't tell his father of Leila's imminent visit. Most likely his silence was due to the declining health of Yusuf's mother. However, Gabe made their lives difficult, threatening not to allow Karima out of the house or Leila in. Amal told Karima of Leila's visit.

"Your mama smiled and said she would take care

of Gabriel," Amal said. "She has been waiting and planning for her *habibtee* to come home for a long time. You see, Leila, everything happens in due time."

In due time? The time she desperately needed her family passed three and a half years ago.

"Lala, did you hear what Mama said? Everything will be all right," Niveen said.

Were Amal and Niveen drunk? Everything wouldn't be magically delicious. Life didn't work that way. "I heard what *Tante* Amal said. I appreciate all your efforts. I'll email you my hotel information, but don't concern yourself with picking me up, I'll make my way to you. And no, I haven't changed my mind. I won't bring Mia." Leila stood, scooped up the pile of sweaters, and picked her way toward the closet, tripping over the shoes, sandals, and flip-flops littering the floor. The room appeared as if a bomb exploded.

"You're family," Amal insisted. "Family doesn't stay in a hotel. We have plenty of room, and all the men will be away. Why pay for a hotel?"

"Thank you, but I've already reserved a room." Leila navigated the detritus surrounding her, putting away winter shoes and clothes.

Amal wanted to pick up where they left off—before they knew she was pregnant. She wanted to forget all the harsh words exchanged and the tearing of flesh and scarring of the soul that resulted. Leila wasn't a saint or martyr. She couldn't do what her aunt wished. To reach a place of forgiveness and trust, she must travel many miles.

"You insist on keeping us at a distance." Amal sighed. "Perhaps we deserve this harsh treatment, but what about the child? How can you leave her on her own? Who will take care of her?"

Leila stopped and shoved the hair off her face. This conversation exhausted her. How would she survive being in the same house with all of them again? She forgot how pushy and dramatic her aunt was. Part of her behavior could be blamed on culture, but the majority was her aunt being her aunt. "We've been through this matter before. I'm not bringing Mia this time. I have family here who will take good care of her."

"Family?" Amal screeched. "What family? Are you married? Why did you not share this joyous news before? How wonderful."

Oh, dear Lord. Why didn't she keep her mouth shut? She didn't have the time or energy to redefine the word family for Amal. For Leila, family wasn't limited to the people who shared her DNA or a marriage certificate tying two people together. Family were people of all colors and cultures who gathered around her, protected, and loved her through good times and bad. Over the last few months, her family expanded to include AJ, Tyra, and Aiden. But Leila wasn't prepared to share her newly formed family with her old one.

"*Tante* Amal, stop. Please, I…" Leila rubbed the back of her neck. "Look, I'm grateful for your help—both of you. I would like to see you and Mama and make peace with the past. But understand, forgiveness and peace will take time. Until I'm assured my child will be safe and welcome, I will not expose her to anything or anyone who could cause her an ounce of pain. This topic is not up for negotiation. And no, I am not married, and I'm not going into the particulars of my life now. I'll see you on Saturday for dinner."

After a few minutes of awkward conversation, Leila ended the call and once again sank to her bed—drained. She was more anxious about seeing her family than excited. The entire trip would be painful. She didn't tell Amal or Niveen she would fly in on Thursday. She would try to see Eric on Thursday or Friday night, wander New York City, visiting her favorite places, and then spend a few days with the family.

Glancing at the clock, Leila focused on packing. She despised packing. The simple act of choosing the right outfits to wear in her family's presence stressed her. She wasn't the same frightened and sheltered young woman they last saw. Now, her dresses and skirts were shorter and flirtier. She wore shorts and showed the occasional cleavage, and she never straightened her hair.

She made a huge mess choosing the right outfits, but what she wore or how she looked shouldn't matter. Family should love you from the inside out. She straightened her spine and packed clothes she felt pretty, confident, and comfortable in.

Thirty minutes later, Leila finished packing, and her room was half-way orderly. She needed to complete one more task before she finished preparing the food. On purpose, she waited until the last minute to call Eric. She didn't want him to inform Gabe of her request to meet. With shaky hands, Leila dialed Eric's number and waited—expecting to receive his voicemail.

"Hello, this is Dr. Dixon."

His deep baritone voice filled her ears. Opening and closing her mouth, Leila was unable to force the words past her lips. Her breaths were shallow, and her entire body trembled.

"Hello?"

Her hands fisted tightly—nails cutting into her palms. "Hello, Eric," she croaked.

"May I ask who's speaking?"

Clearing her throat, Leila sucked in air. "Leila—Leila Solomon."

The conversation that followed was stilted and short. Where once they knew each other well, now they were strangers. Leila informed him she would travel to New Jersey on business the next day and needed to discuss an important issue in person. Although several times he asked what they were meeting about, she refused to elaborate.

"Fine, Leila." He sighed. "But our meeting must be short. I'll see you at the diner across from the clinic at three. I have dinner plans."

"Thank you." Exhaling, Leila slumped her shoulders. "That plan sounds fine. But Eric, please don't mention our meeting to Gabe."

"Fine," he clipped. "He's not in town anyway. Yesterday, Gabe cancelled all his appointments and took his family to Cape May for the next ten days."

By the time she ended the call, Leila was drenched. She flopped on her bed. How would she survive an in-person meeting if she could barely speak on the phone without losing control? Eric didn't sound like the man she knew. He used to be warm and personable, but now he was cold and detached. Perhaps he was shocked to hear from her.

Leila glanced at the clock again. She was late. Taking a deep breath, she stood, and for the next forty-five minutes, she cleared her mind of everything having to do with her trip and concentrated on preparing the food. She kneaded together the ground beef, onion, parsley, and spices and shaped the mixture into thick fingers of *kofta* to be grilled. She prepared the *fattoush* salad, mixing crispy lettuce, crunchy baked squares of pita, diced tomatoes, cucumbers, green onion, garlic, lemon, olive oil, and mint. Last night she marinated the chicken breast with fresh onion she liquefied in the blender along with salt, pepper, lemon, garlic, parsley, and five spice.

Finished with the food, she returned to her bedroom and searched through her swim suits, finding the black, barely-there bikini Deena bought her for her birthday. She slipped on the scraps of material and studied herself in the mirror, taking in her toned olive skin, ample breasts, long midnight curly hair, and hazel eyes. She looked good—pretty even.

Leila tugged on a short red sundress and slid her feet with their bright red toenails into sandals. Loading the car was quickly accomplished as was the short drive to Aiden's. She parked behind his car, opened all the car windows, and switched off the ignition. All day, she ran around and needed a few minutes to sit in silence, catch her breath, and gather her thoughts.

Scanning the vicinity for Deena's car, Leila didn't see it anywhere. Before she closed her eyes and rested her head against the headrest, she noted Tyra's vehicle parked in front of a sleek sports car most likely belonging to doctor Jayden Meyers.

The return of Jay in Tyra's life was one of the few benefits of Gina's appearance. To avoid Gina, Tyra had escaped more and more to Jayden's apartment. She appeared daily to make AJ breakfast and tuck him in at night but then disappeared. Leila was concerned about Tyra's behavior, but Aiden was delighted Tyra and Jay were back together.

"Wake up, sleeping beauty. You've been dozing in your car for fifteen minutes. Who are you hiding from?"

Leila opened her eyes, and she smiled. "Hi, sweetheart. Sorry I'm late." She opened the door and stepped out. Stretching and balancing on her toes, she wrapped her arms around Aiden's neck and buried her face in the side of his neck, breathing him in. For the rest of the day she would oust Gina, Eric, and her family from her mind. Instead, she would take every opportunity to snuggle in Aiden's arms and memorize the feel of his hard body against hers so when life came at her hell-bent on taking her to her knees, she'd be strong enough to withstand the blow. After all, they survived Hurricane Gina. What could be worse?

He held her close then gently held her away. "Everything okay"

"Now I'm here, everything is perfect." She brushed her lips across his. "Where is everyone?"

Kissing her nose, he released her and turned to the car. He opened the trunk and stacked the containers filled with food. "The kids are destroying the family room, building some sort of fort, and Jay and Ty are walking on the beach. They've been gone awhile and should return soon. Deena's on her way. She called and said she received an offer on the property next door, and she's negotiating the terms with the owners."

"Oh, that's awesome." Leila clapped. "I bet she closes the deal. The owners moved to The Keys and are motivated to sell. Oceanfront Manor is quite a house.

Hope you get good neighbors."

As Leila unloaded the containers and prepared dinner, she told Aiden of her conversation with her aunt and cousin as well as her conversation with Eric.

"Let me come with you to New Jersey. I'll stay in the wings for support if you need me."

"I love you for offering, but I need to settle the past and attempt peace with my family on my own." She smiled.

Aiden nodded. He kissed her then handed her a glass of wine and grabbed a beer. "Let's start the grill and relax on the deck for a while."

Leila cajoled the kids from their fort, while Aiden started the grill. They barely settled on the deck, listening to the children giggling and splashing in the pool when, hand in hand, Tyra and Jay climbed the deck stairs. Tyra's smile was huge, extending to her eyes. Jay's smile was identical to hers.

"Thought you two were lost. Want a beer?" Aiden rose from his chair.

"I think champagne is probably in order." Deena strode onto the deck from the kitchen, carrying a bottle of champagne.

Turning, Leila noticed Deena carrying a bottle of the champagne they gave buyers at closing. She glanced from Deena to Tyra, and then to Jay whose smile grew.

Jay nodded. "Definitely a champagne moment." He gathered Tyra close and kissed her.

Winding her arms around his neck, Tyra surrendered to the kiss.

"What am I missing here?" Aiden asked Leila and Deena.

Pulling away from Jay, Tyra held out her left hand, showing off a large princess cut diamond engagement ring.

"She finally said yes," Jay said.

"He made me an offer I couldn't refuse."

"Congratulations, man." Aiden grinned and shook Jay's hand. "How did you finally catch the girl?"

"I bought her the largest, gaudiest ring I found, sweetened the deal with the house next door, and promised her a lifetime of my love."

Shrugging, Tyra grinned. "The ring sold me, of course."

Aiden pulled Tyra in his arms and kissed her cheek. "You found happy. I'm thrilled for you, Ty."

Standing back, Leila studied her friends. As Tyra and Deena hugged and admired the ring, Aiden returned to the kitchen for glasses, and Jayden wrestled with the champagne bottle. She turned her attention to the children playing in the pool—joyous and carefree. Life was good. She was blessed with everything she dreamed of—a man who loved her and Mia, two beautiful children, and good friends who always supported her. She was the luckiest woman in the world. She lost her original family, but she built a new one from scratch.

A few short months ago, she stood below this deck with her baby girl in her arms. She was bereft as she swayed to a song now on her favorite's list and admired a couple and child holding each other. She closed her eyes and with Mia in her arms, swayed and dreamed she was in the strong and capable arms of a man who adored her.

Music filled her ears and Aiden's arms snaked

around her. She didn't startle. Leila was accustomed to the feel of Aiden's strong arms. She settled against him.

He kissed the top of her head and swayed with her in time to the music.

She turned in his embrace, wrapped her arms around his neck, and kissed him. This moment—right now, right here—was the definition of happy.

Chapter Twenty-Three
Collapse

With his cell phone to his ear, Aiden paced. Occasionally, he paused, leaned against the deck railing, and took a swig of his scotch. He stared at the calm ocean and the setting sun dipping below the horizon, a sight he never tired of.

"I'm sorry you were worried, Aiden. Please don't be angry. I'm dealing with a lot right now, but I'm fine." Leila sighed.

"Baby, I'm not angry. When I couldn't reach you, I was concerned. You said you were meeting Eric at three, and now it's eight." He placed the crystal tumbler on top of the wooden railing and raked his fingers through his hair. "I'm glad you're okay. Tell me about your day."

"I don't have much to tell. Anyway, I'm wiped out, and I have to call Mia before she falls asleep. Can we talk tomorrow?"

Not much to tell? Today, she met with the man who was Mia's father and informed the dumbass he fathered a kid. She had plenty to talk about. What the hell happened? Leila didn't sound like herself. From the second they started chatting, her answers were short and evasive. Why was she ending their conversation without sharing what must have been a stressful event?

At the crack of dawn, Aiden drove Leila to the

airport. He engaged her in conversation, but she answered with one or two words. The next few days would be difficult and life-changing, and he wanted her to know she had his support.

He scrubbed a hand over his face and prayed for patience. "I know you're drained, but let me share the day with you. Tell me, how is the hotel? How was your talk with Eric?" He picked up his glass and took another swallow of the amber liquid.

"The hotel is…a place to lay my head at night. The room isn't great, but it's inexpensive, and I'm not moving in permanently. As for Eric, I…I'm not ready to relive our meeting—not now."

Aiden researched her *hotel*. The place was a cheap fleabag motel located in the outskirts of Newark close to the train. The motel was a dump, and over the last week, Aiden failed to convince her to let him pay for better lodgings or stay with his brother at the Manhattan penthouse.

Leila was a strong independent woman. Aiden loved her self-reliance and courage. He adored her fierce protective streak and deep love for her daughter and his son. He appreciated her stubbornness even when it revealed itself in the most inopportune times. But she wasn't on her own anymore. They should take care of each other and their newly formed family.

Families were precious. They, like any structure, were strong if their infrastructure was meticulously built with the best and strongest of material. However, if the foundation was newly laid and wasn't given the opportunity to solidify, any dwelling built on top would develop cracks that could easily lead to collapse. To save the home, all hands must be on deck—watchful and willing to do anything to protect the precious dwelling.

Aiden stopped pacing. Not long ago, he constructed the image of the perfect family—his family—AJ, Mia, and Leila. He first pictured them as he sat on the beach with Leila, asking for her forgiveness after he stood her up. He searched his memory banks, recalling the image. His breath hitched as his brain hiccupped and the picture focused with such clarity his hands shook, and the crystal tumbler slipped from his fingers, shattering on the deck and spraying scotch across the wood.

Rapunzel stood on the beach laughing with her gorgeous midnight curls flowing down her back, holding their boy's hand. AJ's green eyes sparkled with mischief as he held Mia's tiny palm, and she grinned up at him. Aiden closed the circle, holding Leila's hand in one of his and Mia's in the other. Each member of his family was unique. They didn't resemble each other, but that fact didn't matter because their hearts were in sync. The ties binding them together were invisible yet strong as steel.

"Aiden? Are you there? Are you okay?"

Aiden blinked. Before the image completely receded, however, strong winds battered his family, tearing their hands apart, breaking their circle, and fissuring their foundation. Gasping, he focused on the shards of glass surrounding him.

No matter what either of them did, or how hard they resisted, gravity drew them together. But could the awesome force of gravity be defied? He glanced at the red, white, and blue helium balloons Jayden brought the kids. They were tightly secured to the wrought-iron table. Like any object with mass, the balloons were pulled to Earth by gravity, but inside them swirled an imperceptible secret weapon—helium. If the powerful ocean breeze weakened their ties, the balloons would defy the gravitational force.

Aiden listened to his gut. He and Leila were in trouble. He couldn't leave their fate to the Universe. Leaning against the railing, he hung his head. "I'm here, and I'm fine. I understand you're not ready to talk. Call Mia and rest. We can chat tomorrow."

"Thank you, Aiden." Leila exhaled. "Sleep well."

Relief was evident in her voice. "Leila?"

"Yes?"

He swallowed past the lump in his throat. Whatever happened today shook their foundation. Where was the intimacy, trust, and joy they shared twenty-four hours ago? Adrenaline coursed through his bloodstream, and his pulse accelerated. His relationship with Leila was tender, and deep in the infrastructure of the home they built a tiny fissure formed.

Now was the time to be proactive before the crack grew and spread to the main structural components of the house—affecting the supporting beams, misaligning doors and windows, sloping floors, and bowing walls— and threatening all the inhabitants. Right or wrong, he must rally his troops and save his family. He cleared his throat. "I love you. Sweet dreams, baby."

"You too, Aiden."

Her voice was ragged and filled with unshed tears, and her pain clawed at his heart and his sanity. He disconnected the call, shoved aside his worries, and utilized the adrenaline and the cell he gripped like a lifeline to gather intel and make plans.

"Hi, Aiden. Is everything okay?" Deena answered on the second ring.

"That's what I need to know. Have you spoken to Leila today?" He shoved a hand through his hair. "I did, and she sounded terrible. What's going on?"

"I spoke with her, but I can't discuss what she and I talked about. I understand you're worried, and you care for her. Still, I can't break her confidence."

"I don't just *care*." Aiden clenched his jaw. "I love her. She and Mia mean the world. If she's in trouble or hurting, she needs my help. If you won't tell me what's going on, tell me what to do."

For a few seconds, Deena was silent. "I don't think you can do anything. She must deal with Eric in her own way. This is her journey...not yours. Leila knows you love her, and she loves you, but..."

"But what?" he growled.

"Look, the situation with Eric isn't as simple as she believed."

Aiden's stomach clenched. Were all Middle Eastern women cryptic and stubborn? He closed his eyes and prayed for patience. "Deena, you're a good friend. I understand and respect your position, but I can't help if I don't know what's going on. What happened with Eric? Was he an ass? Leila's completely shut down."

"I've said too much already." She released a long breath. "Leila has a lot of decisions to make. The best advice I have is...give her time and space. I'm sorry, but Mia's awake and asking for her mommy. I have to go."

For a few minutes, Aiden sat motionless, replaying Deena's words. He stood and cleaned the shattered glass then went inside to text another of his trusted warriors, hoping this one was more helpful.

—I need you.—

Although most nights Tyra now spent at Jayden's condominium, she was never far from her cell.

—AJ?—

—No. Me.—

He shook his head, feeling guilty for pulling Tyra from whatever she was doing with Jay.

—On my way.—

Aiden smiled. He could always depend on Tyra just as she could him. They might not always agree, but the love they shared for one another and for AJ was steadfast. They'd been insanely busy, and what he needed now was his best friend's support, as well as her ability to distract him until he could race across the country after Leila.

As he made reservations, texted his brother, and packed, he talked with Tyra deep into the night. Tyra was happier than he'd ever seen her. Although she would always be an integral part of his family, she and Jay built a separate life.

"I need to send Gina a big thank-you gift for showing up and making us all temporarily insane. Hey, when you're in Manhattan can you stop by the Hershey Store and send her one of those giant chocolate kisses from me?" Tyra asked with a wide grin.

"Let sleeping dogs lie." Aiden shook his head. "I need her to stay gone and you to stay sane while I run after my woman. But while we're on the subject of relationships, you surprised me a bit—a lot actually. I'm thrilled for you and Jay. Want to tell me what tricks he used to convince you to come to your senses?"

"No tricks, A." Tyra studied the rock on her finger. "I guess I finally woke up and found the world changed. AJ is growing. You have Leila and Mia, and Jay's patient but not a saint. He reached his bullshit limit. I was terrified I'd end up alone."

"Ty, are you serious?" Aiden stopped packing and focused on her. "You will always be a part of our family. Alone is not something you should ever worry about. We're adding, not subtracting, to our village. I only pushed because I was certain you loved Jay as he did you. You deserve a full life."

"I know. I do love Jay. I needed a kick in the pants." She shrugged. "Gina and Leila provided that." Tyra met his gaze. "Jay understood I couldn't be away from my boy—not after everything we've been through. You, Leila, Mia, and AJ needed to bond, but I struggled. Jay believed in us, when I couldn't, and he devised a great compromise. I'm good now. How about you? What's the situation with Gina?"

"Leila was right." Aiden shrugged. "Gina harbored delusions of us reuniting. I disabused her of that fantasy. But the visit with Klein sealed the deal, and she ran. You should have seen the shock and horror on her face when Klein laid out AJ's medical history and probable future." He shook his head. "She didn't ask a single question. After he finished speaking, she stood, walked out, and drove away."

"Now what?" Tyra tilted her head and frowned. "Is she coming back?"

"I don't know." Aiden thinned his lips. "I've updated Mike. He said to give her some time. If I don't hear from her in the next few weeks, I'll call. This time, though, I won't leave AJ vulnerable. Mike is drawing up papers to terminate her parental rights. I'm pretty sure she's gone for good."

"Thank-God," she whispered. "Can I ask you a question?"

He nodded as he packed

"What about AJ's biological father?" She cleared her throat. "Did you two ever talk about the elephant in the room?"

"Yeah, we talked. The situation is as I suspected. AJ's biological father was a passing patron in the bar. Gina was drunk and high. She can't remember his name or what he looked like. He's not a threat."

"Wow, you and Leila have had a lot to deal with. How is she handling all of the stress and drama?"

Aiden stopped packing and met Tyra's gaze. "We've been surrounded by kids and constant activity." He opened and closed his mouth then shook his head. "We haven't spoken in specifics about my conversations with Gina or what happened at Klein's office."

"Aiden, don't you think…"

"I know. I know." He held up a hand. "Leila and I have a lot to talk about. We were both thrilled when Gina disappeared, but time simply wasn't on our side to have deep conversations. We've operated in survival mode for weeks. But she knows I love her and Mia. As soon as this drama with her family is resolved, and we have a chance to breathe, we'll talk."

"A, stop being a moron." Tyra glared. "In the past, Leila was burned by every man in her life. Although she knows Gina is out of the picture, she can't be certain if that situation is temporary or permanent. You didn't communicate." She placed a hand on her hip and shook her head. "Don't make assumptions about how she feels or what she thinks or knows. She has never been in a healthy relationship with any man—let alone an American man. Your relationship is unchartered territory."

"I thought Gina's and my actions spoke for themselves. Leila never asked any questions. I know our relationship scares her at times, but I…" A knot formed in the pit of his stomach. Did Leila doubt their relationship? He didn't think so. If she harbored doubts, she didn't let on.

He hung his head. Without clearly stating his intentions for their future, he let her walk into Eric's arms. He wanted to marry her…and Mia. Could she be easily persuaded to leave him and AJ?

Expelling a long breath, he shook his head. No way. He didn't believe Leila was that weak. Even if she found peace with her family—and he hoped she would—under no circumstances would she walk away from him and into Eric's traitorous arms.

"I know you love her. Each time you speak about her or she walks into a room, your face lights up." Tyra walked to him. "No one has ever fought for Leila. She's learned to accept what life gives her without asking for more." She scrutinized him. "I've been chatting with Deena. She won't say much, but…Leila's in for a rough time, A. Handle her with care. She sees the world through a different lens, and her experiences and beliefs have colored her worldview. I have faith in you, though. Go play super-hero and win back the girl…but be gentle." Tyra hugged him, kissed his cheek, and left the room.

Aiden stayed awake the rest of the night replaying

his conversations with Leila, Deena, and Tyra. Although Deena might know Leila better and longer, she was wrong. Space was the last thing he could give her.

Early the next morning, Aiden tiptoed into AJ's room, kissed him goodbye, and drove to the airport. As soon as he settled in his first-class seat, he closed his eyes and drifted off. When the plane glided on to the tarmac at Newark Liberty International Airport, he jolted awake. Aiden stretched, yawned, and then he checked his watch—twelve-thirty p.m. Two and a half hours passed quickly.

Newark Airport was frenzied and packed full of people. After he flagged down a taxi, he sat back, gave the driver the address to Matt's place, and called Leila. She didn't answer. He called her before he boarded the plane, and he texted several times, but she never returned his calls or texts. Although he knew the address to her motel, he wasn't certain of her plans. She said she would wander the city, and he wanted to meet up and spend the day reconnecting.

With no word from Leila, Aiden dropped his bag at Sphere, the luxurious seventy-two story tower where his brother occupied a palatial penthouse. Sphere was located between Hell's Kitchen and the Hudson Yards District. The place was a few blocks from the High Line, Hudson River Park, the Theatre District, and most importantly, West Chelsea's Art Galleries where the Stone Gallery was located.

As he strode to the Gallery, Aiden texted Leila again.

—Hi. Haven't heard from you today. I'm worried. You okay?—

—Fine. Sorry I haven't answered. Busy day.—

The dump truck sitting on Aiden's chest shifted gears and moved. He inhaled deeply—his chest fully expanding for the first time since Leila boarded the plane. He checked his watch. The time was almost three.

—What are you up to? Did you sightsee?—

She didn't reply for almost five minutes.

—No. Eric wanted to meet and talk again. Just returned to the hotel. Exhausted and have a lot to think about. Need a nap. Will call later.—

When he read her response, he stopped short. Pedestrians grumbled and threw him dirty looks as they maneuvered around him. Aiden blinked and reread the message. What the hell happened? What was she not saying? Leila normally wasn't secretive. But in the last twenty-four hours, she excelled in the art of evasion.

Deena said the situation with Eric was complicated. What did she mean? The man was Mia's father, but he was married and probably had a family of his own. Leila didn't need anything from him. She only wished to inform him he fathered a child.

Aiden broke out in a cold sweat. They were both idiots. Why didn't they discuss what they would do if Eric demanded to see his child? Did Leila consider this possibility? She was a smart woman. Of course she did. He wanted to kick himself. He'd been too wrapped up in his own messy life and never asked. He hung his head—ashamed and alarmed.

He attempted another deep breath, but the dump truck was back with a heavier load. Dialing Leila's number, he moved out of pedestrian traffic and gazed upward, surprised to see he stood outside the Stone

Gallery. He sheltered under the awning, waiting for her to answer.

"Aiden?"

Her voice was hoarse. Was she crying? Aiden swallowed passed the lump in his throat. "Leila, baby, what's wrong?"

"Nothing is wrong." She sniffled. "I've had an emotional day. That's all."

"Talk to me, baby. Let me help, please."

"I can't right now." She cleared her throat. "Anyway, we should speak in person."

"Okay. Sit tight." Aiden scanned the street for a taxi. "Depending on traffic, I'll see you in about forty-five minutes."

Leila gasped. "What? You're in Jersey?"

"Close enough." Aiden hailed a passing cab. "I'm in the city at the Gallery in Chelsea. Hold on a sec." He gave the driver the address to Leila's motel.

"Oh, Aiden. Why are you here? I told you I would be fine, and I will be."

"You're not fine. Not at all." He ran a hand through his hair.

"I-I'm not in a good place right now." She sniffed again.

"I know, baby." Aiden closed his eyes and laid his head against the seat. "Pack while you wait. I'm taking you with me to Matt's. We can drop your things at the penthouse, and then we can have a quiet dinner and chat. We're finally on our own, and we can catch up."

"I'm not referring to the motel. I'm not in a good place in my head. I can't have this conversation now."

"I understood what you meant." Aiden opened his eyes and gazed out the window. Traffic was a bitch, and getting out of the city would take forever. "But we need to talk. I'll be at your motel as soon as I can."

"Okay."

"Okay?" He quirked an eyebrow, expecting an argument.

"Yeah, Aiden. See you soon."

Aiden noted the resolve in her voice. He straightened and his pulse hammered. Yesterday, he perceived a tiny crack in their foundation. By the tone of Leila's voice, he was certain that fissure expanded horizontally and vertically throughout the *entire* substructure, and they were on the verge of structural collapse.

Chapter Twenty-Four
Time

Leila paced her stifling motel room from end to end, wearing a path into the threadbare carpet. Aiden was on his way, and although he deserved an explanation, she wasn't ready to rehash her time with Eric or the turmoil their conversations provoked. She loved Aiden, but her world turned upside down once again, and she needed time to think before she leapt. Any decisions she made would affect many people—most importantly Mia. Bone-weary, she dropped to the edge of the bed and closed her eyes, sifting through the events of the last two days.

As planned, yesterday afternoon she'd met Eric at the diner across from the clinic. The haggard, hunched over man who shuffled into the diner didn't resemble the handsome, cocky man she used to know. His thick blond hair was replaced with thinning silver strands, and his face was pale and gaunt—ravaged.

"The last few years were tough. But time has been generous to you." Eric's lips tilted in a small smile as he sat across from her. "I'm sorry, but I don't have a lot of time. How can I help you?"

Questioning the wisdom of her plan, Leila opened and closed her mouth. The waitress arrived to pour coffee for him, giving Leila a chance to consider her next move, but she froze—unable to move or think. She felt as if she was in a movie scene on television and someone pushed pause. The only detail she registered was his lack of a wedding band.

"Leila, I'm not sure what this meeting is about, but as I said I don't…"

Startled, she blinked. "You have a daughter," she blurted. "*We* have a daughter. Her name is Mia. She's three, and she's beautiful." The second the words left her mouth, she slammed a hand over it and met his wide, shock-filled eyes.

Eric dropped his mug to the table, splattering coffee everywhere.

God, what had she done? Her pulse hammered. With trembling hands, she grabbed napkins from the dispenser. She opened the door to the past, and she must walk through—the choice to turn and run was no longer an option. "Mia looks like you. I don't expect anything from you. When *Baba* and Gabe find out, though, I don't know how they'll react and…"

Shaking his head, Eric blinked repeatedly. "Say it again…slowly," he whispered.

"I got pregnant the night we were together." Licking her lips, she took a deep breath, and told him everything, starting with the day she found out she was pregnant to her plans to see her family.

Grabbing her cell, she scrolled to a recent photo of her baby girl wearing a pink and white ruffled bikini and a toothy grin. "This is Mia." She had spent the next three hours showing him pictures and answering questions on every aspect of their daughter's childhood.

The incessant sound of a car horn beeping and a woman's voice shouting from the room next door startled Leila back to reality. She shook her head and scanned the filthy motel room. She loathed sleeping in the bed or walking on the carpet barefooted. Standing, she paced once more. She must clear her mind and prepare for her conversation with Aiden. The second he entered the room, he would lose his mind as Eric had. Just as she refused Eric's offer to relocate to an upscale hotel, she would refuse to move to Matt's penthouse.

For years, the Solomon men ruled every aspect of her life. Now, she was on her own and made her own decisions. Leila wasn't pleased Aiden didn't honor her decision to handle this trip on her own. But she wasn't proud of her behavior over the last two days. If she communicated openly, he wouldn't have chased after her, but she was overwhelmed.

Lately, almost every single day was a shit-show. At times she lay in bed, afraid to open her eyes in the morning, wondering what train, plane, or automobile would hit her next.

She examined her face in the bathroom mirror. She appeared as she felt—wasted. As she splashed cold water on her face, she heard knocking at the door. Drying her face and hands, she shuffled to the door and peered through the peephole. She opened the door and feasted on the sight of Aiden's tall, powerful body looming above her.

Without hesitation, Aiden wrapped an arm around her waist. As he closed the door with his foot, he gathered her to him and buried his face in her hair.

Leila held on, burrowing close. On auto-pilot, she tilted her head.

He captured her lips in a long drugging kiss as he buried his hands in her hair.

For a few minutes, her world righted before she

remembered where she was and why she was there. Breaking the kiss, she pulled away. She stepped back and wrapped her arms around herself.

Running a hand over his face, Aiden exhaled. He surveyed the room. Frowning, he focused on her and opened his mouth.

Leila raised her hand. "Don't. I know this place is a pit and should be burned to the ground, but I'm staying." She shook her head. "Please, don't argue. We have a lot to talk about. If you don't want to talk here, you can meet me at the diner across the way. I just have to change."

Aiden studied her for a few seconds. "We'll stay. What's going on, baby? You're worrying me." He pulled out the desk chair and sat.

"I know. I'm sorry." Leila sat on the edge of the bed. "I...I met with Eric. He..." She wrung her hands. "He's not the same man I knew."

"Is that a good or bad thing?" Aiden tilted his head.

"He was married, and they had a child...a little girl...Sarah Jane." Leila's eyes filled with tears. "She resembled Mia—a carbon copy actually."

"Go on." He swallowed hard.

"She died, Aiden. She was fifteen months when she contracted RSV—Respiratory Syncytial Virus. Five days later, she was gone. The loss of his child destroyed his marriage...and him." When Eric showed her pictures of the petite pixie so like her own baby girl, waves of pain wafted off him and slammed into her. If she wasn't sitting, she would have fallen.

"How did he react when you told him about Mia?" Aiden leaned forward, resting his elbows on his knees.

"He fell apart." She licked her lips. "For a long

time, we sat in a diner as he studied pictures of Mia and asked a million questions—desperate to know every detail of her life…our lives. Then we strolled and chatted. We met up again today." She shook her head. "He insists on paying child support and called his accountant to set up regular payments. He transferred a ridiculously large sum of money into my account for back child support."

"Well, sounds as if your meeting went better than you predicted. But you have more to tell me. Right?"

"He wants to meet Mia and be a part of her life." Her mouth was dry, and she reached for the water bottle on the night-stand, unscrewing the lid with shaking fingers and gulping down most of the water.

"How do you feel about that plan?" Aiden straightened.

Leila stood, strolled to the window, and stared at the grimy parking lot. How did she feel? She was undone. For a long time after she moved to Florida, she fantasized of calling Eric and telling him she was pregnant with his baby. She dreamed he would be over-joyed, leave his fiancée, run to her side, and they would be a family.

When she shared her ridiculous fantasy with Deena, she received a lecture and a reality check. Eric did not want a long-term relationship. She was a notch on his belt. He enjoyed the chase, and when he captured the prize, he was no longer interested.

But the man who Leila spent hours with yesterday, and most of today, was different than his younger version. This Eric was soft-spoken and kind. He was thoughtful and deeply regretted his behavior. He wasn't sure how he would have reacted if she told him she was pregnant, but he admitted he probably wouldn't have been supportive. Gabe informed him she was accepted to a university out of state, and he didn't question the weak explanation and was relieved he didn't have to see the hurt in her eyes daily.

Leila faced Aiden and cleared her throat. Although he initially appeared calm, his anger and frustration levels were rising. He was a smart man and could easily read her every emotion. "If you asked me a week ago, my answer would be different. But now, everything has changed. He's lost one child already, and I can't deny him the privilege of knowing Mia. She also deserves a chance to know her father and to be loved by him. I don't know how he will fit into our lives, but I'll do anything for Mia. I need to pave the way and set a good example."

"Something tells me Mia is not the only person he wants in his life. Am I wrong?" He pierced her with his gaze.

She couldn't lie. Eric was always charismatic and easy to talk with, but now he was more genuine. He told her all about his ex-wife and their contentious break-up after Sarah Jane's death, and she shared all the details of her life, including Aiden, AJ, and Gina. While Leila loved Aiden, she found she liked this new and improved Eric. She was confused, exhausted, and tired of being interrogated.

No doubt, some chemistry still existed between her and Eric. Leila's feelings for Eric, though, were different than those for Aiden. Like old friends, she and Eric reminisced about the lunches they used to share, the overindulgent patients the clinic catered to, and the excitement they experienced when they first opened the clinic.

He updated her about recent family events but admitted he and Gabe were at a crossroads and were dissolving the practice. Eric's heart was no longer in concierge medicine. Instead, he built on an idea she worked on for one of her classes. He was opening a series of clinics for the indigent and asked her opinion about locations and how to attract immigrants.

The water Leila gulped down threatened to make a reappearance, and she took deep breaths to control her churning stomach. "He asked for time—with me and Mia." She closed her eyes and recalled all the times she curled up alone on her bed, dreaming of having a man in her life. Now she had two. Deena warned her not to act foolishly. Aiden was a gift—everything she needed.

Leila predicted what Niveen and her mama would say if she asked for their opinion. Family is what matters most. Eric was Mia's father, and he'd changed. They both made mistakes, but they matured. Shouldn't she explore a relationship with him—if not for herself then for Mia? Leila opened her eyes.

"I understand he wants time with Mia, and if you think he will be good for her, I respect your decision. But how do you figure into this equation? Hasn't that ship sailed? How can you have any feelings left for him, and what about us?" Aiden clenched his jaw. "What did you tell him?"

"I love you, Aiden. You and AJ are the best thing to happen to me." She hung her head. "But...I...Mia..."

Aiden stood and pulled her into his arms. "Leila, for God's sake, you know I love you and Mia, and you say you love me. Don't throw us away. Our lives have been crazy, and we haven't talked. If you're worried about Gina, don't be. She means nothing to me and isn't interested in motherhood. Mike is drawing up papers to terminate her rights, and I think she'll sign." He gulped in air. "If Eric wants to be a father to Mia, that's fine. I don't understand why you must be part of the equation."

"You're right. We haven't talked." Leila dragged herself out of his arms. "That's not your fault or mine." She clenched her fists. "Since we've met our lives have been in complete chaos. I don't know if I'm coming or going anymore, and I have to deal with my family tomorrow." She dug her hands into her hair and closed her eyes. "Every single damn day my head feels as if it might explode." She opened her eyes and dropped her arms to her sides, feeling defeated. "Aiden, I know I am blessed. But lately, every day I wake up hopeful the soap opera that is my life will somehow become less complicated. Instead, the exact opposite happens. I'm not blaming you. That's my life right now. I can't handle everything coming at me at once anymore."

"Baby, what do you need? Tell me. I don't want to lose you." Aiden dropped his head. He cleared his throat. "How can I help you?"

She knew what she needed. Aiden wouldn't understand. She was about to hurt him in a way she never thought she was capable of doing to another human being. She took a deep breath. "Today was the first day in a long time I breathed…drama free. One secret revealed, and for the first time in years, I was weightless." As predicted, pain slid across his features and immediately sliced through her as well, but she gritted her teeth and continued. He pushed her to share her feelings when she wasn't ready. Now, he would hear every thought—raw and unfiltered.

"You know, Aiden, when I was a child, I used to have a recurring dream where I possessed the ability to fly. I was powerful and flew anywhere and did anything I wanted—completely untethered and jubilant. I have no idea what tomorrow will bring." She shrugged. "I hope when I leave New Jersey, I will be free of my entire burden and will breathe easy. I long to fly free for the rest of my life."

"What does that mean for us? Are you saying I am holding you down?" He rubbed his forehead with a shaking hand. "Do you think being with Eric will give you the freedom you crave? How can you choose to be with a man who slept with you, stole your innocence and trust, then scraped you off like garbage? Where's your self-respect?"

Leila flinched.

"Leila, I…" Aiden stepped toward her.

"No." She moved away. "You're not listening, Aiden."

Shaking his head, his lips thinned. "I hear you. Eric wants you and Mia," he spit out. "He's lost everything. You and Mia are a beautiful, ready-made replacement family. Surely, you're not that gullible? Are you ready to throw us away after a day with him?"

She hurt Aiden, and he lashed out. But his words tore into her—arrows piercing her skin. The pain was familiar. Her flesh tore, gaped open, and she bled. Angry and hurt, people rarely chose their words with care.

Unable to breathe, Leila pressed her hands to her chest and gasped. She needed space. Confused and distraught, she backed away farther. She asked Aiden to give her this week, and he chased after her, cornering and stifling her. She loved Aiden and AJ, but sometimes, love was toxic and blind. And sometimes love wasn't enough.

Right or wrong, she couldn't stop the words from passing through her lips. "I love you with all my heart," she croaked. "But what I need is something you can't seem to give me without throwing my past in my face, hurting me, or trusting me to sort out my life. You asked what I need and what I want. *Time*. I need time…away from you and from us."

Chapter Twenty-Five
Lion-Tamer

Watching Aiden open the motel door and walk out of her life was devastating. Leila resolved not to run after him. He pushed her too far, and for once in her life, she shoved back. Wrung out, she collapsed on the bed and fell immediately into a fitful sleep to be awakened by the ringing of her cell—Niveen. Her cousin called to confirm their meeting at four the next day. The second she heard Leila's hoarse voice, however, she refused to hang up until Leila promised to tell her everything tomorrow.

Over the last few months, Leila spoke to Niveen about her growing and complex relationship with Aiden and AJ, but she didn't mention Eric. Niveen never asked who Mia's father was. On several occasions, she asked for pictures of Mia, but Leila always conveniently forgot or lied and said her telephone misbehaved. Niveen was an intelligent woman and stopped asking.

Leila slept off and on for the rest of the night replaying her conversation with Aiden and worrying about her reunion with her family. She hated the way she and Aiden parted, but she felt cornered. She admitted how overwhelmed and confused she was, and instead of supporting her, he was accusatory and judgmental. She loved him, but he hurt her.

By six a.m., she was desperate for fresh air. Woodenly, she rose, showered, and dressed. Pale, with dark circles under her eyes, she appeared as if she suffered from a terminal illness. Grabbing her purse, she trekked to a nearby diner for caffeine and a bagel. As she added extra honey to her hot tea and picked at a bagel, she once again replayed her interactions with Eric and Aiden—inadvertently comparing the two. She lost a man she loved and gained a man she lost.

Her life was a hot mess. She glanced at her watch—eight a.m. Hopefully, Deena was awake because she desperately needed her. Paying her tab, she trudged back to her room and called her confidante.

"Leila, you're hurt and angry, and you have a right to be. But don't come to any final conclusions. I know he acted like a dick, but Aiden loves you and was out of his mind with worry."

"I've experienced that type of love before, and it degrades and suffocates." Leila shook her head. "I can't let anyone hold me back from living my life. Old habits are hard to break, but I must break them because, Deena, I deserve better as does my daughter. I cannot be in a toxic relationship."

"Here's what I suggest." Deena sighed. "Compartmentalize what's happening with Aiden and Eric. Focus on your meeting with the family. Survive the next few days, and when you're home and rested, we'll sift through this mess together. You and Aiden have been under a great deal of stress, and when all this drama concludes, you'll see your relationship differently."

"But he…"

"No, listen to the words you used. These words

don't describe your relationship with Aiden. Those terms, and the accompanying emotions, are leftovers from the past. Please, take some time to deal with the present and live in the moment before you make any permanent decisions about your future."

Leila spent the rest of the day failing miserably at living in the present until three-fifteen p.m. when she boarded the train to Jersey City. She sat and closed her eyes, surrendering to the train's rhythmic shudder and shake as it pulled out of the station, taking her closer to her childhood home.

Out of desperation for the caffeine hit, she held tightly to the five-dollar Styrofoam cup of iced tea she bought. The filthy train was stiflingly hot and humid in the mid-day heat, and she took a few sips of the quickly diluting drink. The train-car was almost empty, save a couple of teenagers making out a few seats in front and an older Asian couple with large plastic shopping bags behind.

The lack of passengers surprised her given the time. Perhaps everyone was at the shore or on their way to the city for a fun evening instead of voluntarily submitting to a family inquisition in Jersey City. Exhaustion overwhelmed Leila to the point she considerd calling to cancel until Sunday, and she closed her eyes and rested her head against the window.

As the train came to a jerking stop, Leila banged her head against the window. An automated voice announced the Journal Square stop. Pulse racing and head aching, she stood on wobbly legs and exited the train, climbing the numerous stairs leading to the busy Jersey City streets. She was five blocks from her childhood home, and as she scanned her surroundings, she shoved all thoughts of Aiden and Eric to a corner of her brain. Childhood memories, good and bad, battered her.

She walked toward her home and her mama—one step after another—as her pulse bounded, limbs trembled, and beads of sweat sprouted on her upper lip and forehead. Lost in memories of the past, she recalled the numerous times Karima held her hand and crossed these busy streets on their way to *Baharat*, church, and *Tante* Amal's house. How many times did she, the *tantes*, cousins, and Mama board the train to the city to purchase their Christmas or Easter dresses from the huge department store on Thirty-Fourth Street, laughing all the way?

Her entire childhood was *not* a nightmare. Leila smiled. Karima did her best to show Leila joy existed, even if they didn't have a lot of money, lived in a tiny, cramped house where often angry, accusatory voices and drunken rages echoed.

Despite the ugliness Yusuf forced into her world, he hadn't succeeded in wiping out all the beauty of family life. Leila remembered music, family dinners, days at the beach, and holiday celebrations. She recalled the strength and love of her mother's arms, the adoration shining from her eyes when she studied Leila, and the special moments they shared before bed each night. Where had these memories hidden for so long? Why did she remember the pain but not the joy? Didn't some variety of joy and pain exist side by side on these streets and in her home as they did for every person in the world?

Leila glanced up, surveying the rundown, two-story blue house she stood in front of—*home*. Iron burglar bars guarded the windows and front door. She peered at the open second floor window. Yellow curtains with white ruffles bellowed through the bars each time Mother Nature sent a tiny breeze, swirling the dense humidity about. Leila smiled. She couldn't believe the curtains she fashioned in her seventh grade sewing class still hung. How many times did she and Mama take them down, wash, repair, press, and rehang them?

Hearing the creak of the front door, she gulped in air then glanced at the porch—Niveen. Of course, Niveen would greet her. She understood Leila, like a condemned prisoner being led to the executioner, needed a strong arm to guide her past the rusted chain-linked fence, up the cracked concrete steps, and through the entryway.

Without hesitation, Niveen raced down the stairs and path leading to the fence. She threw open the gate and gathered Leila into her arms, holding her tight. "Lala," she whispered. "Dear God, is this beautiful woman really my Lala standing tall, strong, and brave?"

As she circled her cousin with her arms, Leila leaned into Niveen's embrace. She blinked and forced away the tears. She must stay strong. "I've missed you, my sister," she said in Arabic.

"Not as much as I missed you, *yah ell-bee*." Niveen pulled away and inspected every millimeter of Leila's face. Her smile faded. "You've been crying yourself silly, haven't you?"

Leila opened her mouth but closed it when she noticed movement at the front door. "*Tante* Amal," she whispered.

Niveen turned and grasped her hand. "We'll talk

later. Now, though you have returned to the arms of the people who never stopped loving you. Later, we'll have time to fix what ails you." She squeezed Leila's palm and hauled her behind her. "Trust me. You'll be fine. By the end of the day, you'll feel better than you have in years."

Seconds later, Leila was engulfed in Amal's arms.

"You are loved," Amal whispered. She held Leila's shoulders and held her away. "Remember, the past isn't always as clear as you remember. Promise me, you'll now listen and understand with the heart and mind of an adult and mother…not a child drowning in pain, confusion, and disappointment."

Leila stared into her aunt's beseeching eyes. Overcome with emotion—fear, as well as anticipation, love, and an unexpected relief to finally be in the arms of her people—she was incapable of producing any words. She nodded.

Sandwiched between Amal and Niveen, Leila stepped over the threshold and froze. She surveyed the vicinity. Not a single detail of the house changed since the night she slipped out the backdoor like a thief. She followed Amal down the hall leading to the formal living room. The heavy ceramic cross still hung over the door, family pictures lined the hallway walls, and the wood floors gleamed. Not a speck of dust was in sight. Permeating the air was the scent of furniture polish, garlic, onions, and a hint of her mother's perfume.

"Leila?" Niveen squeezed her shoulder.

She nodded. On trembling legs, she stumbled down the hall until she stood at the entrance of the cramped living space. The room was decorated with hand-carved, opulently upholstered Turkish furniture and heavy, gold drapes. This ornate room was her mother's pride and joy, and Karima rarely let family utilize it. Only special guests were granted access.

Engulfed by large, gold tasseled pillows, Karima sat in the middle of the large couch appearing thin and gaunt—her complexion blending with the creamy background of the couch. Her hair, once long, thick, and dark, was thin, short, and white.

Leila gasped, searching for signs of the woman that used to be her mama. When her gaze connected with Karima's warm eyes, she stilled, and her breath stuttered. She sank to the floor at her mother's feet. "Mama. Oh, Mama. What have you done?" Leila moaned as she picked up her mother's boney hand and kissed it over and over again.

For a few minutes, only the sound of Leila's and Karima's weeping filled the room.

Karima ran a hand over Leila's hair. "Come, sit next to me, *habibtee*. We have much to talk about." She squeezed Leila's hand.

Drying her face with the handkerchief her mother provided, she positioned herself next to Karima, noticing the other women disappeared.

"We will not waste time," Karima said. "I have much to say, and my energy is poor. First, may I hold you?" She opened her arms wide.

Leila threw herself into Karima's embrace, holding close her now-fragile, cachectic frame and burying her face in her mother's neck. She breathed in Karima's rose scent. In her mama's arms, she was home, and she couldn't remember why she ever left. Sobs overtook her, and she wept for the days, weeks, months, and years they'd wasted.

Thank God she'd come home. If she lost her mother before they put the past to rest, she would be crippled with guilt and regret for the rest of her days. In light of Karima's obvious illness, the past no longer mattered. Karima carried Leila under her heart for nine months. She loved, nurtured, and protected her to the best of her ability. No one would ever take Karima's place.

Taking a shuddering breath, she gently leaned away and wiped her mother's wet cheeks with her hands. "Mama, I know you're sick. Let's talk about your health first. Nothing else is important now. Why won't you accept treatment? Are you scared of surgery? I don't understand."

"No, we will not start at the end." Karima tugged Leila's hands off her face. "We must start at the beginning."

"But…"

"No." Karima squeezed Leila's hands. She straightened her spine and squared her shoulders. "You will listen. I'm still your mama, and you must do as I ask."

Leila tried not to smile. She remembered her mother's stubborn tone and piercing stare that heralded an argument was imminent. She recognized who Mia inherited her stubborn streak from. No matter the passing of time nor the distance separating them, she and Mia carried part of Karima deep within them—DNA strands passed from generation to generation permanently embedded in every cell.

Karima wiped her eyes and nose. "You were young when you left, but now, you are a mother. I am hopeful you will understand my past actions. Leila, parents do not always make the right decisions, but they do the best they can with each obstacle they face, using their life experience and the knowledge they possess. The best for you and Gabe was to send you away—"

"But…"

"You will listen." Karima glared.

Leila held her mother's gaze and nodded.

"Do you think I am stupid because my English is not perfect, and I believe in the old ways?" She shook her head. "I knew you carried Eric's child."

Leila gaped, and her pulse ratcheted. "What?" She snatched her hands from her mother. "How?"

"How?" Karima clucked her tongue. "Who else caught your eye, romanced you with pretty words, and fed your need for a man's approval? You don't remember me visiting you at the clinic, finding you flushed and giggling over some silly nonsense he said? Do you not remember my warnings not to flirt with him?"

Leila's mouth hung open. Dear God, she'd forgotten Karima's frequent visits to the clinic. She and Eric never knew when she would show up. Leila was infatuated, and she didn't notice Karima was more vigilant than usual. As for lectures about flirting, Mama, *Baba*, or Gabe always admonished her about something. Leila slowly nodded.

"I see you now remember…hmm?" She thinned her lips. "I worried you were too naïve and inexperienced to be involved with such a sophisticated man. He wanted only one thing. I didn't do enough to protect you." Karima wrung her hands. "When you said you were pregnant, I put together the pieces, and I knew

I must protect you and the baby. At the same time, I needed to protect Gabe and your father from themselves."

"Why didn't you tell me?" Leila shook her head.

"What difference would that have made?" Karima tilted her head. "You did not trust me enough to tell me when you first found out you were pregnant. You handled everything on your own. Your head was in the clouds. You decided to break every rule I taught you, but you didn't consider the long-term ramifications of your actions. You dropped the information on us like a bomb. What did you expect?" She threw up her hands. "Holding this family together and keeping everyone safe fell on me alone. I was the mama." She jabbed a finger into her chest. "You, the child carrying a child." She pointed at Leila.

Standing, Leila paced. All the jagged pieces of her life story were coming together in unexpected ways. Karima was much wiser than she gave her credit, and she carried a heavy burden. She'd never stopped loving Leila, but Leila had rebelled, gotten into serious trouble, and stopped trusting the one person who loved her unconditionally. She hurt Karima deeply. "I understand I made terrible mistakes." Leila hung her head. "Believe me, I've paid for them. I'm sorry I hurt you, and I didn't confide in you, but, Mama, I didn't see how you could help me beyond telling me to kill my baby."

"You will never know what I would have said or done to protect you and my grandchild." Karima shook her head, expelling a long sigh. "I protected my family the best way I could. If you stayed, our family would have exploded," she whispered. "Don't you understand what your father and Gabe would have done?"

Leila stopped pacing and dropped next to Karima again. She swallowed hard and studied her hands. "I *do* understand," she whispered. "But explain to me one more thing. Why did you always make excuses for *Baba*'s behavior and protect him? He hurt me—with his words and actions. He despised me. You said and did nothing."

Karima's eyes filled with tears. "Oh, my child, my *habibtee*, you have no knowledge of what I did or didn't do. What you must understand is we all have choices. My choice was to marry your father and stay married. I honored my vow to him and God to be a good wife and to obey. These are our customs and our beliefs. He is the head of the house. I did my best to protect you." Grabbing Leila's hand, she squeezed and swallowed hard. "I know my best wasn't enough."

Leila shook her head. What good would come from blaming her mother for her father's sins? Part of Leila wanted to scream at Karima she could have done so much more to protect her. The other part of her acknowledged the truth. Given her upbringing and circumstances, Karima was limited in her ability to behave differently. The past was the past, and the present was all that mattered. Raising her head, she met her mother's watery gaze. "Mama, you did the best you could. I understand now. But I want you to know you have choices. You live in America and you have me. You can…"

"No, *habibtee*. I could be on the moon or the sun, and I would still honor and obey my husband. I have always known I had choices. Those choices are for other women—not for me. If I left, where would I have gone with you and Gabe? What would I have done without your father, the store, and my family? This life…" She surveyed the room. "This is the only life I know. You are different. You are stronger and smarter. I am sorry I failed you." Karima broke down and wept.

Leila's heart ached. She held the weeping woman in her arms until her sobs quieted, and her tears dried. "Mama, you didn't fail me."

"I did." Karima shook her head. "I know I did. But what you don't understand is from the second you were conceived, you were and are, my love—the reason my heart beats. I cannot live with my actions or lack of action. I hurt you. Without you, why should my heart beat?"

Leila froze. Agony sliced through her. Karima was killing herself purposefully. She must convince her she and Mia had a good life because of her sacrifices. Karima carried a heavy burden her entire life, and now Leila would do her best to remove some of that weight. Karima wasn't weak. She was the strongest of women. "Mama, I understand now why you sent me away. Don't worry about me. I am fine, but you're not, and I…"

Karima patted her hand. "First, I need to know all about your life. I am told you have a child, a career, and a man who loves you. Yes?"

"Yes." Leila hesitated. She didn't want to mislead her mother, but she also couldn't burden her with her troubles with Aiden. "Because of your many sacrifices, we have a beautiful life. Please, can we talk about your health?"

"First, may I see a picture of my grandchild?" Karima smiled.

Nodding, Leila pulled her cell out of her bag and clicked on Mia's album. She handed Karima the phone.

Karima scrolled through the many pictures, smiled, and nodded. After she viewed a large number of pictures, she glanced up. "She is you, *habibtee*."

"No." Leila shook her head. "Mia is Eric."

"How did you choose her name?" Karima tilted her head to the side. "What does her name mean?"

"In Florida, a large Hispanic population exists. I once met a child named Mia at the clinic I worked. I loved the sound of the name and its meaning. You see, in Spanish, Mia means mine." Leila laid a hand to her chest. "I wanted my daughter to have a unique name— not Egyptian or American—and to always know I loved and wanted her."

"The name fits her. She is beautiful like her mama. I can see her heart." Karima swallowed hard. "She is good and kind. She is patient and loving. She will have a good life—one that is better than mine and better than yours because she will be loved by many."

"How can you be certain?" Leila furrowed her eyebrows.

Karima peered at the cell once more. "Do you not see the joy radiating from her in every picture?" She traced Mia's face with a finger. "She knows she is safe and loved. If you do your job well, you will help shape her into an extraordinary person. I did better than my mother and brought you to America. You have opportunities I never did, and Mia will have even more opportunities." She looked into Leila's eyes. "You will make mistakes, and she will make mistakes because we are human and are limited by what we know, what we experience, and how we love. But don't forget to teach her about family."

"The family she has is growing." Leila nodded. "For a long time, Deena was our only family, but now…" She swallowed hard, remembering her village might have shrunk yet again. "We are better and happy. Eric…"

"Does he know he has this beautiful child?" Karima frowned. "He has changed. Life has not been kind."

She nodded and twisted her fingers together. "I didn't know about his divorce or the death of his child. I stayed away and never told Eric about Mia because I didn't want to cause trouble for Gabe or deal with *Baba*." She straightened. "Although I still worry about Gabe and *Baba*, I met Eric on Friday. He had to know." She chewed on her lower lip, recalling Eric's first reaction when he saw a picture of Mia. "He wants desperately to know his child and wants to be a part of her life."

"Good." Karima patted Leila's hand. "But do not worry about Gabe. He will not be a problem any longer."

"I don't understand." Leila frowned.

"Your brother has grown too big for his clothes." Karima shrugged.

"What?" Leila laughed. "He gained weight?" Her mother rarely used English slang and sayings correctly. Sometimes she translated Arabic sayings into English and that adaptation was worse.

"No, no, *habibtee*." Karima smiled. "He thinks too much of himself, and I needed to teach him a lesson. He knows about your child and Eric."

"Oh, my God. Mama, he'll kill Eric." Leila gasped.

"No, he will do no such thing." She reclined against the cushions. "He has retreated to Cape May with his tail between his legs. All these men think they are in charge when they are nothing without us." She shrugged. "I reminded him he failed in his duty as your brother. You gave up everything to build his practice, and he didn't protect you. He was too full of himself and put you in harm's way. That is not how a man behaves. You left to save him and his precious practice. He doesn't know I made you leave, and he will not know this fact."

"Oh, Mama, I fell for Eric's charms. I was young, stupid, and rebellious. My actions were my own." Leila wrung her hands.

"Yes, but his job was to protect the women in this family. He failed. He has other problems now…his wife. I took the opportunity, while your father is gone, to tell my son he is a disappointment. He cannot continue behaving as his father, because he is not married to a woman who will tolerate his nonsense. He must be a better man, father, and husband." She lifted her chin and tightened her jaw. "We had a difficult conversation, but he is my child, and in the future, he will honor his mama."

"And *Baba*?" Leila raised an eyebrow. "What will we do about *Baba* because I won't lose you again? I cannot live without my mama."

"*Habibtee*, I, too, have grown and found my voice." Karima grasped Leila's hand and patted it. "Your *baba* and brother are lions." Smiling, she straightened and slapped a hand to her chest. "I am the lion tamer. For as long as God lets me breathe, I will be your mama, and you and my granddaughter will not lose me."

Leila smiled, relieved Karima found her voice and made a stand—in her own way. "A lion-tamer, huh? This family is in desperate need of one. But if we're to have a future, you must accept medical treatment." She met her mother's gaze. "I need you. Mia needs her *teta* to teach her about our traditions, and Gabe needs you to learn to be a better man. You have sacrificed enough. You are the glue holding us all together. Please don't leave us. Remember, family *is* everything, and without you, we are not a family."

Chapter Twenty-Six
Wait

After his disastrous conversation with Leila at her motel, Aiden spent a sleepless night at Matt's Manhattan penthouse, getting wasted while being lectured to by his dear brother. He left for Florida the next morning. Hung-over, sleep deprived, and heart-broken, he arrived in Florida to find AJ at a friend's house and Tyra waiting.

Tyra ripped into him the second he opened the door to Harbor House. Apparently, while he was drinking away his troubles, Leila called Deena, and Deena called Tyra. Then Tyra, who had a colorful vocabulary, called him every name in the book. He was on the shit list of all the women in his life, and he wasn't sure he blamed them.

Aiden needed to lick his wounds in private while he figured out what to do about Leila and why her words triggered the green-eyed, feeble-brained monster. He couldn't think clearly. He screwed up, but he wasn't ready to deal with the barrage of emotions—anger, disappointment, and shame—barreling at him all at once.

"Stop screeching, for God's sake." He closed his eyes and gritted his teeth. His head would explode if Tyra didn't pipe down. "I can't discuss Leila with you or anyone right now. I'm sorry, Ty, but I need to disappear. I've booked a flight to Thailand, and I'm taking off for a few weeks."

"Are you stupid?" Tyra opened and closed her mouth. Placing her hands on her hips, she glared. "Did you learn nothing from the past? Packing your shit and disappearing is not the way a responsible adult behaves. Stop and think before you ruin your life."

He stalked to his room and packed—Tyra on his heels.

"Aiden James Stone, don't you dare ignore me. I swear to God *I* will pack *my* shit and disappear, leaving you to deal with AJ and your messed-up life."

He froze. He didn't have the time or desire to explain his actions, but he needed Tyra to stay with AJ. Dropping the clothes in his hands, he turned. "Ty, I know I behaved badly. I need time to figure out shit and make a plan. I've got to go. I can't talk to Leila or anyone else right now."

Running a hand through his hair, he dropped his gaze and sank to the edge of the bed. "She asked for time and space, and I'm complying with her wishes. Yes, I could have handled the situation better, but I can't be the only person fighting for us. From the beginning, I chased her, begging and pleading for a chance. I deserve a *partner* who's not scared of life and knows what she wants." He met Tyra's gaze. "What I don't need is a woman who's afraid to live life to its fullest, accepts abusive behavior as a norm, and settles for crumbs when the whole damn cake is in front of her." He threw up his hands. "I love her, but my love is *not* enough. Now, *I* need space."

Despite his deep guilt over leaving AJ without much preparation, early the next morning, Aiden boarded his flight. For two weeks, he lived a solitary life traveling throughout Thailand. He snapped pictures and considered his relationship with Leila. He barely spoke to another soul other than AJ and, on occasion, Tyra. During AJ's conversations with him, he often mentioned Mia. Aiden and Leila were on pause, but his son continued his love affair with Mia. When Aiden spoke with Tyra, he suggested AJ spend more time with Miles and less with Mia.

"A, I understand you screwed up your relationship with Leila, and you're unhappy and sulking. You're both adults. Don't punish AJ and Mia for your choices. You've been gone for a while, and AJ is miserable. He doesn't understand your sudden disappearance, and Mia distracts him. Enough is enough. Get your ass home and parent your child. Now."

Aiden wasn't proud of his behavior. He was a father of a special needs child, and he let his personal problems skew his judgment. For the second time in AJ's short life, Aiden ran away. Although AJ didn't have a memory of Aiden's first disappearing act, now his memory was sharp.

The next day, he hopped a flight home. Moping done, he was ready to clean up his attitude and make amends to the people he hurt—starting with AJ. Over the next two weeks, he spent time with him and bought his forgiveness with a hundred-gallon tank filled with tropical fish that they enjoyed filling together and learning about.

Although Tyra gave Aiden grief when he first returned, she backed off. She was happy and wanted Aiden to be the same. She and Jayden planned to be married in a small chapel in Vero Beach, and Aiden offered to host and cater their reception at the gallery. He hired the best caterer, harpist, and florist money bought.

One person, the one he was incapable of living the rest of his life without, was left to apologize to. Apology, however, was not enough. He must find a way of righting their world. He had no clue how to make them all happy. Mia deserved to have her father in her life, and Leila deserved the time and the latitude to fly free and make her own decisions. Aiden longed to see Leila's face and gauge the damage he caused and his chances of reentry into the beautiful life they built.

Two weeks after he returned from Thailand, he and AJ had just finished eating lunch at the Dancing Dolphin and were leaving when Leila, Mia, and a man he assumed was Eric strolled in. The children embraced as if they hadn't seen each other in decades when they regularly met for play dates facilitated by Deena and Tyra.

Aiden's pulse accelerated, and he stared at Leila. Her smile faded, and she paled. Silence ensued as he scrutinized every inch of her. She was as beautiful as ever, but she was thinner. He caressed her with his gaze—over her now more prominent cheeks, across her full pink lips, and down her wild mass of thick curls.

His gut clenched and the muscles in his arms spasmed—readying to grab her and haul her to him. In his entire life, he never longed to act on his instincts as he did at that moment. For a month he was lost, stumbling blindly in the night unsure which direction to travel. But in her presence, with Eric looking on, Aiden was finally home.

Tears filled Leila's eyes, and she looked away.

Emotion tightened his chest until he was breathless. God, how he'd hurt his girl.

Eric cleared his throat. "Hi, you must be Aiden. I'm Eric Dixon."

Although his gaze stayed on Leila, Aiden shook his hand. He crouched. "Hello, Mia. I…"

Mia's smile fell. She released AJ's hand and ran to her mother, sobbing.

Aiden hung his head. Discouraged and ashamed of his past behavior, he bribed AJ with a visit to the pet store so his boy would agree to leave. In a matter of minutes, he brought both his girls to tears. He had to find a way to repair the damage.

Evidence of Mia's and Leila's unhappiness was clear, and he could no longer deny the inevitable. He and Leila had lost their way, but they needed each other to be complete again. That night, and every night for the next two weeks, he dreamed of Leila and often woke to the sound of her pleading, "Aiden, please wait."

While his nights were filled with dreams of Leila and Mia, his days were a whirlwind of activity. Change was the theme of his life. The Gallery was incredibly busy, and Aiden spent more time there than usual— freeing Tyra to prepare for her wedding and furnish her new home. For the most part, AJ responded to the upheaval better than Aiden or Tyra imagined.

But on moving day, all hell broke loose. As Aiden, Deena, Jayden, Tyra, and Tyra's friend, Alisha, moved Tyra's belongings from Harbor House to Ocean Front Manor, Aiden tripped over one of AJ's toys and almost fell down a flight of steps, carrying boxes. His boy was a handful all day. Giving up, he and AJ went for a walk on the beach.

AJ insisted on walking in the direction of Leila's house.

"Peanut, the waves are high today. Only your feet can touch the water." Aiden increased his stride. AJ would listen for about five minutes before he tested the boundaries. Pushing for control over his world and making his own decisions were new and healthy behaviors, but the adults had to keep a close eye on him. With his hand, Aiden shielded his eyes from the sun and kept his gaze on AJ. He lost his favorite sunglasses somewhere in the Andaman Sea off the west coast of Thailand where he photographed the Surin Islands, a breathtaking collection of rocky islets with crystal blue water.

AJ slowed and picked up a starfish. He held the fish for Aiden to see then placed it in the ocean.

Smiling, Aiden glanced at the tumultuous ocean. He thanked God his boy was happy, healthy, and unfazed by the many changes in his life.

"Mommy. Mia," AJ screeched.

Peering in the distance, Aiden caught his breath.

AJ ran toward Mia and Eric who strolled hand-in-hand.

At a distance, Leila sat under an umbrella.

Aiden glanced at Eric who smiled and nodded. Trudging to where Eric and the kids stood, he cleared his throat. "Hello, Eric."

"Aiden." Eric nodded.

Aiden smiled toward Mia. "Hi, Sunshine." He squatted next to the little girl who studied him with her father's startling azure eyes. "How are you, sweetheart?"

Mia shrugged but didn't smile. She scooched closer to Eric.

How did he forget to add her to the list of people he must make amends to? Children were forgiving, but he must do the work. He missed her as much as he missed her mother, and Tyra was right, he shouldn't have involved the kids in his mess. "I know we haven't seen each other in a long time. You did nothing wrong. I'm sorry. I miss you, Sunshine, and I promise, I won't leave again. Okay?"

Mia stared for a few seconds before she nodded, smiled, and launched herself in his direction.

Laughing, Aiden caught her and toppled to his ass. He hugged her and kissed the top of her head then met Eric's gaze.

Eric smiled. "Mia and AJ, let's build a castle while Aiden talks to Mommy." He gently guided Mia out of Aiden's arms. "Why don't you go say hi to Leila?"

Confused, Aiden studied Eric. What was the man up to? When he saw them at the restaurant, Eric's arms were around Mia and Leila, and he appeared content. Aiden tilted his head and frowned.

"Go to her. You're who she wants and she needs. I blew my chance a long time ago." Eric shrugged. "Even if she might be unsure and scared, she's yours, and my gut tells me she always will be."

Aiden froze, and his breath stuttered. He hung his head, feeling like he'd been sucker-punched. As his heart overflowed with gratitude and joy, his chest ached. He didn't deserve this miraculous turn of events and thanked God, the Universe, and anyone else he could think of. Eric wouldn't be another obstacle he would hurdle to get to his girls.

Swallowing hard, he raised his head and nodded. Grasping Eric's outstretched hand, he shook it as he scanned the beach. Leila was no longer in view.

"She's hiding in the house." Eric grinned. "Go ahead." He lifted his chin. "I'll watch the kids."

Eric *had* changed. Perhaps losing a child and a marriage made him a different man…a better man. Aiden also learned a few lessons, and he hoped his hurtful words and deeds didn't do permanent damage. He needed to earn Leila and Mia's trust and show them he too was a better man—the kind who would love and cherish them for a lifetime.

"Thanks, Eric." He cleared his throat. "Just keep your eye on my boy. He's a bit too brave for his own good at times."

After striding to the house, he climbed the few steps to the deck and faced the sliding door leading into the kitchen. Exhaling hard, he rested his forehead against the glass, closed his eyes, and searched for the right words to convince her to give him another chance. Taking a deep breath, he straightened, knocked, and waited.

Leila opened the door, wearing a white short sleeveless dress over her bathing suit that accentuated her tanned skin and skimmed the top of her thighs. Her hair was braided down her back, and she was barefoot with bright-orange toenails.

She studied him for a few seconds, and then stepped aside.

Stepping into the air-conditioned house, Aiden felt goose bumps sprout on his arms and legs. He closed the door behind him.

She poured a glass of iced-tea from a pitcher.

"Would you like some?" She raised the glass in his direction.

He shook his head. "Can we talk?" His mouth was dry, but the thought of swallowing anything was nauseating.

Nodding, Leila settled at the kitchen table.

Aiden sat in front of her. He swallowed past the cotton balls in his mouth and throat, took a deep breath, and released it. "I'm sorry. I owe you an explanation."

"You don't owe me anything." Leila shook her head.

He was taken aback by her detached voice. She sat stiffly—staring past him. Her face was blank, and her expression unreadable. Aiden ran a hand through his hair. He wished he knew what she was thinking. The aloof, seemingly uninterested woman sitting in front of him, wasn't his warm, caring Rapunzel. But he deserved everything she dished out.

Nightly, in his dreams she begged him to wait, and he would until she was ready to listen. Yes, his imagination might be operating in overdrive, but he also believed some part of Leila reached out. In the past, he behaved like an insecure jerk. Now, he would take his time, do the work, and wait. "Leila, will you let me explain? You don't need to say a single word. Only listen."

Blinking, Leila shrugged.

He cleared his throat. "After I left Florida, I spent two weeks in Thailand. I've relived every conversation we had—especially the last one. I don't have a good excuse for my behavior except to say I reacted out of fear of losing you." He held her hand, and he was filled with a sense of overwhelming relief. He could breathe easier. Even his heart settled into a peaceful, steady beat. God he'd missed this woman who filled his and AJ's world with love and joy he never dreamed he would experience.

She tugged to free her hand.

Aiden held on. He couldn't let go before he took responsibility for the pain he caused and convinced her of his love. "I love you, baby, but I'm afraid I don't have a lot of good examples to follow where relationships are concerned. You see, my father adored my mother. He tried everything to make her happy. Nothing he did was enough, and in the end, she took off."

Glancing up, she met his gaze.

"Dad was undone. Eventually, anger and despair set in, and he didn't care his children heard his drunken rants or sobs in the middle of the night." Aiden licked his lips. "As a kid, I blamed myself for her leaving. I tried to be good and make her smile, but I wasn't enough."

"Then Gina entered my life, and from the beginning, she and I were a poor fit. She was wild and reckless and craved everything she couldn't have. Still, I held on until her actions forced me to face reality." He squeezed her hand, relieved she wasn't pulling away— praying she would understand his actions, forgive him, and believe in the love he offered. "No matter what I did, neither my mother nor Gina was satisfied. Both eventually took off, looking for someone better."

He hung his head. Never had he admitted his feelings of inadequacy to anyone. If Leila was his future, however, she deserved to know the impact his past made. She shared traumatic past events, and they discussed how those events impacted her decision making and worldview. She deserved the same. "When you were in Jersey, our conversations were brief and rushed. I couldn't see you, but, baby, I heard your distress and confusion. You disengaged, and I was scared to death. You weren't forthcoming about what happened with Eric, and my imagination kicked up. My anxiety soared."

She opened her mouth and pulled to free her hand.

He held on, unable to break their connection, and was terrified if he released her, he would lose her forever. "I'm not blaming or criticizing you. Please listen. I'm telling you how I felt. You told me you reconnected with Eric, and I was convinced you were slipping through my fingers. Although everyone told me to give you space, I panicked."

Taking a deep breath, he exhaled. "You said he wasn't an ass, he wanted you, and you needed space." Swallowing hard, he met her gaze. "I freaked out." He threaded his fingers with her stiff fingers. "I was selfish and only thought about myself. I let my past mess with my head. You were under a great deal of stress, and I didn't give you space. I should have listened and been more supportive, but I'm…"

"Stop, Aiden. Please stop." She ripped her hand out of his. "I understand why you reacted the way you did. Although I'm figuring things out with my family and Eric, my life is chaotic and will stay that way for a long time. You've had complicated and messy, and now you and AJ deserve smooth and easy. We're not good for each other. We come from different backgrounds." She shrugged. "My life will never be smooth and easy."

Aiden smiled, relieved she shared her feelings. Her

reasoning was flawed, but at least now he understood her fears and why she resisted his pleas for a second chance. "I love you as you are. Don't change a single thing. Our differences make us stronger not weaker. We see things from different perspectives, and we will learn and grow from and with one another."

"I don't know how you can say that." She tilted her head and frowned. "We aren't together because of our differences. We folded under pressure. How is that a recipe for a successful future?"

He raked a hand through his hair. Why was she so obstinate? She wouldn't give an inch, and he was running out of material. "Leila, baby, we stumbled because we let the pressure build, and we didn't communicate well. Many couples experience this same problem. We were busy, and life happened. Believe it or not, communication problems are not isolated to a particular culture."

Releasing a long breath, Leila dropped her shoulders.

Aiden cupped her cheek with his palm, and for a second she leaned into his hand. His pulse accelerated. A sliver of hope showed through the darkness, and he rejoiced. "We met as our lives exploded. We did everything ass-backward, dealing with the hard stuff before we ever experienced easy." He shook his head and laughed. "Hell, I don't think we ever went out on a date without kids. Did we?"

She scrunched her forehead, smiled, and shook her head.

"See, our story is far from done, Rapunzel. We are just getting started. We might think we know a lot about each other, but we don't know the basics. You, like all sane people, love Good God Donuts and hate chocolate—which incidentally makes no sense. Other than those minute details, I don't know anything else…" He shrugged.

Leila widened her smile.

"The list of what I want to know is endless. Every single thing about you fascinates me. What's your favorite book, movie, and color? Which TV shows do you binge watch? What makes you smile? What makes you cry? Are your feet cold at night? Do you like beer or wine with pizza?" He held her hands, unable to tear his gaze away from hers. Leila's exquisite smile and radiant face filled him with a sense of hope and excitement for their future. "Let's start from the beginning. I'm willing to wait for as long as you need. Please think about what I said, and before making any decisions…wait."

Chapter Twenty-Seven
Gravity

Leila and Eric tiptoed out of Mia's room, closing the door behind them. When Eric visited, Mia insisted both parents tuck her in and read her a story. Over the last six weeks, Eric flew to Florida twice, staying for a week each time. At first, Mia was shy and unsure, but Eric quickly charmed her. When he returned to New Jersey, he called or video chatted Mia every day. Eric and Mia's relationship grew stronger.

Grabbing a bottle of wine, Leila followed Eric out to the deck. Sharing a bottle of wine after Mia was down was a ritual they enjoyed.

Eric poured the wine and handed Leila a glass.

Deena was out on her second date with Alisha, and other than the sound of the waves crashing to the shore, the world around them was at peace. Leila lounged on a deck chair lost in thought, replaying her conversation with Aiden from the day before. When she was confused and distraught, she flung away Aiden, but he boomeranged. Now, she must search her heart and make a decision. But first, she would have a truthful conversation with Eric.

Although she was certain of his love and devotion for his daughter, she was equally convinced no future existed for them as a couple. She wouldn't string him along with unrealistic expectations. He would fly to

Jersey in the morning, and they must discuss future visits.

He cleared his throat.

Startled, she glanced up. "I'm sorry. Did you say something?"

He gazed into her eyes. "We need to talk. I…"

"Eric…"

He shook his head and smiled. "Let me. Okay?"

Swallowing hard, she nodded.

"Leila, I'm in love with my child, and I need to be a part of her life. Over the last few weeks, I've been thinking, and I've made some decisions." He gazed at the ocean. "New York no longer holds the key to my happiness. My parents moved to San Diego years ago, and my ex and I are not on speaking terms. The practice has lost its charm, and frankly, if I have to cater to another rich hypochondriac, I might lose my mind." He released a long breath. "I'm moving to Florida."

"What? Eric…" She gasped.

"Hear me out." He held up a hand. "You are in love with Aiden. I shouldn't have asked you for something you couldn't give. You told me you loved him, and I pressured you to give us time when all the time in the world wouldn't make any difference. I can't go back and right a wrong, but I will do better in the future. We both will. I want us to be friends. I don't know what happened between you and Aiden, but I can guess I played an unfortunate role in your break-up."

Eyes wide, she stared, unable to comprehend all he said. He was letting her off the hook where a relationship with him was concerned, but he wasn't withdrawing his attention from his daughter who Leila suspected was also falling in love with her daddy.

Leila's throat tightened. "Eric, yes, you complicated my relationship with Aiden, but you're not to blame for our separation. I am. Anyway, my relationship with Aiden is not your problem. I want you to be in Mia's life. She adores you, and I can see you feel the same way, but moving?"

"Leila, life is damn unpredictable." He held her hand. "Don't wait too long before you right a wrong. Take every second God gives you to love as much and as hard as humanly possible. Nothing else is important."

She nodded. Perhaps Eric was right, and the time had come to be brave and repair her relationship with Aiden.

"I'm moving to Florida so I don't miss a minute more with Mia. She is too young to travel back and forth between us, and she shouldn't be the one making sacrifices. Eventually, when the time is right, I want her to know I am her daddy." Eric squeezed her hand. "Being a good father to Mia is the most important role in my life. She has given me a reason to live again, and I swear to God, I won't let either of you down. I also won't interfere in your relationship with Aiden."

Leila closed her eyes and inhaled deeply. Everything she dreamed for her child came true. Mia had a strong man to show her a father's love, not wrath, and she would grow happy, healthy, and strong. Eric wouldn't raise his voice or his hand to their child. The cycle of violence and abuse ended. Mia wouldn't know shame. She would hold her head high, and even when she stumbled or ran into life's many obstacles, she would have both parents by her side to help her stand once again.

Smiling, she wiped at a wayward tear and met Eric's gaze. "Our girl is smart and sensitive." She cleared her throat. "She has you figured out. I overheard her tell AJ you were her daddy the other day. So, any second now, she'll let the word slip."

He opened and closed his mouth then he grinned.

Eric and Leila used the rest of the evening making plans for his move. Selling his home, separating from the concierge practice completely, and moving his life to Florida would take time and effort. Long after he left, she stayed awake, dreaming what the future might hold for her and Mia.

Leila spent the week catching up on her online real estate courses and preparing for her licensing exam. Searching her heart, she made the decision to no longer deny her feelings for Aiden. She longed to live her life free to make her own decisions, but without Aiden, she was lost—blowing in the wind like one of those helium balloons whipped from here to there. Aiden loved her as she was—without chains, rules, boundaries, or shame.

The time Leila had spent in New Jersey was eye-opening. Karima lived a different life than her daughter, and likewise, Mia would live a different life than her grandmother or mother. Each generation experienced unique challenges and trials, but they also enjoyed opportunities that previous generations didn't. Leila journeyed back to her roots, made peace with her family and herself, and she grew. In many aspects of her life, uncertainty existed, and much work needed to be done to solidify the fragile peace she built with her family.

While she struggled to accept and forgive Yusuf's

Mona Sedrak

behavior and the manner in which he treated her and
Karima, she understood Karima's decisions better. Her
mother wasn't raised to question or challenge her
husband or his actions. He set boundaries she didn't
dare cross. Those boundaries narrowed Karima's world
to family members and friends coming from the same
background and holding the same beliefs.

Since her visit home, she spoke with her mother
daily, and with Niveen and Amal's help, she reunited
with many of her cousins. Often, Karima, Amal, and
Niveen video chatted with Mia, and Mia picked up on
the Arabic language, calling her grand-mother, *Teta*.
Even Karima's health improved, and she was scheduled
for heart bypass surgery in two months.

But Karima wasn't a miracle worker. While she
brought Gabe to heel, Yusuf wasn't as easily tamed.
Leila pleaded with her mother to stop her efforts at
reunification. Leila no longer craved her father's
approval and attention. Karima wasn't easily thwarted.
She insisted, one day her family would be at peace.

The day before Tyra's wedding, Gabe called. Leila
wasn't surprised when she answered the call.

"I owe you an apology," he muttered.

"Okay." She couldn't muster any enthusiasm or
forgiveness.

"Look. I'm sorry I did not protect you as I should
have."

Leila stepped onto the deck and closed the sliding
door. Although Mia was absorbed in a movie, she
possessed overly curious ears. "I don't blame you." She
paced. "Eric and I were consenting adults. The thing
you should be sorry for is the way you treated me when
I needed you."

"No, you were not a consenting adult. He was, but you were…"

"Stop, Gabe." She gritted her teeth. "I'm not interested in rehashing the past. If the purpose of your call was to apologize…apology accepted. Anything else?" This conversation was not healing—as her mother hoped. If they spoke much longer, they would utter hurtful words, damaging their precarious relationship further. Gabe's words were worthless. Only his future actions would help heal Leila's heart.

"Eric and I talked. He's leaving the practice."

"I know." She stared into the distance.

"I'm glad he is seeing his girl."

Leila shook her head. Her brother would forever be a disappointment. "*His girl* has a name—Mia. We have nothing in common, Gabe, and too much time and events have passed for us to pick up again. Consider yourself absolved. Thanks for calling."

"You've changed, Leila," Gabe mumbled. "I don't understand what you want from me."

"Of course I've changed. You don't know me at all." She tilted her head to the heavens. "I don't need anything from you. But you can do something for yourself and your family. *Baba* is a poor role model. He'll never win husband or father of the year. Be a better man."

Leila ended the call proud she stood up to her brother, but also sad for both of them. They lost their way as siblings. She planned to return to Jersey for her mother's surgery. Perhaps if she and Gabe spoke face-to-face, in time, their relationship would improve.

The next day, Leila awoke to an overly excited Mia bouncing on her bed, begging to put on her wedding dress. Rolling to her side, she peered at the bedside clock and groaned. "*Habibtee*, come curl up next to me, and try to sleep. The sun is still snoozing."

"Nope. Nope. Nope. Time to get married, Mommy. AJ's at church waiting for me. He has wings."

"AJ is not at church yet, and yes, he will have rings, but not for you. Remember, the rings are for the bride and groom?" She grinned and focused on her daughter.

Mia frowned. "Sure?"

"Yes, *habibtee*, I am certain." Leila held her daughter in a tight embrace. "One day, you will be a beautiful bride, and you will have a big wedding and wear a special wedding dress made just for you. Eric will walk you down the aisle, and the church will be gorgeous—filled with flowers and all the people who love you."

"A lot of people love me?" Mia furrowed her brow and tilted her head.

"Yes." Leila's swallowed past the knot in her throat. "A lot of people do love you. Don't worry, we will find a huge church."

"And wings? Can I have wings?" Mia giggled.

Laughing, Leila pushed aside the covers. Her energy-filled daughter wouldn't rest until late tonight. Time to get up. "Yes, my love. You shall have wings that sparkle in the sun."

Hours later with hair and make-up done and minimal jewelry on, Leila sprayed jasmine perfume behind each ear. She gazed in the mirror and smiled. She chose a deep burgundy, sleeveless, floral-lace dress with a sweetheart neckline and sheer handkerchief hemline for the occasion. The dress was the most elegant and revealing she owned. She was hesitant to purchase it, but the lady at the thrift store insisted the dress was made for her and took off an additional thirty percent. Leila took a picture of herself and sent the photo to Niveen and Mama. Both insisted she looked beautiful.

Grabbing her shawl and clutch, Leila searched for Mia. If they didn't hurry, they'd be late. Since Mia and AJ were in the wedding, Tyra would transform into a bridezilla. Instead of bridesmaids and groomsmen, Tyra and Jayden elected to have the children stand by their side, holding candles throughout the service—a common Middle Eastern custom. Leila decorated the long flameless LED candles with ribbons and flowers.

She strode into the family room, relieved Mia sat on the couch with her hair and dress intact. She left her twenty minutes ago, electronic tablet in hand, speaking with Eric. "Mia, we need to go. Say goodbye to Eric now."

"He like my dre'th." Mia grinned.

"Of course." Leila smiled. "You look beautiful, and you did a good job staying clean. Now, say goodbye." She held her hand out for the tablet.

"Bye. Talk tomorrow?" Mia held tight to the tablet.

"Of course, Buttercup. Bye now. Be a good girl for your mommy."

Mia nodded and gave Leila the tablet.

"Thanks for keeping her busy. We have to run. We'll call tomorrow." Leila disconnected the call, guided Mia out of the house, and into the car for the short ride to the chapel. Parking the car in the crowded lot, Leila took a deep breath. Aiden's car was located a few slots over. She switched off the ignition and closed her eyes. Butterflies danced in her stomach, and her pulse accelerated. She must control her nerves, pull up her big girl panties, and talk to Aiden.

A week ago, when they sat in the kitchen, and he poured out his heart, he was clear the ball was in her court. He wanted them to start again—fresh. He was right. They already climbed Mount Everest, and now they must backtrack and learn to crawl and walk together—hand in hand.

Over the last two months, Leila's and Aiden's lives changed. A few days ago, Deena, Alisha, and Leila treated Tyra to a popular Middle Eastern restaurant with live music and a belly-dancer to celebrate her upcoming nuptials. Over dessert, she casually mentioned Gina's attorney informed Aiden the newlywed Mrs. Giorgio Pessina now resided in Rome and no longer wished to have any contact with AJ or Aiden. She signed the papers relinquishing all her parental rights.

"Mommy. Mommy. Let's go."

Leila startled and glanced at her daughter bouncing in the backseat. They were both a bundle of nerves but for different reasons. Today was the day Leila would take charge of her life and right her world. Aiden was her future. Although they had a lot to learn about one another, they loved each other. She would not be ungrateful and frivolous and throw away such a love. Today was Tyra and Jayden's day, but the day was also Aiden's and Leila's.

Hand in hand, she and Mia strolled to the chapel. Her child was a delicious cream puff in a pale peach organza and lace sleeveless dress that fell to her ankles in layers. Mia's wispy blonde hair was swept in a ponytail with a matching bow, and Leila, although admittedly biased, didn't think a more beautiful child existed.

Throughout the short service, Leila sat in the front pew, watching Mia fidget next to Tyra. Aiden, breathtakingly handsome in a tux, sat across the aisle, watching AJ squirm next to Jayden. The children did remarkably well, but Leila was happy she chose flameless candles instead of the traditional wax candles. Her heart and mind were already aflame, waiting for the opportunity to speak to Aiden. The last thing they needed was one of the munchkins setting fire to the chapel.

When the service ended, a flurry of activity followed as Aiden snapped wedding pictures at the chapel and on the beach. By the time he finished, he was the only one smiling. He had taken his time, and the bride was ready to kill him.

The kids were *done*. AJ took off his jacket, vest, and bowtie, and Mia threw off her sandals and yanked out her hair bow. The kids chased each other on the beach as Aiden and Leila gathered their belongings.

In the parking lot of the gallery, Leila did her best to clean up her sandy, sweaty child. Little could be done to put her back to the state she was in before the service, but Leila didn't care. For the kids, the hard part of the day was over. They would most likely disappear into AJ's teepee for the duration of the reception along with Miles who was also present.

Luckily, Tyra hired Miles's older sister to chaperone the children during the reception.

Mia firmly in hand, Leila stepped into the gallery and froze. The Stone Gallery was transformed. High-top tables were elegantly arranged with breathtaking flower arrangements spread throughout. A harpist played in the corner, and formally dressed servers greeted guests at the door with long-stemmed champagne flutes. Leila strolled from room to room. Each room offered guests a delicious treat—cocktails and a champagne fountain, desserts complete with a chocolate fountain, a carving station, and hors d'oeuvres of every kind.

Leila settled Mia with the baby-sitter then nabbed a glass of champagne. She wandered to the main gallery where all the action took place. In the center of the gallery, a small dance floor was set. Guests lingered with food and drink, waiting for the bride and groom to make their appearance. Leila searched the crowd for Aiden but didn't see him. They exchanged glances during the ceremony and smiles on the beach but nothing more.

Spotting Alisha and Deena standing close to one another engrossed in conversation, Leila shuffled in their direction. Alisha was a soft-spoken woman with flawless cocoa skin, short, dark curly hair, and a beautiful smile. Deena was cautious but happy, and Leila was thrilled her dear friend was brave enough to risk her heart once more.

Seeing Jayden and Tyra stroll inside, Leila froze. They glowed—love and joy emanating from them and filling the room.

The harpist stopped playing, and the DJ took over. They danced their first dance to John Legend's *All of Me*. Expertly, Jayden twirled his bride around the small dance floor, dipping her and kissing her passionately as the song ended. Not a dry eye was left in the room.

Smiling, Leila wiped her cheeks, hoping one day

she and Aiden would be on a dance floor celebrating their love with their friends and family watching. In all probability, two little troublemakers would be stealing their limelight. Envisioning how different that dance would be compared to the one she witnessed, she grinned. If a wedding was in her future, she would have to accept two pint-sized gremlins photo-bombing her first dance and most of the wedding pictures.

Turning, she scanned each table in the gallery. Time to take her future in her hands and reintroduce herself to the man who captured her heart. Initially, she didn't see him in the crowd, but a tingling sensation spread from her fingers and toes straight to her heart. She sensed him waiting. Spine straight and shoulders back, she strode through the crowd—drawn by a force out of her control.

He stood alone, leaning against a high-top table in the corner of the gallery with a hand in his pants pocket. Two untouched champagne glasses graced the table. He tracked her every movement as she made her way through the crowd.

Seconds later, she stood in front of Aiden—heartrate galloping and breathing shallow. The world around them faded into the periphery, and his beautiful smile and warm cognac eyes filled her vision. Goosebumps sprouted on her arms, and she shivered. "Hi," she whispered as she extended a trembling hand. "I'm Leila Solomon."

Aiden grinned as he took her hand. "Hi, Leila. I'm Aiden Stone." He squeezed her hand, gently gathered her into his embrace, and rested his forehead against hers. "Sounds like they're playing our song. Want to dance?"

Leila closed her eyes and listened as Sarah Bareilles crooned a verse from *Gravity*, "Something always brings me back..." She melted into Aiden's arms. Opening her eyes, she met his gaze. "Yes, sweetheart. I want to dance with you—now and forever."

A word about the author…

Mona Sedrak lives in Cincinnati, Ohio and works as a university administrator and professor. Although she has co-published two academic books, she is now writing mainstream fiction and women's fiction. She is an avid reader and is probably Audible's best customer. Writing and reading fiction is her escape from reality.

Mona lives with her husband of thirty-four years, a geriatric maltipoo, and an Amazon Parrot named Pretzel. She binge watches too many shows to count and she loves fine brandy.

Visit her at:
> http://www.monasedrak.com
> ~
> **Another title by this author**
> *Six Months*